PRAISE FOR THE CASEY HOLLAND MYSTERIES

"The modest but resourceful Casey is a perfect heroine for our times, a combination of thought and action."
—Lou Allin, Crime Writers of Canada

"A traditional mystery complicated by the characters' desires to keep secrets and the self-serving manipulations of others. It's a good read with urban grit and a spicy climax." —*Hamilton Spectator*

"A mystery that fits the bill." —*National Post*

A Casey Holland Mystery

THE
Deep
End

Debra Purdy Kong

TouchWood
Editions

TouchWood Editions
touchwoodeditions.com

LIBRARY AND ARCHIVES CANADA CATALOGUING IN PUBLICATION
Kong, Debra Purdy, 1955–, author
The deep end / Debra Purdy Kong.

(A Casey Holland mystery)
Issued in print and electronic formats.
ISBN 978-1-77151-093-6

I. Title. II. Series: Kong, Debra Purdy, 1955– . Casey Holland mystery.

PS8571.O694D44 2014   C813'.54   C2014-902765-6

Editor: Frances Thorsen
Copy editor: Cailey Cavallin
Proofreader: Sarah Weber
Design: Pete Kohut
Cover image: coolmilo, istockphoto.com
Author photo: Jerald Walliser

Canadian Patrimoine
Heritage canadien

Canada Council   Conseil des Arts
for the Arts   du Canada

BRITISH COLUMBIA
ARTS COUNCIL

We gratefully acknowledge the financial support for our publishing activities from
the Government of Canada through the Canada Book Fund and the Canada
Council for the Arts, and from the Province of British Columbia through the
British Columbia Arts Council and the Book Publishing Tax Credit.

The interior pages of this book have been printed on 100% post-consumer
recycled paper, processed chlorine free, and printed with vegetable-based inks.

1 2 3 4 5 18 17 16 15 14

PRINTED IN CANADA

For my intelligent and incredibly wise son, Alex, whose constant support and excellent cooking skills gave me invaluable writing time.

ONE

"CODE WHITE IN UNIT ONE common area!" a woman shouted through Mac Jorgenson's two-way radio.

Oh, crap. As Casey looked at Mac, her already warm face grew hotter. It looked like her first volunteer shift in juvie was going to be eventful.

Mac put his thermos down and picked up the radio. "Copy that. On my way." He reached for the suit jacket draped over his chair, then apparently thought better of it. While more voices acknowledged the call over the radio, he said, "Did you have a chance to memorize the codes?"

"Yes." Casey followed him out of his office. "Code white means staff need assistance." And Unit One was the girls' unit.

"Good. On day shifts, I have enough staff to assist, but evenings are another matter."

For a two-hundred-thirty-pound man in his late fifties, Fraserview Youth Custody Center's director moved surprisingly fast. He and Casey ran down the corridor, fluorescent tubes flickering above them. Although orientation had taken place only a few days ago, she couldn't remember what was behind every door.

The farther they went, the hotter she became. She should have remembered not to wear anything too warm. Worse, the stench of over-cooked broccoli threatened to curdle her stomach. She remembered that the kitchen was just beyond the girls' unit.

An Asian man charged into the unit. His navy cargo pants and light blue shirt identified him as a youth supervisor.

"That's Winson Chen," Mac said, slowing down and breathing hard. "He's in charge of Unit Two."

As they neared the girls' unit, Casey heard shouting inside. "What can I do to help?"

"I'll let you know." Mac pushed the door open as someone yelled, "Get her!"

Winson and a female supervisor were trying to separate two brawling teenagers. Some girls clustered together were watching the action with amusement. A strawberry blonde stood next to the unit's entrance, checking her nails and glancing at the fight with a bored expression. As the door closed, she peered through the small, thick pane of glass.

The brawlers grunted and cursed, ignoring the supervisors' orders to break it up. A tall girl with light brown skin yanked her opponent's dark blond dreadlocks. Dreadlock girl howled. Casey stayed near Mac, prepared to jump in if asked. He knew about her skills and some of the things she'd been through at work. Dreadlock girl stomped on the tall girl's foot. Tall girl swore and recoiled, losing her balance.

Winson caught her before she fell. "That's enough, Mercedes."

"Let go!" She tried to twist away from him.

"First, you calm down, all right?"

"*Sí, sí!*" Her shoulders slackened. When Winson released her, Mercedes straightened up and ran her fingers through her black curls.

The unit's supervisor, a petite, muscular woman, let go of Dreadlock girl. Scowling, she retrieved a tissue from her pocket and placed it over her bleeding hand.

"What happened?" Mac asked the supervisor.

She started to answer when Dreadlock girl blurted, "Mercedes stole my money and I want it back!"

"Liar!" Mercedes shouted.

"They both need some down time, Mac," the supervisor said, dabbing her hand. Her subdued tone didn't match her harsh expression any better than her flaming cheeks matched her bleached, spiky hair. The woman inspected the front of her navy pullover, presumably checking for blood.

"How much is missing, Roxanne?" Mac asked Dreadlock girl.

"A twenty-dollar bill."

Casey caught the furtive looks the girls exchanged.

"Why wasn't the money in the lockbox?" Winson asked the girls' supervisor.

The supervisor didn't acknowledge him, but looked at Mac instead. "Roxanne neglected to tell me she had it."

Mac turned to Roxanne. "Where did you get the money?"

The anger swirling around Roxanne was so strong that Casey half expected an electrical charge to zip around the room. "I got it from Mercedes, only she took it back."

"I didn't!"

"You two will wait in the Special Unit until we've found the money," Mac said. "But first, I'd like everyone to meet our newest volunteer, who I trust will stick with us despite this inauspicious start. Casey's a criminology student and an experienced security officer."

And that was all Mac would say. Casey had been cautioned not to share her last name or any contact info with residents. Casey flashed a smile and hoped she didn't look as awkward as she felt. The girls' stares were wary. Winson gave her a brief nod.

"You'll work with Mia tonight," Mac said to Casey.

"Welcome aboard." Mia barely looked at Casey as she continued to dab her wound.

"Thanks."

"Winson, could you escort the ladies out, please?" Mac asked.

"Why should I go?" Roxanne shot back. "I was the one ripped off!"

"You also broke the rule about fighting," Mac replied.

"She made me!" Roxanne pointed at her enemy. As Winson started to lead them out of the unit, Roxanne added, "You'll get yours, bitch."

Mercedes muttered something in Spanish.

"Stop it," Winson said to her. "No one's going to poop on anyone's head. And you two know the rules about swearing and disrespect. Do you want to lose all privileges for the next week?"

"How do you know what I said?" Mercedes asked, but the door closed before Casey heard a response.

"Were you scratched or bitten?" Mac asked Mia.

"Gouged is more like it."

"Do you need medical help?"

"Just a bandage."

"I'll get it. Casey, let me show you the first aid room."

Back in the corridor, Casey gagged again on the broccoli stench. Her sweater clung to her sweaty back.

"I guess you now realize that I wasn't exaggerating about the frequent violence in here," Mac said, wiping his brow. "Juvie is a stressful, negative place filled with kids who have serious issues. Most have never lived a structured life. Some take to it. Others don't."

Casey had felt the oppression the moment she stepped into the building. "The only thing that really surprises me is the heat in this place."

"The furnace is always in overdrive, but since this old building will be demolished soon, the powers that be won't spend a penny to fix it."

"I heard the new center is opening in six months. You must look forward to moving."

"I'm too close to retirement to move anywhere. When the wrecking ball hits these walls, I'll be boarding the nearest cruise ship." Mac removed a large key ring from the belt around his ample waist. "The one perk to working here is that no one pays close attention to us. Fraserview's simply a holding pen for the overflow of kids waiting to be transferred to Burnaby Youth Custody Services, or the new facility once it opens. Since none of the twenty-five residents are supposed to be here for more than a few days and the government's on yet another cutback binge, we lack sufficient staffing and programs. Mind you, lack of program funding has been a problem for all facilities for years." He unlocked the door. "I cope by managing things a little differently, trying to keep the atmosphere as relaxed as possible. As you've just seen, I often fail spectacularly."

"I don't think the failure's yours."

"The buck stops with me." Mac switched on the lights. More fluorescent tubes flickered as if reluctant to get to work. "When people confuse a relaxed environment with a lax one, there can be a backlash."

Was he alluding to staff as well as residents?

"Still, I firmly believe in an open-door policy for everyone," Mac added, "which is why I don't keep my office locked. Of course, my computer's password protected and the filing cabinets are always locked. After all, why tempt people?"

Casey wandered past a spotless sink, labeled cupboards, and a narrow bed. "Is there anything specific I should do in the girls' unit?"

"See if anyone wants to chat while Mia and I search for the money."

Mac had said that many residents simply want someone to listen to them. One or two girls might confide in her if they decided she was trustworthy.

"After your orientation, another girl was brought in, and she too is now under psychiatric care," Mac added as he started out of the room. "That makes three out of the eight girls, so I'm sure I don't have to tell you to tread lightly. Teenaged girls with legal and family problems, among other things, are hypersensitive."

"So I've learned."

"Right. You've encountered difficult teens through your work, correct?"

"Yeah, and I think I mentioned that I'm also the legal guardian of a thirteen-year-old girl. Drama isn't new to me." The truth was, Summer had been a gigantic pain in the ass lately.

"Oh, yes, I remember." Mac locked the door. "Should none of the girls wants to talk, feel free to search the common room for the money. If you aren't comfortable with that, don't worry. We'll do it. Oh, and one more word of advice: don't watch the girls too closely." Mac jiggled the door handle, as if checking to ensure the door was locked. "Once they realize we're serious about the search, it's quite possible the money will magically reappear."

Across the corridor, a woman pushed a cleaning cart out of a room. Her gray poodle perm matched the color of her polo shirt. The woman stopped to adjust the black cardigan partially hanging off the cart.

"Phyllis, this is our new volunteer, Casey."

The woman peered at her through large glasses with light blue frames. She looked to be in her late sixties, early seventies.

"Hi," Casey said. "I'm surprised you need a sweater in this place."

"I mop the pool room," Phyllis answered in a British accent. "It leaks. Cold in the basement too. It floods."

"Sounds like you've got a lot of work."

Phyllis nodded to Mac. "She'll do." And then she moved on.

"For Phyllis, that's a glowing endorsement," Mac remarked.

On their way back to Unit One, Casey said, "This place seems too large for one cleaner. Does she have help?"

"There's a fellow working in the other wing, plus more cleaning staff during the day. Phyllis prefers the slower pace of evenings, and no one makes her clean the basement. Her younger colleague does that."

Casey had spent only a short time in the other wing of this L-shaped structure, but she knew it contained Unit Three, which was the second boys' unit, as well as a classroom and an admissions area for new arrivals. At orientation, a boy was brought in, handcuffed and shackled. His personal effects were taken, a government-stamped towel and clothing issued, disinfecting shampoo handed out. It had been depressing to watch.

Casey followed Mac inside Unit One, where Mia was saying, "I repeat, no one goes to their rooms, opens their lockers, or leaves the common area until I say so." She pointed at Casey. "The volunteer will ensure you comply. Understood?"

Casey cringed. She'd just been labeled an enforcer. She glanced at the strawberry blonde, who was now sitting at the table nearest the door. She stared at the tabletop, still uninterested in what was happening. The girls seemed oblivious to her as well.

"If we don't find the money," Mia went on, "we'll be forced to resort to full body searches. Smoking privileges will also be canceled for a week."

Mac looked at Casey. "Shout if you need us." He followed Mia down the narrow hall to the back of the unit.

A group of four girls whispered to one another as they studied Casey.

"You're kind of old to be in school, aren't ya?" one of them said, as they ambled closer.

"Probably. I'm thirty-two."

"My mom's that old," another remarked. "You have cool violet eyes. Are they contacts?"

"They're real."

"Those curls don't look natural," a third girl noted.

"They're not. It's a loose perm."

"You should get rid of that shitty paper-bag color," the first girl said, "or put highlights in." She glanced at the music video playing on the TV. "Oh my god, I love this song!" The girl grabbed the remote and cranked up the volume. When her friends joined her on the sofa, all four began singing.

Casey turned to the strawberry blonde, who stood and again looked out the small window in the door. Was she seeking a chance to escape, or waiting for someone? Visiting hours were underway. The girl could be expecting a visitor, except visitors weren't allowed in the units.

While Casey pretended not to watch the girls, she strolled around the room, wondering how many arguments these yellow-painted brick walls had absorbed over the decades. Pink and black anti-bullying posters hung next to the door. Other drawings brightened the adjoining wall: distinctive red-and-black Haida Gwaii art, vivid watercolors, and pen-and-ink drawings of flags, flowers, and places. The corner of each picture contained the artist's name, country of origin, or ethnic background. At least twenty countries were represented.

The song ended and the volume went back down. Casey could almost feel some of the girls watching her, probably trying to figure out why anyone would come to Fraserview voluntarily. The strawberry blonde was still looking out the window.

"Hi," Casey said, approaching her. "I noticed that there's a half-finished jigsaw puzzle on that table in the corner. Do you like puzzles?"

The girl kept her gaze on the corridor. "No."

"Are you waiting for a visitor?"

"No."

Since she clearly wasn't interested in conversation, Casey wandered toward the supervisor's office. Windows in the upper half of the wall provided a full view of the common area. Aside from the computer, phone, and in-basket, only two files sat on the desk.

Casey started back across the common room. She spotted a

twenty-dollar bill on the floor, partially hidden under the back of the sofa. The cluster of girls sat squeezed together, gawking at a nearly naked rapper swaggering across the TV screen.

The strawberry blonde yanked the door open and stepped into the corridor. "Justin!"

Oh, hell. Was she going to take off? Casey hurried after her and saw flushed, sweaty boys in gym shorts coming down the hall. Winson brought up the rear.

"Justin!" the girl called out. "I need to talk to you!"

A slim boy with large brown eyes glanced at her, then looked at the floor. Wait a sec. The kid looked familiar. Wasn't that? . . . It couldn't be. But he sure looked like Amy Sparrow's grandson. Amy kept his photo on her desk at work. Amy's grandson was named Justin. Casey had met him a couple of times at staff picnics, but the last one was four years ago.

"Hey, Sparrow," a kid said. "Your girlfriend wants it bad."

Oh, crap. Casey watched Justin hurry inside his unit.

"That's enough. Everyone hit the showers," Winson said. "Back inside, Tanya." He looked at Casey. "They're not supposed to leave their unit without permission."

Casey nodded and held the door open for Tanya, who stomped inside.

Did Amy know Justin was in juvie? She hadn't mentioned him in a while, but Amy Sparrow didn't talk about family that often. She was a true professional, the administrative rock who kept the security department on track.

With so many employees having their hours cut over recent weeks, Amy had barely been around since Christmas. Maybe that was a good thing. The confidentiality agreement Casey had signed meant she couldn't reveal who was inside Fraserview. Amy adored Justin. If he was in trouble, she would want to know. Yet, who would be the one to tell her?

TWO

CASEY SAT IN FRONT OF Stan Cordaseto's desk and tried not to cringe at his neon orange shirt and plaid jacket. The older Mainland's security supervisor got, the more hideous his clothing choices became. His wife had given up the battle to coordinate his wardrobe ages ago. Despite the distraction, Casey had managed to get the gist of her new assignment.

"I'm not clear why GenMart's loss prevention officer recommended you to her manager," Stan said.

"Kendal Winters is an old friend who knows I live near the store."

She'd also partied with Kendal on New Year's Eve. Kendal had told her about the young shoplifters targeting GenMart Department Store, then escaping on Mainland Public Transport buses. Kendal's proposal to have GenMart work with MPT security had intrigued Casey; however, she knew there were protocols to follow. Casey noticed the way Stan was rubbing his trim gray beard. She'd worked with him long enough to know that the gesture meant something wasn't right.

"Is there a problem?" she asked.

"Marie was up for the next assignment."

Casey had spotted Marie Crenshaw down by the ladies' locker room a little while ago. She was probably still milling about, attempting to gather stronger employee support for unionization.

"I'm giving you this one because of your location and availability." Stan slid a folder toward Casey.

"Thanks. Are the police okay with us doing surveillance?"

"Seeing as how the investigating officers believe these kids are part of a larger crime ring, yeah, they are. In fact, they want us to note which stops the kids exit at and which direction they go."

"Given all the cutbacks Gwyn's dumped on us, I'm surprised he's allowing this."

"Our illustrious president is doing the police and GenMart a favor by offering our resources. I'm sure he'll cash in eventually," Stan replied. "You can follow any of the suspects off the bus for a three-block radius, but that's all. No confrontations or arrests unless you see them commit a crime. As usual, just observe and report, okay?"

"Understood." Note taking wasn't Casey's favorite part of the job, but she'd learned to appreciate it the first time she needed to consult her notebook while on the witness stand in court. Even with cameras on the newer buses, detailed notes were still essential.

"Since the punks usually strike after school and in the evening, you'll be on call from 3:00 PM until the store closes," Stan said. "I doubt you'll be called more than once a week, and even then it should only take a couple of hours."

Thankfully, both of her criminology classes were in the morning. "How do you want me to approach this?"

"As soon as the suspects are spotted in the store, the loss prevention officer, or manager on duty, will phone your cell. Drive to GenMart and park in their lot, but don't go inside. Just head for the bus stop right out front and wait for the boys to board." Stan nodded toward the folder. "The police file number and contact info's inside, and GenMart has camera footage of the suspects you can look at."

"Good. I'll call Kendal." She stood and opened the door, glancing outside. "I haven't seen Amy in ages. Is she here?"

"On her lunch break." Stan tapped his pencil on the desk. "Gwyn's cut her hours to three days a week, so she's working her butt off to help with the annual report."

Amy Sparrow had worked with Stan for a long time and they treated each other like family. Stan wasn't the most talkative, cheerful person in the world, so Amy's quiet, studious nature suited him. Did he know about Justin?

"Everything else okay with her?" Casey asked, keeping her tone casual.

Stan dropped the pencil. "Why?"

He knew. "It's just that this is a miserable time of year, what with cutbacks and Christmas bills coming in. Think I'll go say hi."

Marie appeared in the doorway, her stare fixed on Casey. Casey wasn't particularly surprised. She and Marie had never clicked and never would. Professional rivalry was a tough habit to break. Marie's unreciprocated feelings for Lou, who'd moved in with Casey two months ago, didn't help either.

Marie's mouth developed a mean little twist. "What are you doing here, Casey?"

"Catching up with Stan."

As Casey started to leave, Stan said, "Don't go yet."

Marie snatched the file out of Casey's hand. "Is this the GenMart assignment?"

"How did you know about that?" Stan asked.

"I overheard you and Gwyn talking in here, so I thought I'd wait around till your meeting ended. Obviously, Casey beat me to it."

"I asked her to come by," Stan said.

Marie swept thick red hair away from her face. "You said the next assignment would be mine."

"I'm giving it to Casey only because she lives five minutes from the store and getting there fast is crucial. She'll be expected to drop everything at a moment's notice. You're a twenty-minute drive from GenMart, and your kids are too young for you to just take off."

Leaning against the door, Marie sighed. "Anything else on the go? My stupid ex is defaulting on child support again, so I need more hours."

"We've had several complaints about graffiti artists, and I'm waiting for Gywn's go-ahead. Meanwhile, I have a question for both of you." Stan folded his hands on the desk. "What have you heard about attempts to unionize staff?"

Crap. Casey exchanged a blank stare with Marie.

"This isn't an interrogation," Stan added. "But supervisors have been hearing things, so I'm just asking what's up?"

Afraid her face would give too much away, Casey strolled toward Stan's window, which overlooked the yard. This small, privately owned company had always been cash strapped, which was why employees were paid so little. She didn't understand how Mainland, a company designed to cover the routes that TransLink's enormous fleet didn't usually serve, had wound up in direct competition with TransLink, whose workers were unionized and better paid.

"What have supervisors been hearing?" Marie asked.

Waiting for Stan's answer, Casey looked directly below the window. There were fewer cars in staff parking these days. The yard looked abandoned and grim in the pelting rain.

"Nothing much." Stan cleared his throat. "Look, I know things are tough and people are upset about salary freezes and reduced hours. I'm just trying to get a handle on the best way to sort this all out."

"If we told you anything," Marie said, "would you report it to Gwyn?"

"Nope. I'd rather he didn't know I was asking."

"Sorry, Stan," Marie replied. "Can't help you."

"What about you, Casey?" he asked.

What was she supposed to say? If she sold out Marie, she'd destroy an already strained relationship, which would make her working life hell. On the other hand, Stan was a good guy who'd stood up for Casey more times than she could count. He deserved loyalty.

She turned around. "I got an email asking if I'd be interested in unionizing, but I didn't respond."

"Who sent it?"

Ignoring Marie's stoic face, Casey focused on the dwarf jade bonsai sitting on the corner of Stan's desk. The plant was supposed to help relieve stress. It sure in hell wasn't helping now. "I don't want to cause trouble."

Stan drummed his fingers on the desk. "Cards on the table, ladies. Gwyn's about to start a witch hunt, so if either of you is involved in a bid for certification, I'd be real careful who I discussed it with."

Casey had clashed with Gwyn only once in eleven years, and that was just three months ago. He was a stubborn man perpetually trapped between providing excellent customer service and meeting the payroll. Keeping employees happy had slid down Gwyn's priority list, and she'd lost respect for the man.

"Employees can barely pay their bills, Stan," Marie said. "Why wouldn't they want to earn the same as Coast Mountain drivers?"

"I sympathize," Stan replied, "but how would they survive if there was no MPT at all? Union wages and benefits, not to mention the possibility of strikes, could bankrupt this company."

The skepticism on Marie's face was obvious. "Fine." She marched out the door.

Casey didn't follow, preferring to give Marie some space. She didn't want to face accusations about disclosing union issues to management. She hadn't, but Marie probably assumed she had. The woman hadn't let the truth get in the way of badmouthing Casey in the past.

"Think I got through?" Stan asked.

"I hope so." Though she wasn't sure.

"Concentrate on the GenMart thing, okay?" Stan blew out a puff of air. "Just between you and me, Gwyn can find plenty of reasons to lay people off."

Casey knew this. So did Marie, yet she'd chosen a risky venture anyway.

THREE

A FEW MONTHS AGO, MAINLAND'S lunchroom had been filled with laughing, chatting employees. Today, only four people were in the room when Casey entered, and no one was laughing. An accounting clerk had her elbow on the table and her hand on her forehead as she murmured into her phone. In another area, two drivers mumbled to each other between bites of food. The lack of camaraderie was sad, but not surprising. Those who had openly complained about the cutbacks wound up with verbal reprimands and further reduced hours. Censorship and uncertainty filled every molecule in this room. It was an unsettling contrast to the photos of company picnics and Christmas parties past still hanging on the back wall.

Part of Casey blamed Gwyn for Mainland's financial troubles, but, in truth, they weren't entirely his fault. It was common knowledge that Gwyn had gone into huge debt to start this business. Stricter government regulations demanding fuel-efficient buses had forced him to spend far more on newer buses than anticipated. Plans to expand routes farther east and into the Fraser Valley had been thwarted by more obstacles than anyone had bargained for, so Gwyn made do. Long-term employees had remained loyal to the company, but these days loyalty was strained.

Amy, the fourth person in the lunchroom, sat on the far side of the room, in front of the row of windows that looked out onto Lougheed Highway. She had her back to both entrances, and her head was lowered as if she were reading something. Clutching her *Juvenile Offenders in Canada* textbook, Casey strolled between the round, white tables. She'd brought the book as a way to explain her presence at Fraserview. She'd tried to come up with a good opening line, but everything sounded so inadequate.

Casey cleared her throat. "Hi, stranger. Mind if I join you?"

When Amy looked up, the many new lines on her face shocked

Casey. She'd never seen Amy without light pink lipstick and rouge before. Her usually tidy curls resembled a storm-battered bird's nest.

"It's good to see you." Amy removed her glasses and let them dangle from the chain around her neck. "Have a seat."

Casey pulled out a chair and placed the textbook on the table. "How have you been?"

"The year's not off to a great start, but what can you do?" Amy shoved her paperback aside and removed a can of juice and a mug from her *Pirates of the Caribbean* lunch kit. "Are you all settled into domestic bliss?"

"Is there such a thing?" Casey's laugh sounded more like a snort. "I knew Lou liked to collect things, I just didn't know there'd be so many hockey magazines, CDs, DVDs, lava lamps, beer mugs, and—get this—bags of bottle caps."

"It's only been a couple of months. Adjusting takes time."

"You know that patience isn't my strong suit."

"Indeed." Amy smiled and then gazed out the window, her amusement fading. "Another miserable January."

"No kidding." The dark, wet days had made Vancouverites irritable. Horns honked twice as often and people with glum faces wandered down streets and through the malls. Bus passengers not preoccupied with electronic gadgets stared, zombie-like, out the windows. It was as if people had forgotten how to chill out, even for a few moments.

As Amy poured juice into the mug, she glanced at the textbook. "Are you taking another course?"

"Two, actually. It's a lot of work, but if I don't step it up I won't get my criminology degree until I'm forty-five." She held her breath as Amy put her glasses on and read the title. Amy's tiny frame seemed to shrink. "I started volunteering at Fraserview Youth Custody Center on Friday nights."

Amy removed her glasses again. Her mouth started to open, then closed. She cleared her throat. "Justin is there."

"I saw him." Casey tried not to cringe under Amy's stare. Since Amy was the one who brought up Justin, Casey hadn't broken confidentiality. Still, she couldn't offer much information.

"Did you talk to him?" Amy asked. "What was he doing? Is he okay?"

"We didn't talk. He was walking down the hall with other boys after a basketball game, but he seemed fine. Much taller than I remember."

"Justin's grown a lot, in many ways." Amy lifted her mug with both hands. "What's the center like?"

She hadn't been there? Given how close she and Justin were, Casey was surprised. "It's old. In fact, Fraserview's closing in a few months. Only twenty-five kids are there now, so overcrowding isn't an issue, and the director's nice."

Amy raised the mug to her lips, but her hands began to shake and she put it down. She was one of the calmest, most unemotional people Casey knew. It was unnerving to see her like this.

Amy rested her hands in her lap. "Justin and I used to be best friends. When he was five, I'd take him to the park and he'd tell me all the things he wanted to be when he grew up." Her eyes glistened. "Whenever he stayed over, I read him *The Very Hungry Caterpillar* over and over again. I still know the words." She wiped a tear away.

"I'm so sorry, Amy." Casey touched her arm. "You don't have to tell me anything."

"You're one of the most discreet people I know," Amy replied. "Besides, you know Justin and that place." She lowered her head. "His trial's not until March, and he's already been there three weeks."

Good lord. What had Justin done? Casey glanced around the lunchroom. No one was close enough to overhear them. "I'm assuming Justin hasn't been in detention before. As I understand it, juveniles aren't incarcerated unless they've been charged with a really serious crime or have threatened to hurt others."

The corners of Amy's mouth drooped. "The first one."

Casey sat back. "Oh, Amy."

"Justin's girlfriend, Tanya, is also in Fraserview, so I'm not sure he'd be eager to leave her behind even if he could get out. The boy thinks he's in love. His lawyer tells me that this isn't Tanya's first time in custody."

The strawberry blonde. Casey couldn't tell Amy that she'd met the girl.

Amy sipped her juice, then put her empty sandwich container away. "Do you know why I use this silly lunchbox?"

Casey shook her head.

"It was the first present Justin ever bought me with his allowance. I took him to one of those pirate movies way back." She looked at the box. "He wanted me to have a memento of a truly wonderful day together." Amy reached for the mug. "The worst part about all this is the horrible realization that my grandson doesn't trust a single adult in his life."

Not even his grandmother? "How did it come to this, Amy?"

"An excellent question. Lord knows I've spent hours trying to figure out where everything went so wrong." She drank the juice, and then sighed. "The trouble probably started around age ten, when his mother and my son Anthony started fighting constantly. Kirsten walked out on Anthony two years later. Justin was devastated."

"How old is he now?"

"Fifteen. Last year Kirsten moved in with a man Justin despises. This Carl person has two kids who live with him, a boy and a girl. Tanya is friendly with Carl's daughter, Didi, which is how Justin met her."

"Does Justin live with Kirsten?"

"With Anthony. Kirsten has him on weekends. The visits usually end in disaster."

"Does he fight with his mom or with Carl?"

"With all of them, except Didi. Justin has never felt a part of that family, not since day one." Amy frowned. "I'll never forgive Kirsten for putting her needs above his."

"Have his parents visited him at Fraserview?"

Amy lowered her head. "Anthony did once, but I don't know about Kirst—"

"Hi, Amy." Marie plunked into a chair and looked from Amy to Casey. "Am I interrupting?"

Casey frowned. Marie damn well knew she was.

"We were just catching up," Amy said and finished her drink.

"On what?"

"Nothing much." Casey picked up her textbook as Amy put her mug away.

Marie's mouth developed that mean little twist again. "Were you talking about the union thing?" She stared at Casey. "How you think I'll ruin everything for Mainland?"

The urge to reply with something nasty welled up inside Casey, but she squashed it back. She wasn't in the mood for a sparring match.

"Honestly, Marie," Amy said. "Are you and Ingrid really going ahead with certification?"

"Totally."

"Well, I hope it'll make you happy." Amy stood. "Because you'll be doing far more harm than good."

"You're wrong, Amy. A reliable source told me that this company is making more money than it wants us to know. We're practically being robbed."

"Listen to me." Amy leaned close to Marie. "The only reliable source in this place is Stan, and he would strongly disagree with your viewpoint." She walked off.

Casey trailed close behind, grateful that Marie wasn't following. As they started up the stairs to the second floor, Amy said, "Will that silly woman ever learn to think before she acts? If she keeps stirring things up, she could lose her job."

Casey wondered how true that was. If anyone had insider information, it would be Amy.

Amy stopped at the landing and looked up and down the stairwell. "There's something I wanted to tell you before Marie showed up." Amy hesitated. "I saw the shock and the curiosity on your face about Justin, so you should know that he's been charged with the attempted murder of his stepbrother, Brady, and drug possession. They found heroin in Justin's pocket."

"Oh, no." Casey remembered Justin as a friendly, easygoing kid. However, easygoing kids didn't necessarily become easygoing teens.

"The police believe that Justin pushed Brady down the stairs in their home." Amy looked at the ground. "He'd fought with Brady before. Justin's an angry, frustrated boy, but I can't believe that he would intentionally cause Brady that much harm or try to kill him."

"How serious were Brady's injuries?"

"From what I've heard, there's damage to his neck and head, but I don't know more than that."

"Amy, do you know what triggered the fight?"

"Based on what Anthony and the police said, it seems that Justin, Tanya, and Brady went to a party hosted by a classmate of Brady's. Unfortunately, the host's parents were out for the evening." Amy's lips pinched together for a moment. "Ridiculous, isn't it? Fifteen-year-olds left alone. Justin and Brady argued, and shortly afterward Justin and Tanya left and went to Kirsten's. Apparently, Brady followed them and that's when the brawl really got going." Amy paused. "Anthony says that Brady's a bully who resents Justin's presence."

Casey wondered if Justin was still furious with Brady, if he'd threatened to go after him again. "I take it Tanya's been charged with attempted murder, too?"

"Yes, although according to his lawyer, Justin insists she had nothing to do with it. The police think otherwise. Given her history, I wouldn't be surprised if she was the one who pushed Brady down the stairs. It would be like Justin to protect her."

Tanya had been assertive Friday night—desperate to see Justin, but not overly aggressive. Maybe she wanted to make sure he'd back her up, get their story straight.

"Brady's also known to police, as they say," Amy added. "He had a reputation for fighting long before Justin came on the scene. I wish I knew more, but my son says that now Justin won't talk to his lawyer, or anyone else, which is baffling. All of it is." She resumed climbing the steps. "Three months ago, after Justin had returned from another stressful weekend with his mother, he ranted to me about hating drugs. Anthony's never had complaints from the school or the police about Justin. Honestly, Anthony's been more of a problem than Justin ever was."

Amy had only mentioned Anthony's drinking problem once, when he wound up in hospital after a near-fatal binge. "Is there anything I can do?"

"Truthfully, that's why I'm telling you all this." Her voice faltered.

Casey had been wondering why all this candidness was coming from an essentially private person.

"Can you make sure that Justin's all right?" Her voice faltered. "And please tell him I'll do whatever I can to help him. It's important that he knows this."

"I'll try, but there are confidentiality rules at Fraserview. Given that I know Justin, I might not be allowed to see him."

"Please try. I need to know why he won't talk to me, and what really happened in the house that night."

Gaining access to Tanya would be easier. It would be interesting to hear what the girl had to say about their predicament.

FOUR

CASEY ENTERED HER APARTMENT, KICKED off her boots, and spotted the light blinking on the phone. Not many people called her landline anymore, except Rhonda from prison and telemarketers. One of these days, she'd get rid of the phone. At least she'd finally banished her old answering machine in favor of voice mail.

Casey headed for the phone but stopped when her foot struck something hard. Wincing, she glared at the unpacked box Lou had been using as a side table for his remotes. This was the second time she'd smacked into that damn box. What did he keep in there anyway?

She slumped onto his ancient easy chair, opened the box, and gaped at . . . a pile of fist-sized rocks. Was he joking? Rock collecting too? After Lou moved in, her spacious third-floor suite in this big old house had begun to resemble a junkyard. He'd promised to put everything away, but that was a month ago. She'd already had to store her stationary bike and some other belongings in the basement to accommodate his furniture. Casey massaged her stinging toes. She'd known Lou for over ten years, and until four weeks ago, she'd had no idea that he was such a procrastinator when it came to household chores.

Casey glanced at the blinking light. Probably someone wanting to sell her something. She was already behind on homework. The message would have to wait. She hobbled to the kitchen table and shrugged off her coat, determined to finish reading this week's chapter before her next class. She flipped to the bookmarked page in her text and read, *Fifteen-year-old delinquents are boisterous, rebellious, and unpredictable. They are prone to criminal acts, disrespectful of authority, and generally hostile.* Was this Justin? Had he completely derailed, or had he been swept up by circumstances and a cute strawberry blonde with a criminal record?

Someone pounded up the staircase. Summer flung the door open and charged inside, startling Casey. Summer had been told numerous times that she didn't need to knock before entering the apartment, yet she rarely came up these days, not since Devon invaded her life. Summer's golden retriever, Cheyenne, followed her inside.

"Did Mom call you?" Summer's expression was a mix of anxiety and anger.

Tail wagging, Cheyenne trotted up to Casey, who scratched the dog's head. "I just got home and haven't checked messages yet, and please don't stomp up the stairs. I don't want the tenants complaining about noise again."

Before Devon came on the scene, Summer had been more courteous. Casey was still embarrassed about the fact that both of the university students she rented to had complained in December about Summer's loud music. Although their studio suites were at the back of the house, they shared the second floor with Summer.

"Whatever," Summer grumbled. "Anyway, you were wrong when you said Mom would be glad that I told her about the party. She, like, totally freaked."

"I didn't say she'd be glad. I said she'd appreciate being kept in the loop," Casey replied. "You should have told her about the party *before* you went."

"I didn't have time."

Yeah, right. Summer and Rhonda hadn't been getting along since Rhonda told her, in a phone conversation before Christmas, that thirteen was too young to have a boyfriend. Casey had heard Summer mutter that her mother couldn't do much about it from prison. Rhonda and Summer had lived apart for eighteen months now. Casey had a sinking feeling that they were growing apart emotionally as well. She wasn't sure how she could help. Duties as Summer's legal guardian and caretaker of this big old house—still owned by Rhonda—not to mention courses, work, and a new living arrangement with Lou, kept her too busy to help sort out a complicated mother/daughter relationship.

"She hates Devon and she hasn't even met him!" Summer walked to the bay window and plunked down on the cushioned seat. "It's not fair."

"Maybe she'd think differently if they met." Casey doubted it, though. Devon had too much swagger for a fourteen-year-old. Worse, he thought it was cool that his girlfriend's mother was incarcerated. The kid had been hanging around Summer since mid-December. Casey didn't like the way he showed up every single day, mooching food. Worse, she'd spotted them kissing last week. Summer had looked embarrassed. Devon, on the other hand, thought it was funny. Why couldn't Summer have stuck with the boy who had facial piercings and a mohawk? At least Jacob had been polite, and so inexperienced with girls that he had been more of a friend than a boyfriend.

"How was your math quiz today?" Casey asked.

Summer got up, went over to Ralphie's cage, and lifted him out. She didn't pay much attention to Casey's guinea pig, except when he became a handy distraction. "All right."

"What does that mean?"

While Summer stroked Ralphie, Cheyenne sniffed the critter. "I got nine out of twenty."

Damn it. Four points lower than the last quiz. Summer was spending far too much time with Devon. "Do you have math homework?"

"Only to fix what I got wrong. Devon's coming over to watch a movie tonight."

She wasn't even asking now? "I think you need a break from socializing to focus on school work and finish your chores."

"I emptied the dishwasher," Summer answered in a defensive tone.

"But you didn't refill it with the dirty dishes that are stacked all over the kitchen. It's a mess, Summer, and you haven't stuck to our bargain." Casey struggled to stay calm. "I agreed to let you make your own food in the downstairs kitchen provided you kept it clean, remember?"

"Fine." Summer put Ralphie back in his cage.

"Then you can vacuum the living room like you were supposed to do yesterday. And don't forget the week's worth of dog poop in the yard." How many bloody times did she need reminding?

"Whatever!" Summer stormed out of the apartment, Cheyenne close on her heels.

Casey leaned back in her chair and sighed. Brooding about that child wouldn't help. She returned to her textbook. *Thirteen-year-olds can become sullen and withdrawn. They are tense, critical, and highly self-conscious.* Casey grimaced. Especially if their mothers were serving a life sentence for second-degree murder.

Lou stepped through the still-open door. "Why does Summer look so mad?"

"I told her to finish her chores."

"Good. Stand your ground." He shut the door, then tossed his damp coat on the rocking chair. Raindrops glistened on his brown hair. "She's becoming a real problem."

Casey wiggled her sore toes. There were problems, and then there were problems. "What are you planning to do with the box of rocks I just smashed my foot against for the second time?"

"I was going to make a rock garden in the spring."

"Until then, would you mind not leaving them in the living room? We don't have enough floor space, Lou."

"I'll stash it downstairs." He grunted as he lifted the box. Lou wasn't a huge guy, but there were impressive muscles on his lean frame. "Can you open the door?"

"Sure." She hurried across the room and swung open the door. "What have you planned for dinner?"

"I thought I'd wait to see what you wanted," he replied.

"You know I'm not fussy. You could have chosen whatever you felt like."

"You don't want to cook?"

"No, Lou. I really don't. I have homework and then I need to see Kendal about a new assignment."

He put the box down. "What's it about?"

As Casey filled him in, she thought she heard footsteps on the stairs. She was about to peek out the door when Cheyenne trotted into the apartment once more. Summer then reappeared, with Devon right behind her. The beanpole had a smirk on his pimply face. He nodded to Lou but barely acknowledged her. Honest to god, Casey had no idea what Summer saw in this creep. Other than the thick brown hair and unusually light brown eyes, he wasn't even that good looking. Baggy pants hung so low on his hips that they threatened to fall down. Worse, the kid smelled of cigarette smoke.

"Devon popped by and wants to help clean," Summer said.

In exchange for another free meal. Casey stared at the boy. "You can help if you like, Devon, but you'll have to leave right after dinner. Summer has to do extra studying until her math grade improves."

Summer's facial muscles tightened. Her mouth opened as if to say something, but she apparently thought better of it.

"No problem," Devon said.

"I'll pick up some takeout." Lou put on his coat and lifted the box of rocks.

Great, more takeout. The second time this week. As the three headed downstairs, Casey shut the door. She noticed the blinking message light again and figured she might as well see who'd called.

"I heard about the party." Rhonda's irritated voice made Casey cringe. "And I'm pissed that you let Summer go. She needs a stricter curfew, Casey, and if her math grade doesn't go up, make an appointment with her teacher. Also, find out all you can about this Devon kid. I'll call in a few days for an update."

Rhonda was barking orders now? Four months into her sentence, Rhonda had suddenly decided she should stay involved in her child's life, especially after she learned that Summer was getting into trouble at school. In the fourteen months since then, Rhonda had been the one who chose the disciplinary measures. Casey hadn't welcomed her new role as enforcer, nor did she like being told to report on all of Summer's ups and downs. She felt more like a spy than a caregiver. Rhonda had no idea how much energy it took to cope with a surly, self-absorbed teen.

Casey turned back to the textbook and realized that distractions had caused her to read the paragraphs out of sequence. Now she read, *Fourteen-year-olds suddenly become social extroverts—the center of their world shifts dramatically from home to peers.* It had already happened in this house, and Casey sensed a battle looming. It wasn't one she intended to lose.

FIVE

CASEY GRINNED AS KENDAL WINTERS gave her a big hug and said, "Two get-togethers in less than a month. Does this mean you're back on track?"

"I hope so." Casey regretted the lapse in her social life over the past twenty months. There'd been too many long weeks spent unraveling her father's secretive past, then coming to terms with Rhonda's imprisonment and guardianship of Summer. All while building a deeper relationship with Lou. Somehow, her life had become consumed with work and responsibility and commitment to others at the expense of fun with old friends.

"You should come running with me this weekend," Kendal said. "I'm training for the marathon in May."

"I haven't run in years. I was doing yoga for a while, then I kind of lost interest." No wonder her friend looked so fit. Kendal's long hair made her face seem more rectangular than ever. The hip-hugging jeans lengthened her torso, and those three-inch heels on her boots put her at six feet. "You're probably still the best athlete our high school ever had."

"You weren't so bad yourself." Kendal grinned. "So, welcome to GenMart's loss prevention office, or the security closet, as we call it." She spread her arms to encompass the tiny, windowless room. "I'm really glad we'll be working together."

"It's rare for MPT to team up with businesses, but whatever works."

"Pull up a chair."

The place barely fit the second chair, let alone the filing cabinet and desk. A short bench had been fastened to the wall opposite the desk.

"I'm guessing that the tiny room beside the bench is a holding pen for violent shoplifters?"

"You got it. More of them are tweaked out on drugs these days, and things can get crazy. A coworker got his nose busted a few months back."

"Sounds like the job's getting more dangerous. Are you sure you want to join the RCMP?"

"Absolutely." Kendal clicked the mouse and four images appeared on a wall-mounted screen. Two of the images showed a boy with light blond hair. "I still think you should consider police work. There can't be many more promotion opportunities at MPT."

Kendal had already raised the subject on New Year's Eve. Casey thought she'd explained this. "Like I said at the party, being second-in-command is good enough for now. Stan treats me well."

"You really are the world's most loyal person."

Or the most undecided. Thirty-two years old and she still didn't know what she wanted to do with her life. Casey studied the screen. "Tell me about your setup."

"We have a dozen closed-circuit TV cameras." Kendal moved the cursor to the menu on the left side of the screen. "I can create a total of sixteen panel images on the screen. The cameras are stationary, so I can't pan or tilt them, but I can zoom in. We can see every corner of the store, with at least two cameras each in electronics and jewelry, plus one for cosmetics."

"I gather the blond kid is one of the shoplifters?"

"Part of the trio, yeah. Here's footage from a few days ago." Kendal clicked the mouse and brought up an image of the electronics counter. "Watch Blondie grab two iPods from a box behind the counter. The sales associate wasn't supposed to leave the box out in the open, but he's new. One of Blondie's cohorts keeps the associate busy at the games display case." She clicked on another image that showed a stocky boy with olive skin and short, dark brown hair talking to the associate.

"How long did the boy keep him busy?"

"Five minutes." Kendal brought up a third image. "This skinny, freckled kid is the lookout. He hovers in front of the counter, scoping things out. If he sees any staff or customers watching him or Blondie too closely, he signals them on his cell."

Casey scribbled notes about the suspects. "Do the same three boys always show up?"

"Yeah." Kendal clicked the mouse. "On this occasion, Blondie takes the iPods to boys' wear, picks up a couple of T-shirts, then heads for the men's fitting room."

"Aren't there change rooms in the kids' department?"

"We have an attendant there. In menswear, the door's kept locked and customers ring the buzzer for service. Since associates don't have time to hang around after they've unlocked the door, the kid waits for a customer to come out, then grabs the door before it closes." The screen showed Blondie doing exactly that. Kendal fast forwarded the footage. "He stays in the change room for seven and a half minutes before reappearing without the T-shirts. He left them in the room on top of the discarded iPod packaging."

"Clever."

"Once we realized what was happening, I reviewed archived footage and found the same three kids in different parts of the store six weeks earlier. They zigzag their way through the aisles to see if they are being followed and glance at the cameras periodically."

"Wouldn't they want to try and hide their faces?"

"We think the boys aren't overly worried about it. After all, they're minors who would have to be caught red-handed. So far, they've been too smart to let that happen."

"Stan said they might be part of a larger crime ring. I guess they're hitting electronics the most?"

"As well as jewelry, clothing, and shavers."

"Shavers?"

"Surprisingly, they're a popular target at many stores," Kendal answered. "We now keep them locked up."

Casey had read the file before meeting Kendal and was surprised to learn that over a thousand bucks in merchandise had been stolen in less than two months. How had the boys gotten away with so much? Kendal was an experienced loss prevention officer. Still, she couldn't be here all the time, and who knew how competent her colleagues were?

"Half the time, the boys pay for small stuff like pop and gum," Kendal said. "They like playing games, trying to throw us off."

"You haven't confronted them yet?" Casey saw the flash of annoyance and realized she'd offended her friend.

"How can I when I've never seen them actually take anything? The footage I showed you happened while another LPO was on duty. Loss prevention officers can't touch anyone unless we see them pocket something and walk out of the store. We're not even allowed to do checks at the door because it's not customer friendly."

"Do the boys have a set routine or pattern?"

"Not really." Kendal closed the images. "They tend to hang around other departments before strolling to electronics. The visits usually last about twenty minutes."

"Do they always board the bus together?"

"They have the two times I've seen them."

Casey closed her notebook. "Once I get your phone call, I'll drive over and park in GenMart's lot, then head for the bus stop."

"Good. I just hope I can nail these delinquents before they do more damage."

"Speaking of delinquents, I just had a thought," Casey said. "I know you're volunteering with the community police, but would you like to add more volunteering to your résumé?"

"If it doesn't swallow up a lot of time, sure. What do you have in mind?"

"Fraserview Youth Custody Center. I've just started there Friday nights, and they need more help. It would only take a couple of hours a week."

"I've heard of that juvie center. It's the old building near Boundary and Marine Drive, right?"

"Technically, it's in Burnaby, but yeah, Vancouver's part of the neighborhood."

Casey told her about Mac, and how teenagers as young as twelve were sent there to either await trial or serve a sentence for a serious crime. "A lot of the residents have a parade of social workers, psychiatrists, probation officers, and lawyers working with them. A teacher comes in during the day for classes, and they're supposed to have extracurricular sports and crafts available, but government cutbacks put a lot of programs on hold."

"So, what do the kids do to unwind?"

"Watch movies, listen to music, and play basketball if the staff are willing to referee," Casey answered. "Most of the residents are bored out of their minds, though. Few have visitors, so Mac relies on volunteers to talk with them, or play cards, or whatever else is available."

Kendal's eyes sparkled with mischief. "Maybe we could teach those kids a thing or two."

"Maybe." But Casey had a feeling it would be the other way around.

SIX

A SHIVER TINGLED ACROSS CASEY'S shoulders, and she was filled with a sense of foreboding. Justin wasn't in his unit like he was supposed to be. Since the gymnasium's bathroom was out of service, Winson Chen had let him leave to use Unit Two's bathroom. When he didn't return, Winson sent Casey to bring him back. So, where the hell was he? As far as Casey knew, the only unlocked rooms during visiting hours were the living units, visiting area, and Mac's office.

She hurried down the corridor, marching past a janitorial cart. Spotting the cleaning woman's black cardigan hanging off the end of the cart, she figured Phyllis was nearby. Mac and Kendal stepped out of the visitors' area. Casey rushed toward them, happy that her friend's volunteer work with the police department had enabled her to fly through background checks and paperwork. An ally around here would be welcome. Mac was so eager for volunteers that he was combining Kendal's orientation with her first shift. Casey had thought it strange that the director conducted orientations, until he confided that he didn't want staff passing along bad habits.

Casey drew nearer as Mac was saying, "The Special Unit is a bit barbaric compared to living units in newer centers, but this is how segregation operated fifty years ago, and there've been no upgrades worth mentioning here."

"Are many kids in the Special Unit?" Kendal asked.

"It's been empty lately. If residents are a danger to themselves or others, or if they deliberately break rules, then we have to separate them. We try to correct the behavior and assess when they can rejoin the others." He gave Casey a brief nod. "If these kids don't learn to be accountable for bad choices, how will they learn? Who will teach them?"

"Good point," Kendal remarked. "Where is the unit?"

"It's the last door on the right at the end of the corridor, across from the swimming pool, which is no longer used, thanks to budget cuts."

Above the Special Unit's entrance, another flickering fluorescent tube was about to die. Casey figured the whole place would be in darkness before it closed. A blue bucket sat next to the fire exit at the far end of the hall to catch drips from the leaking roof.

"The next door up from the pool is the gym," Mac added, "which is where Casey's been enjoying a rousing game of basketball, I gather." He smiled at her, then turned to Kendal. "There's no budget for a recreational director, so youth supervisors do what they can to keep the boys busy."

"Justin Sparrow was supposed to use Unit Two's bathroom then come straight back, but he hasn't," Casey said. "Have you seen him?"

"With my permission, he's having a quick chat with Miss Tanya in the visitors' lounge. She's upset about being transferred to another facility tomorrow and Justin has a calming effect on her. I radioed Winson about it a couple of minutes ago."

"Thanks." Casey noticed the heavy bags under Mac's eyes. He looked exhausted; however, she needed to do this now. "I didn't get a chance to talk to you earlier, but I thought you should know that I work with Justin's grandmother." Mac's expression darkened. "I didn't know Justin was here until I caught a glimpse of him last week. Amy asked me to check on him now and then."

"Did you tell Justin's grandmother that he was here?" Mac asked.

"No. She brought his name up when she heard I was volunteering here. I didn't tell her anything because I don't know anything."

Mac seemed to think about this for a moment. "Did Tanya's name come up?"

"Amy referred to a girlfriend who's in here, but I didn't tell her that I'd seen Tanya."

"Good," Mac replied. "Confidentiality is vital here. There are many rules and boundaries inside juvie. If they're not followed, our dysfunctional little family could unravel into something quite ugly."

Dysfunctional little family? An odd way to put it, Casey thought.

"Confidentiality agreements and privacy come under the rules category," Mac went on. "Whatever Justin says to you must stay between you two, especially if it concerns legal matters. Many volunteers have one-on-one conversations with residents that must remain confidential, unless something comes out that might harm the resident or others."

"What if Justin wants me to give his grandmother a message?" Casey asked. "Or she wants me to say something to him?"

"That's a boundaries issue," Mac replied. "Personally, I have no hard and fast rule about passing messages between parents and guardians and our residents, as long as you're very discreet. You mustn't be viewed as Justin's pipeline to the outside, as other residents would then expect you to get messages to their relatives."

"Understood," Casey replied. "It's just that Justin's never been in trouble before and Amy's frightened for him."

"All the same, it's best if you're not assigned to Justin's unit after tonight. Since his time with Tanya's nearly up, though, you may escort him back to the gym," Mac said. "Make sure Miss Tanya returns to her unit as well, and be careful what you say in front of them." He turned to Kendal. "You can start in the girls' unit, and we'll see how it goes."

"Sure." Kendal removed a granola bar from her pocket and began to unwrap it.

"That doesn't have nuts in it, does it?" Mac asked.

"Actually, it's a honey nut bar. I came straight from work and didn't have time for dinner," Kendal answered. "Does someone have an allergy?"

"I forgot to tell you that Winson has a serious peanut allergy. All food should be left with your personal belongings at reception."

"Sure. I'll just pop back to my locker and stick it in my purse."

"Actually, ask our receptionist, Rawan, to hand you your purse. Volunteers aren't allowed past the counter to access personal belongings," Mac said. "Unfortunately, we've had security problems with volunteers taking home things they shouldn't."

Casey spotted the girl with the dreadlocks—the one who'd been fighting last week—standing in the corridor, watching them.

"Do you need something, Roxanne?" Mac called out.

"Where's Tanya?"

"She'll be back in a minute. Inside your unit, please."

"I need to talk to her."

"You can when she returns."

"It's visiting hours," Roxanne replied. "Why can't I wait in the hall?"

"Because you don't have permission," Mac replied. "Inside, please."

The girl scowled. "I hate you, you dirty old man!"

Casey glanced at Kendal, who shrugged.

"What have I said about name-calling?" Mac's voice was calm but firm.

Roxanne ran back inside the girls' unit.

"Some days, you can't win." He sighed. "Lashing out with name-calling and accusations is common, ladies. Don't take it personally."

"I get a lot of that in the store," Kendal said.

"On the buses, too," Casey added.

"Good to know. Tanya's the only friend Roxanne's made in here, and she's not happy about Tanya's transfer either." Mac turned to Kendal. "However, like I said, there has to be accountability, so I need to have a word with Roxanne. Kendal, why don't you join me after you've put your food away?"

The receptionist Casey had met at orientation, Rawan Faysal, stepped into the corridor. Her dark, blond-streaked hair flowed over her shoulders. "Mac?" She waved a folder at him. "A new admission's arriving within the hour."

"Thank you." He sighed and, for a brief moment, placed his hand on his chest. "It's going to be one of those nights." He headed toward Rawan.

Kendal shrugged at Casey, then followed Mac.

Casey entered the visitors' area and counted six residents, each with an older adult. Half of the families were watching a hockey game, while others talked quietly at tables. A fiftysomething man was playing ping-pong with a boy who looked about twelve. Most of the adults seemed pensive. The reason was probably the corrections officer observing everyone from behind his desk.

Casey recognized Mercedes, the Spanish-speaking girl Roxanne brawled with last week. Her head was lowered and she looked depressed. A Latino man with thinning hair, possibly in his mid-thirties, patted her back while glancing around the room. There was some resemblance, though he looked a little young to be her father. He could be an older brother. When the man caught Casey watching him, she turned her attention to the worn, mismatched sofas and chairs. The yellowing blue and gray linoleum looked like it had been waxed a million times. A bookcase was filled with dusty board games and puzzles.

To her right, Justin and Tanya sat at a table in the corner. Tanya dabbed her eyes and looked over her shoulder at the Latino man while saying something to Justin. As Casey strolled toward them, Tanya looked up and glared, as if to warn her off.

"Sorry to intrude," Casey said, "but Mac wants both of you to rejoin your units now."

Justin's brown eyes blinked at her and he tilted his head slightly. "I know you, right?"

Oh, boy. "I work with your grandmother."

He sat up straight, shoulders rigid. "Did Nana send you here?"

"No."

Justin stood.

"Don't go." Tanya grabbed his hand. "There's something I gotta tell you."

Casey frowned when Justin sat down again. The girl looked at Casey, as if expecting her to leave. Not bloody likely.

"Justin, we really have to go," Casey said.

He got to his feet more slowly this time.

"Justin." Tanya's frosty tone made him hesitate.

"I'll get in trouble," he said.

"Please," Tanya begged.

"I don't know what to do." The kid looked miserable.

"How about you talk on our way back?" Casey suggested.

Despite her scowl, Tanya rose. No one spoke as they walked down the corridor. Tanya glanced at Casey a couple of times. Whatever she wanted to tell Justin was obviously too personal to say in front of a volunteer. Casey spotted Phyllis mopping the floor outside the conference room. Phyllis looked up and gave her a quick nod.

When they reached the girls' unit, Tanya again reached for Justin's hand. "You *have* to, Justin. There's no other way."

Justin looked like he wanted to disappear through the floor. What on earth did Tanya want him to do? "Come on," Casey murmured, but he simply stood there.

"Justin!" Winson yelled from the gym entrance farther down the hall. "What are you doing?"

"Mac said I could talk to Tanya."

"Not for this long. Back in the gym, bud."

The girls' supervisor, Mia, emerged from her unit. "Tanya, back inside, *now*." The same angry eyes Casey saw last week were there again. "You didn't have permission to leave."

"You were on the phone."

"And you just happened to see Justin in the corridor?"

Casey figured that the girl probably made a habit of standing by the door, waiting for chances to talk to her beloved.

As Tanya shuffled to the doorway, Casey and Justin continued down the corridor.

Winson turned his attention to the game and blew his whistle. "Stop that!" He darted back inside the gym.

"Don't touch me, bitch!" Tanya yelled from behind them.

Justin grimaced but didn't look back.

"Excuse me?" Mia's voice was almost menacing.

Once Tanya was inside, Casey said, "Amy asked me to tell you that she's standing by you, no matter what."

A heavy woman with puffy cheeks and a stained apron emerged from the kitchen. The woman's narrow eyes glinted and her down-turned mouth puckered with disapproval as she waddled past Casey and Justin, carrying two buckets.

"I need out," he mumbled.

"I'm sure you do. Amy's been confused about why you won't see her."

Justin glanced at Casey. "Would you want your family seeing you in this shithole?"

Winson re-emerged. Justin hurried past him into the gym, but

Winson seemed more interested in watching something behind Casey than joining him. Casey turned and saw the big woman with the apron lock a door next to the kitchen, then head toward the main entrance.

"I gather she's the cook?" Casey asked.

"Oksana, yes. I'd say don't get on her bad side, but Oksana doesn't have a good one, so just stay out of her way. Here's another tip," Winson said. "Don't let girls and boys mingle. Didn't Mac tell you that?"

"He did, but he also gave those two permission to talk."

"He shouldn't have," a male voice said from behind her. "And I'll have to speak to Mac about supervisors leaving volunteers alone with residents."

Casey turned to find a muscular man with a receding hairline and cold black eyes. Where the hell had he come from?

"This is our senior youth supervisor, Amir," Winson said. "He's in charge of Unit Three."

"If she's not been properly trained," Amir said to Winson, "then she shouldn't be here."

"I'll deal with it," Winson said. "I was the one who sent her after Justin, and I need to talk to Mac about something else anyway. Maybe you can watch the boys."

"I can't watch both units," Amir shot back. "Get someone else."

Winson let out a long sigh. "Then I guess Casey will have to watch things for five minutes."

"Are you out of your mind?" Amir said. "What did I just say?"

"That you won't help out," Winson said defiantly. "And why are you so suddenly by the book? It's not like you haven't bent the rules before."

Amir glared at him, then looked up and down the corridor. "Have it your way, but one fight and she's toast. I don't know why females are allowed here in the first place."

Casey was beginning to understand why Fraserview had so few volunteers. The building wasn't the only outdated thing about this place. She also suspected that staff shortages in the evening contributed to the lax rules Mac had mentioned.

"There's a two-way radio on my desk if you need help," Winson said to Casey. "You know how to use one?"

"I've used them many times."

Winson entered the gym and blew the whistle. "All right, guys, we're done. Let's go!"

Half of the boys headed for Amir's unit in the adjoining wing, while the others made their way toward Winson's unit.

"Everyone stays inside until I get back," Winson said to Casey. "Understand?"

"Yes." How stupid did he think she was?

Casey took a deep, calming breath and wondered what the boys would try to get away with. As she stepped inside, some of them glanced her way. Others gawked and murmured to one another before turning their attention to the hockey game on TV. What they should have been doing was heading for the showers because the room stank. Justin sat alone at a table by the door.

Casey picked up the radio in Winson's office and sat at the table next to Justin. The seat, one of five attached to the table with steel support beams, wasn't overly comfy. Unlike the girls' unit, this room had no drawings on the wall, but there was a foosball table. Comic books were stacked haphazardly on a four-foot-high bookcase next to the entrance. She wanted to talk to Justin, learn more about what Tanya wanted him to do, but he turned his back to her. Just as well. It wouldn't be smart to be seen striking up a conversation in front of the others.

Winson returned less than ten minutes later, looking glum and preoccupied as he walked right past her. He didn't even seem to notice the boys.

Casey followed him into his office. "Here's your radio."

He sat down. "Thanks."

"Everything okay?"

"Uh, yeah. Mac wants to see you," he replied, his eyes not quite meeting hers. Either his conversation with Mac didn't go well, or she was in more trouble than she thought.

"I'd better go now."

As Casey left the common room, she noticed the boys' furtive glances. Justin wasn't at the table, which was just as well. She didn't want to be asked for any favors.

Casey headed down the corridor. If Mac was going to let her go, then she might as well get it over with. She knocked on his door and peered through the window. She could see Mac in profile; he was seated but leaning forward as if searching for something on the floor. His thermos was on its side, coffee spilling out of it. Casey opened the door and stepped inside.

"Mac?" The unmistakable sound of retching greeted her.

He gripped the edge of the desk like he was about to keel over. Casey hurried over to him, avoiding the chunky puddle by his feet. She glanced at the door that connected Mac's office to the conference room. It stood ajar, revealing that the room was dark.

"Do you need a doctor? Should I call 911?"

His eyes were unfocused, his expression confused. "My pills."

"Where are they?"

Mac closed his eyes and grimaced. "Jacket."

The jacket was draped over the back of his chair. Casey scrambled through his pockets until she found a small bottle labeled DIGOXIN. "How many do you need?"

"One." He clamped his hand on his chest and mumbled, "Tanya, Justin."

"They're back in their units." As she tried to open the bottle, Mac groaned as if in agony. "Help!" She shouted toward the open office door. "I need help in here!" Casey pushed down hard on the bottle lid, twisted, and pulled. The lid popped off, spilling pills everywhere. "Shit!" She tapped a pill from the bottle and grabbed the thermos. There was just enough liquid left in it to wash the pill down. She placed the pill in Mac's mouth and poured the coffee in. Mac swallowed, groaned again, and slumped to the side.

"Oh, no!"

"What happened?" Rawan said from the doorway, her eyes wide. "I was signing out a visitor when I heard you yell."

"I think Mac's having a heart attack. I gave him the pill he asked for, but I don't think it's working!"

Rawan grabbed Mac's radio. "Code yellow, director's office! Code yellow, director's office."

Casey wished she'd thought of that. Mercedes's Latino visitor appeared in the doorway.

"Is something wrong?" he asked.

"Are you a doctor?" Casey asked.

"No." He stared at Mac. "What happened?"

"Possible heart attack," Casey replied. "We need to call 911."

"I'm on it." Rawan dialed. Once she described the situation to the dispatcher, she turned to Casey. "They want to know what you gave him."

"One digoxin pill from the bottle in his pocket." She checked Mac's pulse. "There's no pulse!" She looked at the Latino. "Can you help me get him on the floor?"

He maneuvered Mac's upper body while Casey tackled his legs. Rawan was still on the phone when Mia appeared with the first aid kit.

"I have level two first aid," Mia said, kneeling next to Mac. "Casey, keep people out of here."

"Okay." She and the man stepped outside.

Standing in front of the door, Casey tried to avoid answering visitors' questions. Oh, god, had she contributed to Mac's condition? Had she not given him enough pills, or the wrong pill? What if there'd been a second bottle in another pocket? She hadn't searched the inside pockets before she found the digoxin. Casey began to feel clammy and lightheaded. The suffocating heat in this building didn't help.

She wasn't surprised to see the fire department arrive. They often showed up first in medical emergencies. Rawan, who'd returned to reception, buzzed them in. Casey waved them over. A couple of minutes later, she did the same for the paramedics. While everyone piled into the office, Casey leaned against the wall next to reception and sank down on her haunches.

"Come to my office," Rawan said to her.

Casey let Rawan help her up and take her to a chair by the desk.

Rawan then collapsed into her own chair. Her olive skin looked flushed. She drummed her long pink nails on the desk.

"I had no idea Mac had a serious heart condition," Casey said.

"We found out a couple of months ago. He has a weak heart muscle or something. I don't know. Mac doesn't like talking about it."

"He looked exhausted tonight."

"I know. He had an attack last month, but the pills helped that time."

Rawan got up and tended to the departing visitors while Casey sat there feeling useless. Should she return to Winson's unit, or wait here for news?

She had no idea how much time had passed when Mia appeared in the doorway, her face ashen. "Mac didn't make it," she said.

SEVEN

"OH, NO." CASEY'S STOMACH ROILED and nausea overwhelmed her. Maybe she should have given Mac more than one pill, given the severity of his attack. Would it have saved him?

"Casey, maybe you can see if Winson needs help," Mia said. The steely determination she'd shown earlier had dissolved into resignation. "Word will be out soon, if it isn't already. The news will send some of the kids off the deep end."

"Where's Amir?" Rawan asked, wiping a tear from her cheek.

Mia's expression hardened. "Why do you ask?"

"He's the most senior staff on duty, so he should be the one to call Mac's wife."

"Indeed," Mia remarked. "We wouldn't want the wife to be the last to know."

Casey saw the icy exchange but didn't care. All she could think about was her blundered attempt to save Mac. She walked past the visitors' area. Judging from the tense, expectant faces, Casey doubted they'd heard the news. The Latino man and Mercedes sat at a table and talked quietly. Paramedics and firefighters still hovered in and around Mac's office, preventing anyone from seeing what was happening. Casey walked slowly, her steps sluggish. Everything felt out of kilter, surreal.

She'd almost reached Unit Two when Kendal stepped out of Unit One. "What's going on?"

Casey moved closer and whispered, "Mac had a heart attack and died."

"No way!"

"I tried to help him." Casey took a deep breath and began to describe what had happened. She stopped talking when Roxanne stepped out from behind Kendal.

"The old man's dead?" the girl asked.

Oh, crap. "Please go back inside," Casey replied.

Roxanne shook her head, her dreadlocks swinging back and forth. "I heard you." Her voice rose. "You said Mac had a heart attack and died!"

Lord, she must have snuck up right behind Kendal.

"Come on," Kendal said to Roxanne, who'd started to sob. "Let's go talk."

As the two stepped back inside the girls' unit, Winson approached from the south end of the corridor. Why wasn't he in his unit? Who was watching the boys?

"Why are you two talking out here?" he asked.

"This is Kendal's first night and she's alone with the girls. She wanted to know when Mia would be back."

Winson's jaw tightened. "Did you mention Mac?"

"Yes." She didn't appreciate the dramatic eye roll.

"Why would you have a highly sensitive discussion where you could be overheard? What were you thinking?"

She was thinking, where the hell had he and Amir been while Mac was dying? "I was thinking that you must have noticed how unwell Mac looked," Casey said. "He was vomiting and keeling over by the time I reached his office."

Winson's dark eyes narrowed. "I don't have to answer to you."

"Not to me, no." Had Winson actually talked to Mac? Was Mac's condition the reason Winson seemed so preoccupied when he returned to the unit? Did Winson have an ulterior motive for sending her to Mac's office, like knowing what was happening, but wanting to dump responsibility on the volunteer?

"Here's a tip," Winson said. "Don't talk in the hall where anyone can hear you."

"We were whispering," Casey said.

"Is that right?" he replied. "Well, look behind you."

Casey turned and saw two solemn boys at Unit Two's entrance. Oh, lord. Had they overheard her as well? Either way, they must have heard Roxanne's outburst.

Winson shifted and stood taller, as if trying to look superior. "Amir hates the volunteer program. If he's put in charge, it will be shut down."

"Mac's dead!" Mercedes shouted from the north end of the corridor. "No!"

Casey spotted Mercedes as she struggled to get past the firefighters who wouldn't let her inside Mac's office. The Latino man said something to her in Spanish. A moment later, Mia rushed up to Mercedes, who collapsed to her knees.

Two RCMP officers entered Fraserview. Why were they here? Casey turned to Winson, who looked unnerved by the police presence.

Amir appeared from the other wing and marched toward them. As he passed Casey, he said, "Go help Mia with that girl."

Casey followed him down the corridor. Mia was trying to calm Mercedes, but the girl's flailing arms kept Mia at bay. The Latino man retrieved his coat from reception, then—glancing at the cops—scurried out of the building. Interesting that he was abandoning Mercedes now. Did the cops worry him that much? Casey approached Mia and the girl, stopping close enough for Mia to see her.

Casey heard Amir talking to the officers. "I'm saying you've been misinformed," he said. "Who the hell reported a homicide?"

Casey flinched. What? The officers observed Mercedes and Mia, and then noticed her. Casey tried not to wither under their scrutiny.

"Is there a room we can use to interview people?" the older of the two cops asked Amir.

"Yes, but residents need to return to their units. Visiting hours are over."

"We'd rather everyone stay where they are until we've had a quick word," the officer replied.

Amir's balding head began to shine and his body grew rigid. "I can send anyone who had a visitor to meet with you."

"How many residents had visitors tonight?"

"The list's at reception."

"We'll talk to visitors first." The officer turned to those who were standing around watching. "We'd like everyone to stay until we've had a chance to speak with each of you. It shouldn't take long."

Amir frowned as he led the senior officer to the conference room adjoining Mac's office. His younger colleague spoke with firefighters and paramedics.

"I can't hang around," a visitor grumbled. "I've got to get to work."

Mia helped Mercedes to her feet.

"Excuse me?" the younger officer addressed Mia. "Are you the one who assisted the director?"

"Not initially." She nodded toward Casey. "The volunteer got to him first."

Casey grimaced. Mia could have put it less provocatively. "I did, yes," she said and then provided a detailed account of what she'd seen upon reaching Mac's office.

"So, the pill you gave him came directly from the bottle. It wasn't one of the spilled ones?" the officer asked.

"Correct."

He jotted something in his notebook. "Stick around, all right?" he said. "We might have more questions."

"Casey, can you help the other volunteer?" Mia asked.

"Sure." Should she have mentioned that Mac's last words were Justin and Tanya's names? If the cop asked whether Mac had mentioned anything other than his pills, she'd tell him. Otherwise, why point the finger at Justin? It just wasn't plausible that the boy, or even Tanya, could have caused Mac's heart to give out.

Casey started down the corridor, drawing nearer to Phyllis and the cook, Oksana, who hovered near the janitor's closet. Oksana said something to Phyllis, who then shuffled toward Casey. She'd put on her sweater and hugged herself as if she were cold. Bad news had that effect on some people, even in an overheated place like this.

Pale eyes blinked up at Casey through large square lenses. "Is it true that poor Mac is dead?"

Casey glanced up and down the corridor, making sure no one could hear. "I'm afraid so."

Phyllis mumbled, "He was the only one who'd give me a job." She gazed into space. "A dark, dark day."

The piercing sound of a fire alarm made Casey jump and cover her ears. God, now what? Staff and residents poured into the corridor and headed for exits at either end. Glancing over her shoulder, Casey saw firefighters, police, and staff directing visitors out the main entrance. As she hurried to help Kendal, she sniffed the air. There was no smoky smell and certainly no sign of flames. Kendal led the girls, some with tearstained faces, toward the exit. Mia and Mercedes joined them.

Mia seemed to be counting heads. She turned abruptly and jogged back toward the girls' unit. Winson yelled something at the boys, but the alarm was so loud that Casey didn't think most of the boys heard him. He spoke into his radio and rushed back to his unit. A scowling Amir and a firefighter marched down the hall. Glaring at Casey, Amir pointed to the exit, making it clear he wanted her to leave. The firefighter stopped to examine the pull station between Unit One and the first aid room.

Amir unlocked the mechanical room and stepped inside. Casey watched him read the fire panel, then yell something into his radio. Seconds later, he opened the panel's glass door and pressed a button. The alarm went silent.

Mia and Winson rushed out of their units.

"Code green!" Winston yelled into his radio.

Holy crap. Code green meant a missing resident, which also meant a possible escape. Casey watched the kids hurry back inside, rubbing chilly arms. Where were Justin and Tanya? Her heart beat faster. Amir relocked the mechanical room door, while Winson checked the swimming pool and gym doors. Both were locked.

"Have you seen Justin or Tanya in the last fifteen minutes?" Winson asked her.

Oh, hell. "No."

Residents loitered in the corridor. Some were quiet, others chattered excitedly. She thought she heard a girl mention Tanya's name.

"Everyone, back in your units right now," Mia called out.

Amir jogged toward the police officers re-entering the building.

"Mia, start in the other wing," Winson said. "I'll do this one."

"Can I help?" Casey asked.

"Check all the doors on that side of the corridor." He gestured across the hall. "If anything's not locked, go in and search the area thoroughly."

"I know Justin's grandmother," she blurted. "If he's out, he might try to contact her. I could give her number and address to the police."

Winson's stare was unreadable. "You know the family?"

"Just the grandmother; she's a coworker. I told Mac about it."

"Let the police know."

Casey felt bad about the extra stress Amy was about to experience, but this was a criminal matter. Information couldn't be withheld now.

"Casey!" Kendal rushed up to her. "I just heard about Tanya and Justin."

"When did you last see Tanya?"

"I'm not sure. I was trying to calm down that Roxanne chick," she murmured. "I've learned some interesting stuff. Call me later."

Casey approached the officer she'd spoken with earlier. "Excuse me," she said. "I have information about the residents who've gone missing."

As she was explaining her connection to Justin, a familiar voice behind her said, "How do we know you didn't help Justin escape?"

Casey turned and stared at Amir. The jerk was about to stomp on her last nerve. His thick black eyebrows were scrunched together, his entire manner bristling with defiance and challenge.

"Because I'm *telling* you I didn't," she replied with enough force to let him know she wasn't about to cower. "Surely surveillance cameras can verify how and when the kids got out, and if they had help."

Uncertainty flickered across Amir's face.

"We'd like to look at the footage," the officer said to Amir.

"The camera at the south end isn't working," he replied. "It was supposed to be fixed three days ago but there was a mix-up."

The officer stared him down. "What about the other exits, or are those cameras broken too?"

Amir's frosty tone barely contained the hostility he obviously felt. "I'll see what I can do."

The officer turned to Casey. "It might be better if you leave after all, Miss Holland. If we need more information, we'll contact you."

"Wait," Amir said. "Two residents are missing. We're in lockdown."

"Exactly the point," the officer replied. "Obviously, there are too many people in here to keep track of. All nonessential personnel who've been interviewed should leave."

Amir shook his head. "I still think you're wasting your time talking to people about a heart attack. Mac Jorgenson was an old man with a serious heart condition called dilated cardiomyopathy. He came to work looking like hell tonight. End of story."

But it wasn't the end of the story, Casey thought. The story was why didn't the digoxin pill help Mac? Why did he mention Justin and Tanya just before he died? And what had been bothering Winson when he told her to go see Mac?

Casey left before Amir started accusing her of aiding in Mac's demise. She dropped off her visitor's badge at reception and signed out. Rawan quietly handed over her coat and purse. It looked like she'd been crying.

Outside, two officers scanned the grounds with flashlights. A third officer was talking to someone in the parking lot. Casey took the icy steps carefully. Out of the corner of her eye, she noticed a small red glow beneath a tree just beyond the building. Someone was smoking, someone short and bundled in black from head to foot. The individual stepped away from the tree and into the pool of light from the building's floodlight. It was the cleaning woman, Phyllis.

"Rough night, huh?" Casey said.

She took a drag on the cigarette. "It is."

"Did you hear that two residents, Justin and Tanya, went missing?"

Phyllis gave a small nod. "Bad seeds every which way."

"You didn't, by any chance, see them sneak off the grounds?"

"Just came on break a minute ago." She tapped the cigarette. "When I was seventeen, I ran off to marry Frank. Some thought we were daft, but I had to get away. My dad . . . Violent bugger, he was. But that's all in the past. Deep waters under a low bridge." She paused. "Sometimes waters rise. Still, you can't go back. Some things can't be undone."

"I guess not." That's what worried her about Justin.

"A storm's brewing." Phyllis gazed at the starless sky. "Inside and out."

Casey hugged herself and glanced at the officers. "What do you mean by inside?"

"Nothing goes together. People aren't where they should be, doing what they shouldn't. It's all pineapple upside down." She crushed the cigarette with her boot and headed for the entrance.

EIGHT

"HONESTLY, CASEY, I DIDN'T KNOW what to do or say."

Casey shivered in the damp, chilly air as she stood at the bus stop and waited for the shoplifters to emerge from GenMart. When she called Amy last night, Amy said the police had already been in touch. Now Amy was telling her that Justin had called this morning. The kid refused to turn himself in because "bad things" were happening in Fraserview, although he wouldn't elaborate. He'd also begged his grandmother for food and cash.

"What do you think he meant by bad things?" Amy asked.

"Good question." Casey paused. "About the time Justin and Tanya escaped, Fraserview's director, Mac Jorgenson, had a heart attack and died. It could be that."

"How awful, although I got the impression there was more than one issue. The director's death could have put Justin over the edge."

"Possibly." Fraserview seemed to have ongoing turmoil. "Does Justin want you to meet him?"

"Yes. Hold on a minute, will you?" Amy said. "I need a tissue."

"I'm on assignment right now, so if the line goes dead, don't panic. It means I'm on the move."

"I'm sorry, I didn't know. Should I hang up?"

"No, the M5 isn't due for five minutes. But if it or the suspects show up early, I'll have to go."

"Be right back."

A gust of wind nearly pulled Casey's umbrella from her hand. It was the last Saturday of January, and, as usual, rain was coming down, sometimes light, other times heavy. She looked behind her. GenMart's entrance was just a few yards down. Kendal had called the moment she'd spotted the shoplifters in the store. Too rushed to leave Lou a note, Casey had asked Summer to let him know that she was on the GenMart assignment and didn't know when she'd be back. Summer had barely looked up from the pizza she and Devon were making.

Now that Casey was freezing her butt off, she wished she'd taken a minute to add an extra layer of clothing. The M5 ran only once every half hour. She hoped the boys planned to be on the next one.

"I'm back," Amy said. "Listen, there's something else you should know."

"Okay." Casey again glanced at GenMart's entrance. Still no sign of the boys.

"Brady died from his injuries yesterday." Another pause. "I can't help wondering if Justin found out. As much as he disliked the boy, Justin wouldn't have wanted Brady to die. He must be terrified that he'll be charged with murder."

"Maybe." If Justin had heard, then he'd probably told Tanya— unless it was the other way around. Was this what she'd needed to tell him so urgently last night? Either way, their legal trouble had become a whole lot worse. Casey wouldn't be surprised if escaping was Tanya's idea.

"I have a huge favor to ask, and I'll understand if you decline," Amy said, "but I'd like you to come with me to meet Justin. With any luck, the two of us can talk some sense into my grandson."

Not a great plan. "I can't, Amy. The police are aware that I know Justin. If I'm in contact with him, I'll be expected to notify them, or risk losing my security license."

"I know. It's the reason I'd like you there. If Justin won't accompany me to the nearest police station, I'll need you to call them." Amy's voice cracked. "I'm not sure I would have the courage to do it."

"Oh, Amy."

"I asked my son, but Anthony doesn't want to turn Justin in."

Casey shifted her feet to keep warm. She glanced at the growing number of people waiting to board the bus. There was still no sign of the shoplifters. "Where are you to meet him?"

"He'll phone this afternoon with the details."

"Let me know when he does, and we'll figure this out."

Amy choked back a sob. "Thank you. I'll be in touch."

So, what were these bad things happening in Fraserview? Was Justin referring to everyday dramas, Mac's heart attack, or something else? How had he and Tanya escaped in the first place, or had staff made it easy for them? After all, Mia had been helping Mac, and Kendal was too busy dealing with distraught girls to notice Tanya's disappearance. The girl had probably been hovering by the unit's entrance again and seized the chance to bolt.

And what was up with Winson? Justin had been sitting at the table by the door when Winson returned to the unit. Granted, she hadn't seen Justin when she left the unit a couple of minutes later. Had he already snuck out by then, or had he taken off after Winson left the unit again? When had Winson left, and why? Had he been searching for Justin? He hadn't called a code green then, so he couldn't have been alarmed. Casey recalled that Winson had been coming from Amir's area of the building when he approached her and Kendal in the corridor. What the hell had Winson been doing down there?

The blond kid Casey had seen on the camera footage the other day emerged from GenMart. He walked up to the curb and, with his back to her, peered down the street. Casey spotted the M5 easing up to the red light a block from the bus stop. The boy was speaking on the phone. He turned and looked at the people waiting to board. Casey tilted her umbrella down to shield her face.

Two more boys joined him. Casey recognized the stocky boy and his freckled cohort from the camera footage. While the boys merged with the other passengers, Casey stepped back so she'd be last on board.

As she entered the bus, the driver, Ingrid, gave her a curt nod. Nothing was said. Nothing was supposed to be said. Ingrid had little respect for security personnel anyway and was probably annoyed to have one on board. The M5 was nearly full. The shoplifters grabbed the seats along the back of the bus. Casey took her time heading down the aisle. Her phone rang and she stopped near the center exit.

"The boys are gone, but I didn't see them take anything," Kendal said. "Are they on the bus?"

"Yeah."

"Sorry I couldn't give you a heads up. I was sidetracked."

"No worries."

"You didn't call last night," Kendal said.

"I was exhausted. Sorry." This wasn't the time to talk about it. "We'll catch up after I'm done here."

"Sounds good."

Every seat was taken, which gave her a good excuse to stand and steal glimpses of the boys. As Casey edged past two other standees, she spotted the boys focusing on what looked like a Smartphone in Stocky's hand.

The bus rumbled through the heavy Saturday afternoon traffic. At the Main and Broadway stop, the boys made their way off the bus by the center exit. Casey stepped down after them. Blondie and Freckles headed west on Broadway. Stocky walked north on Main Street. Since he carried the Smartphone, Casey tailed him. For the moment, it had stopped raining, so raising the umbrella to shield her face wouldn't work.

Stocky's pigeon-toed gait maintained a leisurely pace, as if he had all the time in the world. He removed something from his pocket and stopped. Seconds later, he tossed a pink item into a garbage receptacle. The kid glanced over his shoulder. Casey lowered her head and retrieved a stick of gum from her purse. Reaching into the receptacle, she swapped the gum wrapper for the pink item: a worn change purse with a Hello Kitty logo. Had those little creeps actually ripped off a child? Pocketing the purse, she realized she'd lost sight of Stocky and marched faster.

Based on Stan's parameters, she could cover a couple more blocks. Casey turned the corner onto Eighth Avenue but didn't see the boy. Damn. He couldn't have reached Quebec Street already and turned off, could he? She walked down the sidewalk, studying the old office building across the street and the newer complex beside it. Like much of Vancouver, this section was an eclectic mix of old and new buildings, both commercial and residential. The street wasn't wide, and Stocky could have entered one of several doorways. Adopting a leisurely pace, she walked past a couple of businesses.

She was midway down the block when she spotted Stocky in a donair shop, leaning against the counter and talking to a man with the same olive skin tone. The man appeared to be handling the Smartphone. The man looked up as a couple of customers walked out of the shop. Casey kept moving, hoping she hadn't captured his interest.

NINE

CASEY ENTERED HER APARTMENT AND nearly stumbled over two empty boxes by the door. At least Lou was putting things away, but why leave the boxes there? "Lou?"

No answer. Maybe he'd gone out. According to the note Summer left downstairs, she'd taken Cheyenne for a walk. Casey removed her boots and coat, then headed for the kitchen.

Just as she feared, Lou hadn't started dinner. She should have phoned to make sure he would at least start cooking, but briefing the police about the donair shop and updating Kendal had been priorities.

Kendal confirmed that a customer reported losing a Smartphone and a little girl's mother reported that her daughter had lost a change purse containing ten bucks. Shoplifters weren't usually pickpockets, although this bunch might be an exception. Still, the items could have been dropped or left on a counter. The boys would definitely have made the most of an opportunity.

Casey plunked into a kitchen chair, then brought up the report template on her laptop. She'd managed to write two sentences before Lou came in, carrying large paper bags. "Good, you're home. How did it go?"

"Okay. Is Summer back yet?"

"No."

"When did she leave?"

"I don't know. I've been out running errands for over an hour."

As he plunked the bags on the counter, Casey smelled Chinese food. Takeout again. When Lou moved in, he'd volunteered to do half of the cooking, but his contribution had mostly been takeout food or prepackaged, microwaveable stuff. Would it kill him to cook a little pasta? She picked up her phone and dialed Summer's number.

"Unavailable. She either turned it off or the battery died."

"She should have called to let me know she was going out," Lou said. "That girl's getting more difficult every week. Maybe you should talk to Rhonda."

"What good will it do? Summer's decided her mother can't do much to her from a prison cell."

"The rules need to be stepped up, Casey. Summer's barely following the ones she's got now. Use some tough love."

"That goes for you too, right?"

"Does it?" Lou lifted food containers out of the bags.

"When you moved in I thought we agreed that we'd both be parenting Summer. Shouldn't this be a joint effort? Since Devon came on the scene, you haven't done much disciplining."

"I've tried, but she doesn't listen to me. When you're not here it's like I'm not either." Lou turned to her, his mouth downcast. "Did you ever tell her that parenting's now a joint thing?"

"I assumed she knew. You babysat her countless times before moving in. Why would she think she doesn't have to listen to you now that you're living here?"

"Ask her."

Exasperated, Casey said, "Would you please take those empty boxes downstairs and see if she's back?"

"Sure, boss." He walked across the room, picked up the boxes, and shut the door a little too loudly as he left the apartment.

Was she being too bossy or overreacting from frustration? Casey called Summer's number again. Still unavailable—damn it. Why did she get the feeling that Summer wasn't walking Cheyenne alone? Maybe she should test that theory. Last week, Summer left her phone up here. Acting on some sort of protective instinct, Casey had found Devon's number and saved it on her own phone. She hadn't expected to need it so quickly. She was about to call the kid when the phone rang in her hand, startling her. The number wasn't familiar.

"This is Mia Quinlan from Fraserview. I'm calling to see if you're still interested in volunteering. I realize that last night's shock might have you reconsidering, but I'd like you to stay with us. We could really use the help."

"I was told that the volunteer program might be ending soon."

"Who said that?" She sounded annoyed.

"Winson Chen. He said Amir's not a fan of volunteers and will likely shut the program down."

"I see. Well, the truth is I've been appointed acting director, and the program stays as long as I'm in charge."

"Good to know." Casey smiled. Amir wouldn't welcome this development.

"Some residents are quite upset about Mac, and on edge about Tanya and Justin's disappearance. We could definitely use some calming influences for the girls. Could you volunteer tomorrow evening?"

GenMart wasn't open Sunday nights. "Sure."

"Thank you. I might see you there. Bye now."

Lou returned as Casey hung up the phone. "She's still out."

Casey called Devon's cell. He answered on the third ring. Since he'd probably hang up if she told him who was calling, Casey identified herself as a friend of Summer's. "I was supposed to call her," she said, changing the pitch of her voice, "but I think her phone's off. Anyway, she gave me your number. Is she there?"

Casey noticed Lou grinning as he opened the food containers. In the background she heard a referee's whistle and clapping.

"Hello?" Summer said.

Casey fought the urge to yell. "Where are you?"

A crowd cheered in the background. "How did you get this number?"

"Answer my question."

"I'm at the rec center," Summer replied. "I was walking Cheyenne and bumped into Devon, so we stopped to watch a hockey game for a few minutes."

"Bumped into Devon?" How bloody convenient. "He was here earlier this afternoon, making pizza."

"Well, I had to do my chores, so he left. Then Cheyenne needed a walk, and I wound up here."

The recreation center was only a couple of blocks away; a quick rendezvous point. "Why did you turn your phone off?"

"The battery was low."

"You couldn't have borrowed Devon's phone to let Lou know where you were?"

"I left a note, so what's the big deal?"

Casey took a calming breath. "The big deal is that you stopped to watch a hockey game when you promised to finish your chores, and you've been gone well over an hour. Come home now, please."

"Whatever."

Casey plunked the phone down. *Whatever?* What the hell kind of response was that? "I should ground her."

Lou shoveled chow mein into his mouth while she paced the room. "Have some food," he said.

"Not hungry." Her phone rang again. It was Amy.

"I just heard from Justin," she said, her voice subdued. "He wants me to bring some things to the pedestrian bridge over the Coquitlam River at eight o'clock. It's near my condo. We used to walk along the trails down there all the time. I tried to persuade him to meet me indoors, or at least somewhere with more shelter, but he wouldn't."

"Amy, please think about this. Isn't it in Justin's best interest if the police are notified now?"

"Of course I've thought about it," she answered. "The problem is that if the police show up instead of me, Justin will think I betrayed him, and I couldn't live with that." She sounded shaky. "Casey, I honestly don't know how to handle this. Will you please come with me?"

It wasn't a great plan, yet turning her back on a friend and skipping a chance to return escapees to Fraserview would be worse. "Just so we're clear, Amy, if I see Justin I'll have to call the police."

"Yes." She cleared her throat. "I'm counting on you to do the right thing."

So Amy could absolve herself of that particular guilt? Even though Casey understood, it put her in an awkward position. She glanced at Lou, who was watching her while he ate.

"I'll be at your place at seven-thirty," Casey said.

They'd barely ended their conversation before Lou said, "What's up?"

"I'm trying to be a friend." The more Casey explained, the deeper Lou frowned.

"You're getting too involved," he said.

She knew that. "I can't turn my back on Amy."

"What if she decides she doesn't want you calling the cops?"

"She won't have a choice. You heard me tell her what I'll have to do."

They were still discussing it when footsteps pounded up the stairs. A door shut on the second floor.

"Sounds like Summer's back and shutting herself in her room," Lou said. "Shouldn't she be finishing those chores?"

"Let's have a chat with her, together." Casey led the way to Summer's bedroom on the second floor and knocked on the door. "Summer, I need to talk to you."

Long seconds passed before Summer cracked the door open wide enough to show her defiant face. "What about?" Cheyenne's snout also poked through the opening.

"Don't take that tone with me," Casey said, feeling her temper rise. "You need to finish your chores. Since you abandoned them for a hockey game and didn't have the courtesy to let us know how late you'd be getting back, you're grounded for two weeks." Until this moment, she had no idea those words would come out of her mouth.

"What! Are you serious?"

"Absolutely. You have to learn to face the consequences, Summer, and when I'm not home you're still accountable to Lou."

Summer glanced at Lou, her eyes flashing. "You can't ground me! Mom makes the rules. I'm phoning her."

"Good, because if you don't, I will."

Disbelief turned to alarm. "Why are you doing this to me?"

"She told you why," Lou said. "Now, go finish your chores."

"But Devon and I are busy downloading music."

Summer opened the door wider to reveal Devon sitting on her bed, arms crossed and a smirk on his pimply face. He tossed his head, flicking hair from his eyes. Fury prickled Casey's skin.

"I thought Casey made it clear weeks ago," Lou said. "No boys in your room."

Casey could feel herself losing it but didn't care. "You snuck that boy in here? What is wrong with you?"

Devon stood, the smirk gone.

"I didn't *sneak* him in!" Summer yelled. "It's not like we were trying to be quiet."

"I heard you," Casey shot back. "I didn't hear him. And how many times do I have to tell you not to pound on the steps? You're not the only one living on this floor! Now get downstairs, both of you!"

"I'm outta here." Devon charged past Casey and Lou.

Casey cringed at the stink of stale smoke coming from his clothes. She seethed as the boy made a point of stomping down each step.

Summer followed him, her eyes filling with tears.

"I'll make sure he leaves," Lou said, turning to go after Summer.

"Call me, Dev," Summer shouted on her way downstairs. "We're not finished!"

Too angry for words, Casey followed close behind.

Devon didn't respond to Summer. At the bottom of the staircase, he flung the front door open and barged outside.

"Don't come back!" Lou yelled, slamming the door. "I'm putting on the alarm, so he can't sneak back in."

Casey had the system installed months ago, but Summer had set it off by mistake so many times that they'd stopped using it. Time to restore the habit.

"I hate you both!" Summer shouted as tears spilled down her face.

"We're not too thrilled with you either," Lou replied, "or the way Devon's been hanging around you so much, mooching food. Do you have any idea how high the grocery bill is now?"

"He does that because his mom can't afford to feed him and his brother and sisters," she replied. "Sometimes, a meal here is the only food he gets all day."

Casey wished she'd started the background check Rhonda wanted. It was so like Summer to help people out this way, especially those she cared about. On the other hand, Devon could be scamming her. She hardly ever went to his place.

"Better go finish those chores," Lou said.

Summer wiped her eyes, then looked from one to the other. Casey could almost see her weighing her options until resignation took over and she trudged down the hall toward the kitchen.

Casey retreated to the living room, wondering what had happened to the supportive, understanding guardian she'd tried to be. Every month she seemed to fail this child a little more, or was it the other way around?

"We did what we had to do," Lou said from the doorway.

"Did we?" She looked out the window. "I freaked out and you told the boy not to come back, so now they'll cut classes and come here while we're at work. Summer does know how to turn off the alarm, you know."

"If we tell her not to let him inside anymore, then she had better not. That girl's had it way too easy."

"If we're overly strict, she could run off with Devon. God knows what would happen then."

He let out a long sigh. "I'm going to finish supper. You ready to eat yet?"

"I suppose I should grab something before I leave."

Lou started up the steps, then stopped and turned around. "Before you run off to help others, maybe you should take a closer look at the people who need you right here."

"That's unfair. Summer has been getting more of my time and attention than anyone else—including you—for over eighteen months, and all I've gotten is a mouthy punk who defies authority and disrespects us."

"Then you'll have to try harder."

"And what about you? What will you do, besides criticize from the sideline?"

She brushed past Lou and jogged upstairs.

TEN

CASEY EASED HER TERCEL DOWN Patricia Avenue, passing an elementary school on the left.

"The road ends just up ahead," Amy said, straining forward in the passenger seat. "Then there's forest and a wide trail along the river. You can pull up beside those yellow posts; that's where the footpath to the pedestrian bridge begins."

After Casey did so, she turned off the engine and scanned the area. Justin had chosen the location well. In front of her, the trees and bushes surrounding the tennis courts offered plenty of places to see without being seen. There wasn't a single soul out on this quiet residential street. Even dog walkers wouldn't want to stay outside long on such a frigid night. Wind swooshed through the trees. Raindrops began to spot the windshield.

"The poor boy must be freezing half to death." Amy squeezed the ski jacket in her lap. "I doubt he fetched his coat before he left."

Not left, escaped. Justin had made his choice and needed to live with the consequences. These damn teens always thought they knew better, always acted before thinking. Okay, so maybe the attitude was less than charitable, but her confrontations with Summer and Lou two hours ago were still bothering her. Nothing had been resolved, nor would it be overnight. No point in brooding over it now, though. Her family issues were nothing compared to Amy's.

Would Amy be able to cope once Justin was hauled away in handcuffs? Would they even be able to get him in handcuffs? Since the meet with Justin would happen in Coquitlam, Casey would need to call the RCMP to pick him up. She'd considered calling them before leaving home, but if Justin changed his mind about showing up, the cops wouldn't appreciate the wasted resources. She'd have to call them without Justin's—and perhaps even Amy's—knowledge. If the kid found out, she'd be forced to restrain him in front of his grandmother. Not something she wanted to do, but she'd brought handcuffs anyway.

Casey noticed the lamp standard illuminating a path that led to the river. She opened the car door and waited for Amy to do the same; however, Amy didn't move. "Are you having second thoughts?"

"And third and fourth." Amy gazed at the trees. "I promised him I'd be here. I can't betray Justin's trust."

No, she depended on others to do that. The closer it came to crunch time, the more Casey regretted becoming involved. She retrieved a flashlight from the glove box. "He should be on the bridge now."

"Would you mind terribly if I went ahead of you?" Amy asked. "Justin doesn't know I brought you along. If he sees two people, he could run before I have a chance to talk to him."

She had a point. "I'll stay back, but I don't want to lose sight of you."

"Fair enough." Amy stepped out of the car and hauled a full back-pack off the backseat.

Casey wondered if Amy had stashed money and a cell phone among the clothes and food. It was possible that Amy had decided not to turn Justin in, but didn't want to admit it. Was this the real reason she wanted to see him alone? Casey put on her tuque, then got out of the car and buttoned her coat.

"The footpath intersects the cycling trail a few yards ahead," Amy said. "That's where you'll find the bridge."

"Are you sure you'll be okay trekking off in the dark?"

"Don't worry. I know these trails really well." She switched on her own flashlight. "That's why Justin wants to meet here."

Meaning that he likely knew these trails just as well, and how to make a quick escape. Casey waited only a few seconds before she started down the path, reaching the intersecting trail in less than a minute. The pedestrian bridge wasn't wide. It sloped upward slightly, preventing her from seeing the other end, not that she could see much in the dark. Amy's white hat was barely visible as she moved toward the center of the bridge.

A chilly gust forced Casey to squint. Raindrops plopped on her cheek. She looked up and down the wide trail. Justin and Tanya wouldn't ambush them, would they? What if they had hooked up with friends? What if hungry wild animals were lurking? She told herself to get a grip.

Amy disappeared from view. Casey stepped onto the bridge. Gripping the blue rail, she listened for voices, but the wind and rushing water were loud. She edged forward until the slope leveled out. She spotted Amy's hat and matching scarf. Justin had already put on the ski jacket. Casey crouched down and, staying in the shadows, inched forward until she could hear a few words.

"You have to go back!" Amy sounded desperate.

"I can't."

"Why not?"

"We owe a favor we can't pay back. I'm trapped!" Justin put on the backpack. "Can't even go home!"

Amy gripped his arm. Casey couldn't hear what she was saying but based on her body language she appeared to be pleading with him.

A female voice called out. Justin turned around. It had to be Tanya.

"Justin, there's always a way out!" The desperation in Amy's voice rang out. "I'll help you."

Grandmother and grandson faced each other. Casey held her breath, hoping he'd make the right choice. Couldn't the kid see that his options were almost nil?

"Justin!" Tanya yelled. "Let's go."

Leaning into the railing, Casey reached for her phone as Justin jogged toward Tanya.

"Wait!" Amy shouted. "Please!"

"Tanya needs me!" he yelled over his shoulder.

Oh, crap. Amy was going after him. Casey called 911. After she explained the situation and provide the location, the dispatcher said, "Can you see which way the kids are heading?"

"South on a trail, on the river's east side, but I can't see Justin. He might have turned off somewhere."

"Where's the grandmother now?"

Casey stepped forward, craning her neck. "Still on the bridge." Amy had stopped running and was looking at the path.

"Stay where you are, ma'am. Officers will be there shortly."

"It's starting to pour. We'll wait in my car. I'm parked at the end of Patricia Avenue." She gave the make and plate number, then hurried up to Amy.

Amy slumped against Casey and cried so hard that her whole body shook. Casey wrapped her arms around Amy's tiny frame, afraid the poor woman would collapse if she let her go. "Let's get in the car before we're soaked."

Amy removed a tissue from her pocket. "He wanted to get back to that stupid girl." As she wiped her nose, wisps of hair not bound by her hat blew every which way.

"I know." Casey urged her forward.

As they walked, Amy said, "I don't know what hold Tanya has over him, but there must be something."

"Did he imply anything?"

"It was the way he looked so torn when I asked him to come with me. It was as if he was coming apart." Her voice cracked. "Then that girl called out, and I saw trepidation and fear. Tanya's controlling him. I'm sure she instigated the escape."

"It's possible."

"I shouldn't have involved you," Amy said. "I need to find him myself."

Bad idea. "How?"

"I think he's staying nearby. Homeless kids sleep under the bridge that's part of the Lougheed Highway all year round. It's not far from here."

"Are you sure?"

"I admit it's been a while since I looked. I used to have a dog, and I walked him day and night on these trails. Justin often went with me when he stayed over. At first he thought that sleeping under a bridge would be cool, but then the weather got bad. When he saw how dirty and miserable the kids looked he squashed that idea."

Still, Justin would remember that refuge. "You can't go there now, Amy. It's too dark and wet." Besides, Tanya would likely give her a problem.

"I'll do it in the morning. I have to convince Justin that he can trust me. So, maybe we shouldn't call the police."

Oh, no. How could she change her mind now? "Amy, I already did, like we agreed."

"Oh." She looked away.

What was she supposed to have done? She'd told Amy she could lose her license if the police learned about this meeting.

"Nana!" Justin yelled from behind them.

Both women turned to find him walking toward them.

"Justin?" Amy started toward him. "Are you coming home?"

The boy stopped and his eyes widened when he saw Casey. Looking past her, his face filled with horror. He turned to Amy. "You called the cops?"

"No! It wasn't me!"

Casey spun around to see the red and blue flashing lights of a police cruiser. When she turned back, the boy was bolting over the bridge.

"Justin!" Amy yelled. "Come back!"

The look of anguish and loss on Amy's face made Casey feel ill.

ELEVEN

→

THE MOMENT CASEY STEPPED INSIDE Fraserview, Mia began peppering her with questions about last night's unsuccessful attempt to bring Justin and Tanya in. It seemed the RCMP had given Mia a call to ask about Casey's relationship with Justin. She supposed they had to, but it was still an irritation. Equally irritating was Mia's attitude about last night's failed mission.

"So, you're basically saying that the RCMP didn't want to spend time traipsing through the bushes in a downpour to look for Justin and Tanya?" Mia asked. "And that's why the kids got away?"

"They did look, but I have no idea for how long since I was asked to leave. The thing is, Justin knows all the shortcuts and escape routes by the Coquitlam River, which is why he wanted to meet his grandmother there in the first place."

"I still think the cops should have done more," Mia grumbled.

Casey saw Rawan roll her eyes as she took Casey's coat and purse and placed them in a locker. It appeared that the strain she'd noticed between Rawan and Mia on Friday night hadn't dissipated. Was Rawan still upset about Mac, or were there other issues?

"Since staff rotate weekends," Mia said, "you might recognize some faces."

Casey noted Mia's silk blouse and beautifully tailored jacket and pants. Fraserview's acting director was apparently making the most of life without a uniform.

"I appreciate you telling me about your connection to Justin and his grandmother," Mia added, "but Mac was right. It wouldn't be wise to place you in Justin's unit once he's back. Word will quickly get out—if it hasn't already—about your relationship with his family. The situation could lead to perceived favoritism."

Casey clipped on her visitor's badge. "You sound certain he will be back."

"They always are."

Casey hadn't heard from Amy today and hadn't expected to. Still, she was curious about whether Amy had gone looking for Justin this morning. If she'd found him, Casey doubted that Amy would tell her. She'd been so upset last night that not a word was said on the drive back to the condo. Amy probably wasn't happy with her, which was troubling. Had calling the police permanently damaged their relationship?

"Do you think Tanya will end up here as well?" Casey asked. "She was due to be transferred, wasn't she?"

"If there's still room for her at Burnaby Youth Custody Services, the transfer will happen as planned," Mia answered. "Rumors are flying that she and Justin caused Mac's heart attack. Some residents aren't thrilled about that. It would be ideal if both of them were transferred elsewhere."

Great. More trouble for Justin. "You don't think they had a role in it, do you?"

"I wouldn't have believed it of Justin. Tanya, on the other hand, was furious with Mac about the transfer. She's not only sneaky and resourceful, but quite capable of harming people when her emotions are out of control." As they approached the girls' unit, Mia added, "Ruby's working in here tonight and, a word of warning, the woman loves to gossip."

In the girls' unit, a six-foot tall, bulky woman with wiry salt and pepper hair chatted with two of the residents.

"Ruby," Mia called out, "I'd like you to meet Casey, one of our new volunteers."

"'Ello der." Ruby shook her hand. "Gals are right; your eyes do look like sparkling amethyst."

"Thank you." Casey wasn't sure if her accent was Jamaican, but it was from somewhere in the Caribbean.

"You got a boyfriend, yeah?"

Were staff supposed to be this personal? Casey glanced at Mia who shrugged. "I'm in a long-term relationship, yes."

"Come sit," Ruby said, ushering her into the office.

Casey followed her and Mia inside.

Mia shut the door and said to Ruby, "How is Mercedes doing?"

"No change. Dat gal only comes out for meals. Maybe Casey could cheer her up."

Casey had no idea how she'd accomplish that. "Isn't she the tall Mexican girl who was upset about Mac?"

"Costa Rican," Ruby said. "But mostly schooled in Canada."

"She was also the one who brawled with Roxanne your first night here," Mia added.

"Dread brawls with everybody." Ruby clicked her tongue.

"Ruby," Mia said with a slight frown. "Please use Roxanne's proper name."

Ruby shrugged and waved her hand dismissively. "Dat gal's got real problems."

Two residents began shouting in the common room. Through the office window, Casey saw a First Nations girl pulling on Roxanne's dreadlocks while Roxanne held a TV remote out of the girl's reach.

"See?" Ruby remarked.

"I'll deal with this." Mia entered the common room.

Ruby clicked her tongue. "Uh-oh. She's got her screw face on."

Casey smiled. "Does she take over like that a lot?"

Ruby chuckled. "Dat lady lives for it. Wants to run everythin' and everyone."

Mia pried the girl's hands off of Roxanne's hair, then took the remote from Roxanne. She stood between them.

"Dey hate the lecturin'." Ruby hurried up to Mia and interrupted with, "Tanks, Mia. I know you're busy, so I'll do the rest. Everything's fine, all cook and curry now." Ruby took the remote from Mia and escorted her to the door while assuring her that both girls would be punished. She then turned to Casey. "Let's go see Mercedes." As they headed toward the back of the unit, the air grew warmer and staler. "She's takin' Mac's death hard, so don't mind her nasty side. Dat gal's moods are overworked most times anyway."

"I don't blame her. Mac's death was pretty awful."

Ruby stopped and gave her a curious look. "You found him, yeah?"

Casey nodded. "It was a tough night, what with the escape and the fire alarm going off. Mia says that some of the residents blame Tanya and Justin for Mac's death."

Ruby clicked her tongue again. "Crazy talk started by staff. Worried about looking bad in front of bosses, so dey blame those two. Tanya and Justin aren't killers. Just got more hormones than common sense. Tanya's a smart gal, but needy. Comes from a fancy home with parents in the pharmacy business," Ruby whispered. "Acting out got dat gal plenty of attention. Her first time here, her madda and fadda came and made a big fuss, and she liked dat. Now dey don't come or even call."

Was Ruby supposed to reveal this much about a resident?

"She's an only child and dat's the problem. I have five brudders and two sistas. Never was time for whinin' 'bout attention."

"Any idea how she and Justin got out?"

"Through the south exit about when poor Mac's heart was giving out. Exit alarm was disconnected. Supposed to be checked every week. Someone sure messed up."

Had Mac mumbled Justin and Tanya's names because he'd been in the corridor and seen them leave? If so, why didn't he use the two-way radio to call for help? Or had his heart forced him to return to his office for his pills? On the two occasions she'd worked with Mac, Casey had noticed that he rarely wore his jacket in this overheated building.

"Winson was supervising Justin's unit that night," Casey said. "Wouldn't he have seen Justin leave?"

Ruby snorted. "He *says* he went and saw Amir for a minute." She glanced behind her and whispered, "But dem two's always breaking rules 'cause Mac wasn't big on enforcement." Her wide mouth grew rigid. "We'll see what the big bosses say."

"Have they been here?"

"Soon. Just watch, everybody'll be actin' all proper while pointin' fingers at somebody else."

If it was proven that Winson had left his unit unsupervised, he could wind up in trouble. After the strained conversation between him and Amir Friday night, Casey doubted Amir would cover for him.

"Any idea how the kids managed to leave the property when there's barbed wire on top of the fence?" Casey asked.

"Wooden crates were piled up. Grounds are supposed to be patrolled every day. Another rule broken."

"How would they have gotten over the top without cutting themselves? And who put the crates there in the first place?"

"Dunno." Ruby stopped in front of a room and tapped on the open door. "I brought company, and Casey could use a manicure." She turned to Casey. "It's Mercedes's specialty."

When had Ruby noticed her nails? Mercedes was curled up in a fetal position, her eyes closed. Even in that position, she looked too long for the cot.

"Mercedes, you be nice to dis gal." When the girl didn't respond Ruby clicked her tongue and turned to Casey. "Shout if you need anything."

As Ruby left, Casey stood in the doorway. What was she supposed to say to a sullen teen? Talking about Mac would be a bad idea, but what about Tanya? Residents probably knew more about the girl's disappearing act than staff.

"May I come in?"

Mercedes opened her eyes, yet barely nodded. Casey took a cautious step into the sparsely furnished room. Mercedes's cot was attached to the wall, as was the desk across from the cot. Bars prevented any chance of escape through the small window. Casey strolled to the orange plastic chair next to the desk and sat down.

"Are you really a nail expert?" she asked.

Mercedes blinked at her. "Uh-huh."

"I've never had a manicure in my life, but yours look great." She focused on Mercedes's black and red nails, nails more than capable of gouging Mia's hand.

Mercedes propped herself up. "You tried to help Mac, right?"

At least there was no recrimination in her voice. "Yes."

"Did he say anything before he . . ." Mercedes lowered her head.

"Not really." Had she heard something? "Why do you ask?"

Mercedes shrugged. "No reason." She glanced at the door. "Some people are glad Mac's dead."

Interesting. Casey nodded as if she already knew this. "I heard Roxanne call him a pervert. Was there anything to that?"

"It's bullshit."

"Are you sure?"

Mercedes's expression hardened. "I know what the real deal is, and Mac wasn't it. Roxanne just wanted him to transfer her out of this hellhole, like he was doing with Tanya."

Casey believed her. She felt bad for mentioning what had to be a painful part of Mercedes's past; however, she needed to push the boundaries to find answers.

"Which people are glad Mac's gone?"

"Most of the supervisors."

"I thought he got along with them."

"You're new, *chica*."

Was that derogatory? Casey decided to ignore it. "What was their problem with Mac?"

Mercedes again glanced at the door. "They thought he was too old. Mac would forget things and he was sick a lot," she murmured. "Worse, Mac was gonna fire some of them."

Was this true, or was the girl making up stories? If Mercedes was telling the truth, how would she have found out? "Mac would have had a hard time pulling that off," Casey remarked. "It's not easy to fire unionized employees unless they've committed a crime, and this place is closing in a few months anyway."

"I know that." Mercedes's dark eyes glittered with hostility. "Killing Mac is criminal."

"True." Casey hesitated, then decided to plunge ahead. "Apparently, some people think Tanya and Justin might have had something to do with his death. But Mac had a serious heart problem and hadn't been looking well that night to begin with."

"That's the thing." The girl edged closer to Casey. "I heard Mia tell Ruby that Mac had too much medication in his system. Someone overdosed him. *Homicidio*, got it?"

She got it. She just didn't buy it. Casey had googled *dilated cardio-myopathy* and learned that Mac had an enlarged heart, which made it weak. Digoxin was the correct medication, and she'd only given him one pill. How could he have had too much in his system, unless he'd taken a pill or two earlier? Casey started to comment about an accidental overdose, when Mercedes shushed her.

She reached for Casey's hands and in a slightly raised voice said, "Your nails are disgusting." She looked at the door. "Ruby, can I get my nail kit?"

After several seconds, Ruby poked her head in the door. "Were you callin'?"

"I need my nail stuff."

Had Ruby been eavesdropping? Was this why Mercedes didn't want to continue the conversation? The girl flashed Casey a grim smile as they waited in silence for Ruby's return.

A minute later, Ruby reappeared carrying a small bag. She glanced at Casey with an unreadable expression. How trustworthy was Ruby, and did she also believe that Mac had been murdered?

"Have fun," Ruby said, then left.

Was she still outside the door? Casey listened but heard only distant chatter.

"Bring your chair closer," Mercedes said, sounding a little more cheerful. "What color do you want?"

"I'm open to suggestions." Casey watched the girl rummage through the bag. Keeping her voice just above a whisper, she asked, "Any idea which employees Mac wanted to fire?"

"Practically all of them," she whispered back. "No one cares about their job." She peered at Casey. "You can't trust anyone to do or say the right thing."

"Including the residents?"

"*Anyone*," Mercedes answered, peering at her.

Casey tried to obtain the names of individuals Mac had planned to fire, but Mercedes stopped cooperating. Maybe she didn't know, or maybe she was worried that Ruby would overhear. It could be that she simply liked playing games, holding power over people. The conversation drifted to music and movies, anything that didn't involve Fraserview. Casey tried a few casual prompts about Mercedes's personal life, but the girl diverted the questions with finesse. Clearly, Mercedes was intelligent and sensitive, but there was a dark cloud hanging over her, as if she were resigned to an unhappy fate.

While Mercedes painted her nails turquoise, Casey pondered the possibility of murder. If the police believed Mac's death was suspicious, wouldn't his office be taped off? And who were the people Mac supposedly wanted gone? A union employee worried enough about his or her job to kill Mac would mean that Mac had something really serious on that individual. Non-union staff were easier to let go, but their jobs didn't pay well enough to kill for, especially since the job wouldn't exist in a few more months. Unless the murder—if it truly was—had nothing to do with employment issues.

By the time her nails were finished and the superficial chitchat had run its course, Casey was eager to leave Mercedes to have a word with Ruby. The possibility—remote as it was—that Mac might have been murdered was getting to her. She headed back down the hall and found Ruby in her office.

"Hi, Ruby. Have you got a minute?"

"Sure." She moved away from the keyboard as Casey sat in the chair opposite the desk. "How was your visit? Did she give you trouble?"

"She was fine." Casey hesitated. "Does Mercedes have any family support?"

"No, her fadda's in prison and madda's dead. All she got is her uncle."

"Is he in his mid-thirties with thinning hair?"

"Dat's him, Cristano Cruz." She clicked her tongue. "In Jamaica, we'd say he's a *ginnal*—someone you can't trust."

"Why?"

"Dunno for certain." She shook her head and frowned. "But der's something about him."

Casey recalled the way Cruz had surveyed the residents in the visiting area Friday night, and how Tanya had given him furtive glances. Although he had been helpful with Mac, he sure left in a hurry when the police showed up. There was another troubling issue, one that could force her to reveal part of her conversation with Mercedes, but she had to ask.

"There's a rumor going around that Mac died from an overdose of digoxin. Do you know if it's true?"

Ruby gave her a look, then rubbed her chin. "It'll all be coming out anyway." She paused. "Mia found out—don't ask me how—that Mac had ten times more of dat medicine in his body than he should have."

Casey slumped back in her chair. "But I only gave him one pill."

"Don't worry yourself. Mac hadn't been taking 'em very long. Could have got confused and done it to hisself."

"Maybe." She recalled the overturned thermos, the contents dripping onto the carpet. "You don't think someone could have deliberately overdosed him, do you?"

Ruby's eyes grew round. "What for? Mac was a good man. This place is closin'. Nobody cares 'bout nothin'."

"That's what I thought." Until tonight.

It would be risky to raise the topic of potential firings with Ruby. It was also quite possible that Mac had kept his computer password protected to prevent staff from learning about his decisions. If that was true, then he'd failed.

Casey left the unit, her thoughts swirling. Staff would have had easier access to Mac's medication than residents, and they'd have known that he didn't wear his jacket much. It would be natural to assume that the digoxin was in one of those pockets. God, had Mac really been murdered?

Feeling more than a little uneasy, Casey hastily signed out, then collected her coat and purse from Rawan, who then returned to perfecting her makeup. Outside, she spotted Phyllis shutting the door of a little blue Smart car.

"Forgot my ciggies." Phyllis shook one out of the pack, lit it, and took a long drag. She blew smoke toward the sky. "Dark night in a dark month. No end in sight."

Casey shoved her hands in her pockets. "I've heard that not everyone is sad about Mac's death, and that he might have had problems with some of his staff." Reaching out to the cleaning lady didn't seem as big a risk as it would be with the youth supervisors. "Just between us, do you think it was true?"

Phyllis looked at the ground for a few moments, then peered at Casey through those big, blue-framed lenses. "Sometimes, there's more to what you know, and sometimes there isn't. The hard part's realizing what's what." She took another drag on her cigarette. "My father believed he knew what was best." She blew the smoke out. "Always preached that the Lord was on his side. Thought it justified everything."

A second reference to her father. Was Phyllis stuck in the past? "He sounds a bit fanatical."

Phyllis grunted. "Didn't know I'd married a man just like him until it was too late. But then he died. Took forever, mind you."

"Your husband was religious?"

She barked out a laugh. "No. Not religious." Her amusement faded. "Only thing he believed in was his fists." Phyllis looked up at the sky once more. "We all make terrible choices now and then. Watch out for yours."

A word of advice, or a warning? "I will." Casey hurried to her car.

TWELVE

WITH AN UNEVENTFUL EVENING OF volunteering now over, Casey waited in Fraserview's parking lot for her car to warm up while she listened to a phone message from Amy.

"I'm sorry for my anger last night. I realize you had to call the RCMP." She sounded shaky. "I decided not to search for Justin this morning. As long as Tanya's with him, it would be pointless. I believe he's still close by, though. I gave him food for only two days and no money." She paused. "I'll see you at work."

Casey closed her eyes. Poor Amy sounded so defeated. Didn't Justin care what he was putting his grandmother through? Amy had said that homeless teens slept under the nearby bridge, and thought that Justin might be hanging out there too. A plan began to form.

Casey phoned Lou, but before she could propose her idea he said, "I caught Devon at the back door and told him to leave."

"Damn that kid. Did he give you any trouble?"

"No, and the alarm's on."

"Do you think Summer would have let him in?"

"Tough to say. She saw me running through the kitchen and out the back door, but she looked more startled than guilty. I don't know what surprised her more: Devon's appearance or me running through the damn house."

Casey wished the frost on her windshield would evaporate faster. "I'll talk to her. Meanwhile, how about a little trip tonight?"

"It's already after nine. Where would we go on a Sunday night?"

"Coquitlam. My gut is telling me that Justin's hiding out beneath a bridge on the Lougheed Highway. Apparently, it's used as a refuge by homeless kids. Amy believes he's hiding nearby."

"Come on, Casey. It's not your problem."

"I contributed to her troubles. If I hadn't made my appearance so obvious, Justin might have gone with Amy last night."

"Didn't you say that the girl was controlling him?"

"Yes, but he did go back to see Amy. He might have had a change of heart and decided to stand up to Tanya."

"Or he might have wanted something else from his grandmother."

"Possibly." Once Tanya realized there was no cash in the backpack, she could have ordered Justin to go get some. "Listen, things are strained between Amy and me. I made things worse and now I need to make them right. I could really use your help."

"You didn't make things worse, and what if your plan backfires? Justin could have hooked up with teens who are high, or violent, or both. What if they're carrying weapons?"

"I know the risks." Lou knew how often she dealt with homeless people on the job. She'd had her share of rides through the seedier parts of the city, dealing with people who were high on something and demanding a free ride, or those in serious need of a fix and medical help. "Being a homeless fugitive is a bigger risk for Justin. He's not street smart, Lou." She heard a long sigh. "I think Summer should come too. She needs to see that her life doesn't totally suck when compared to other people's."

"You've got a point there."

"If I exchange food and cash for a little information, I'm sure it'll be fine. Still, safety in numbers, right?"

"What happens if Summer doesn't want to go?"

"She doesn't have a choice. This is her wakeup call as much as it is Justin's."

→   →   →

"I CAN'T BELIEVE you dragged me out here," Summer grumbled from behind Casey. "My boots are muddy. It's freezing. My hood won't stay up in this stupid wind!"

"Lower your voice," Lou said. "We don't know who's ahead."

It had taken an intense discussion to convince Summer that homeless kids might respond better to someone closer to their own age, and that leaving her home alone was not an option. It was a decision Casey was starting to regret. Once they had parked, and a light drizzle began, Summer wanted to wait in the car; however, Casey squashed that idea. Summer tried to argue, but Casey was in no mood for debate and whining. She'd ordered Summer out of the vehicle.

Lou had stayed out of the conversation. In fact, he hadn't said much since they left the house. Didn't need to. She'd felt his trepidation from the moment she arrived home. Still, all things considered, this wasn't a bad trek. She'd googled a shorter way to the bridge—picking up the Westwood trail at the end of Davies Avenue, south from where she and Amy had been. The only glitch in the plan was that the homeless kids could be hanging out on the other side of the river. Though if that were the case, it would be simpler to cross the bridge on foot. She hoped they wouldn't have to do so. The row houses on their left lit the path they were following. To their right, the river, although not particularly high, rushed by with menacing speed.

"Just so you know, I wouldn't have had Devon over while you guys were out," Summer said. "It's not like I have to see him every night."

Casey glanced at Summer. Yesterday, when Devon stormed out of her bedroom, it was as if she could barely cope with his departure. Why the sudden change in attitude? Or was she playing games? Whatever the reason, Casey didn't want to discuss the boy right now.

"I haven't seen your girlfriends in a while, though I guess you all hang out at school." She waited for a response, but none came. "Have you been socializing with other friends, besides Devon?"

"They don't like Devon, and he doesn't like them."

"Oh." Summer's friendships had come and gone a fair bit since Rhonda's imprisonment. To Casey's relief, she had started socializing with a decent group of girls—that is, until Devon appeared on the scene. "Doesn't he have any guy friends to hang with?"

"He says I'm all he needs."

Alarm bells clanged in Casey's head. She glanced over her shoulder at Lou but couldn't decipher his expression in the shadows.

The increasing traffic noise on Lougheed meant they were almost at the bridge. How many people would they find there? How old, how paranoid, and how violent? Casey was starting to second-guess the wisdom of this teachable moment. "Summer, maybe you should stay back a bit."

"I'm *not* waiting out here in the rain."

"Whoever's under the bridge could be hostile. There might be adults as well as teens."

"So? Won't they need food too?" She charged past Casey.

"Come back here!" Casey called out. Why wouldn't that girl listen?

"I'll get her." Lou started to jog but slipped on wet leaves. "Shit!" His arms pinwheeled, causing his flashlight to shine on trees, sky, and ground. His right foot slipped out from under him and down he went, landing on his butt. As Casey helped Lou to his feet, Summer disappeared.

"Crap," Casey muttered, hurrying after her.

At the bridge, the path veered to the right and sloped down. Casey followed it until she was under the bridge and realized that the east and westbound lanes were two separate structures. She found Summer staring up at a fairly wide cement ledge beneath the eastbound lanes. Two people in sleeping bags were stretched out on the ledge, end to end. Their faces were turned away and neither moved. Large boulders covered the slope between the ledge and the path.

Casey moved past Summer and found herself standing back in the rain. She glanced up at the gap between lanes. Spots of light on the other side of a cluster of bushes caught her attention.

"Stay behind me," she said to Summer and Lou, who'd caught up.

The moment Casey stepped past the bushes the lights vanished. Using her own flashlight, she zeroed in on four people to her left. They were sitting upright but immersed in sleeping bags so that only their heads were showing. There was no ledge here, or boulders, and the slope wasn't sharp. The dirt-covered ground offered plenty of room for others. Clothes spilled out of backpacks near the group and garbage littered the ground. Flashlights suddenly blinded her.

"We're not cops and we're not here to hurt you," Casey said, shielding her eyes.

It took a few seconds, but gradually the lights were lowered. Three of the people wore tuques, but she couldn't distinguish facial features. The shortest person, who was closer to Casey, sported a wool cap with earflaps. A scarf covered much of this person's face, making it impossible to determine age or gender, but she was guessing this was a female. The noise from the westbound vehicles directly above them filled the air for long seconds.

Once the traffic had passed, a male voice bellowed, "What the fuck do you want?"

Casey spotted a knife in the beam of his flashlight. She placed her hand in front of Summer and held her breath, praying he didn't throw it at them.

"Are you deaf?" he yelled. "I asked you a question."

Lou stepped in front of Summer and grabbed Casey's hand with his. She gave it a quick squeeze and held on.

"I'm looking for two teenagers," Casey said. "A boy and a girl who were in this area last night."

The person closest to them pulled down the scarf and said, "Why?" Definitely a female, but not Tanya.

"I'm a friend of a relative who's really worried about them."

The traffic noise again thundered overhead. The woman turned to her companions.

When it was quiet again, the woman said, "Got any smokes?"

"No. Sorry."

Summer removed a pack from her pocket. Oh, hell. Hadn't they gone through this nonsense a few months ago? Summer had promised she wouldn't try cigarettes again.

"They're Devon's," Summer said, as if reading Casey's thoughts. "He's not allowed to smoke at home, and his mom checks his stuff."

This could be true. Devon reeked of smoke so much it would be amazing if his mother hadn't noticed. Casey was about to reach for the pack when Summer scrambled up the slope and handed four cigarettes to the girl. Casey stayed close behind her, ready to pull Summer back if necessary. While the kids lit their smokes, Casey got a closer look at the group. Teenagers, who looked to be between fifteen and seventeen years old.

Summer headed back down the slope. Casey saw the revulsion on her face and wondered what had put her off most. The stink of garbage, filthy bedding, and unwashed bodies, or the grime on their faces?

"Did any of you see the couple in the past twenty-four hours?" Casey asked.

The kids looked at one another, and then the girl said, "We don't give out information for free."

They might not have any info at all, and what was to stop them from making things up? Traffic again rumbled above their heads. Still, it was worth a try. Casey took a ten-dollar bill from her pocket and held it high. "This is all we have."

One of the guys snorted. "I get more from panhandling."

Moron. "Look, it's quick, easy money, and I brought food."

The guy with the knife said, "Any beer?"

"No."

"Take it or leave it," Lou said. "We haven't got all night."

The blade glinted. "What's to stop us from just takin' it and kicking your ass out of here?"

"A 911 call to the cops," Lou replied, raising his cell phone.

Casey wished he'd keep quiet.

"Give us the pack," the girl said, "and I'll tell you what I heard."

"I need to verify that we're talking about the right people first," Casey replied.

The kids consulted with one another, and then the girl took a drag on her cigarette. "I heard them fighting yesterday afternoon. The guy wanted to turn himself in, and the chick said if he did, she'd tell the cops he pushed Brady down the stairs . . . whoever that is."

Good. Not a wasted trip. Casey edged closer as she removed burgers, pop, and bags of chips from her backpack. She handed the food to the girl, who passed most of it to her friends. "What else did they say?"

"The guy said the cops think he did it anyway. That's when the chick said she'd make up stuff about him dealing drugs. The guy got pissed off, and then the chick went all emo and said, . . . *because you'll leave me and I love you. You can't leave!* It was hilarious."

"They actually said all this in front of you?" Lou asked.

"They didn't know I was peeing behind the bushes nearby. The chick freaked out when I stood up. It was awesome." She laughed.

"What else did you hear?" Casey asked.

The girl took another drag on the cigarette. "The chick said they should go to Alberta because she has family there."

Oh, no. "When did you last see them?"

"About an hour before the cops came looking for them last night."

If the girl was telling the truth, it meant that they'd spent the night hiding elsewhere. "Have you seen them today?"

The girl turned and was mumbling to her companions when voices on the trail ahead caught Casey's attention. It sounded like a heated discussion. As two people appeared, Casey recognized the blue ski jacket Amy had given Justin. They spotted Casey and stopped. She shone her flashlight on Justin's startled face. Tanya's surprise turned to a scowl.

"Justin?" Casey called out. "It's me, Casey, Amy's friend. I need to talk to you."

Tanya grabbed Justin's arm and tried to haul him back up the trail. He jerked his arm free.

"Come on!" Tanya shouted. "She'll turn us in!"

"Justin, please." Casey stepped forward.

"What do you want?" he asked.

"To help you before things get worse."

"I told you. She'll turn us in!" Tanya grabbed his arm again.

"You can't help," he said. "You don't know."

"Don't know what?"

Tanya started to pull Justin up the curving trail. This time he didn't resist.

"Wait!" Casey shouted, but both of them had taken off running. "Lou, stay with Summer!"

"Casey, don't!" he replied.

She had to. This was her best shot at bringing Justin in. Casey cleared the bridge and followed the curving path. When it straightened out she spotted Justin's jacket ahead. "Justin, please! Let's talk!"

The trail was slippery in spots with mud and wet, decaying leaves. Casey swung her flashlight from the ground to the kids, then back to the ground to keep from slipping. She jumped over a puddle. When she looked up again, the kids had disappeared.

Casey squinted into the darkness, searching for signs of movement, a glimmer of blue. She ran faster, swiping at the raindrops in her eyes. There were plenty of places to hide along the trail. Casey's breathing grew ragged and her blood pounded so hard she could scarcely hear anything. She thought she saw a flash of blue ahead, just off the path. She kept going until Tanya leapt out from behind a bush. Something sharp and hard struck Casey's forehead.

"Shit!" She clamped her hand over the source of the pain and felt the blood pour out.

THIRTEEN

AS THE M5 BUS PULLED away from the stop, Casey shifted uneasily in her seat. What was up with the shoplifters? They'd boarded together, but all three boys now sat separately. Blondie chose the front, the freckled kid went straight to the back, and Stocky grabbed a seat in the middle. Stocky, sitting nearest to Casey, tossed the occasional glance her way. Surely one small bandage on her forehead didn't warrant this much attention. Unnoticeable as she hoped the cut was, she had to admit that after three days it still hurt when she absently touched it. More stinging, though, was her failure to bring Justin and Tanya in.

Watching Stocky, Casey wondered if he recognized her from when she'd followed him to the donair shop on Saturday. The boys couldn't know her reason for being on the bus, could they? This was only her second ride. She'd never been in GenMart while the suspects were there. But following them off the bus today would be impossible.

Casey looked out the window, her senses on full alert, until Stocky eventually pulled the bell cord and headed for the exit. The kid was getting off the bus two stops earlier than he had last time. Stocky sneered at Casey, as if blaming her for his early exit. Was this a test? Were the boys waiting to see if she'd follow?

As Stocky exited, Casey made a point of not looking at him. The bus continued on. Her attention turned to Blondie, who was watching her. He quickly looked away, then departed at the next stop. Freckles exited the one after that. She wasn't surprised to see him also steal a furtive glance in her direction. How had these junior criminals learned about her so quickly? Casey checked her watch. Stan would still be in the office. She hit speed dial and soon found herself grimacing at her supervisor's snarky tone.

"What do you mean they *made* you?" Stan asked. "How the hell could that have happened?"

"I don't know. Maybe when I walked past the donair shop the kid got a better look at me than I thought."

"But why would that arouse suspicion? You only rode with them once, and that was four days ago. What you just described sounds like a pre-arranged plan to test your responses. The kids are either paranoid or they know something."

"That's what worries me." Casey's thoughts swirled. "I wonder if there's a leak inside the store."

"Could be, I suppose. But that's a slippery slope, Casey."

"I know, yet it's the only logical reason I can think of. It also explains why the kids have been so successful." She hesitated. "Should I talk to Kendal about a leak, or would you rather approach the manager?"

"Let's do both. I need to talk to him and the police about it. If they want us to continue surveillance, Marie will have to take over."

Damn. She hated being pulled from an assignment. "I thought she lived too far away from the store."

"We now know where the suspects exit, and it's not far from Marie's home. She won't have to go as far as GenMart to hook up with the bus."

"If I stay on as a decoy, they won't be watching Marie." Paying two security team members for the same assignment would be a hard sell, though.

"You just don't give up, do ya?"

"It's one of the reasons you made me second-in-command, as I recall."

"True. So, let's get to the bottom of this."

→   →   →

CASEY WASN'T SURE if coincidence played a role in fate, but when she entered her apartment and saw Marie Crenshaw cozying up to Lou on the sofa, her head damn near imploded. The woman was as nervy as ever, and, by the looks of things, her feelings for Lou hadn't faded.

Marie sat up. "What happened to your forehead?"

"Just a little mishap." She hung her coat, trying hard to hide her irritation. "What brings you here?"

"Union business with Lou."

That couldn't be done by phone? Casey zeroed in on him, noting that his Everyone Is Entitled to My Opinion T-shirt had grown tighter since he first started wearing it, thanks to diligent workouts. This fact wouldn't be lost on Marie. Casey caught Lou's concerned expression, but whether it was about her assignment or this awkward moment was hard to tell.

When he saw the cut to her forehead after Sunday night's chase, he became angry. Blood had been streaming down her face and she had to admit she'd looked hideous. Lou hadn't said a word on the ride home, nor had he mentioned the incident since, which she'd more or less expected. Whenever Lou was upset about something he opted for silence. Although she respected his desire to deal with things on his own—she often felt that desire herself—she'd begun to wonder if it was the best approach for a couple now living together.

"Everything okay?" Lou asked, sweeping the hair from his eyes.

"Yeah, fine." She wasn't about to discuss this afternoon's setback in front of her rival. "What's the union business?"

"We need one more signature for certification," Marie replied. "Since Lou expressed interest a few weeks back, I came here to see if he'd sign. God knows I'm not getting enough hours to bump into him at work."

Clearly, Stan hadn't yet called her about the M5 assignment. "I thought lots of staff wanted to unionize. Why do you need Lou's signature?"

"They bailed." Marie tucked thick red hair behind her ears and turned to Lou. "If you would just sign in a couple of places, we'll be done and I can deliver the papers to Ingrid."

Then the rumors were true: Ingrid was driving the union bid. Casey headed for the kitchen. It wasn't a good idea for Lou to get involved, but saying so in front of Marie would create tension. She sure as hell wasn't in the mood for an argument.

Casey entered the kitchen and found, to her disappointment, that Lou once again hadn't started supper. She unwrapped a pack of frozen chicken thighs and set the microwave to thaw.

"I need time to read all this before I sign anything," Lou said to Marie.

"Ingrid wants this wrapped up today. She'll give us grief if we don't."

"She either waits or no deal."

Smiling, Casey rummaged through the fridge for a marinade. Lou didn't like being pushed into decisions. The harder people pushed, the slower he moved.

"You won't back out, will you?" Marie said. "You're one of the few people at Mainland whose word means something."

"I never said I was in, Marie. I only said I was interested to hear what you had to say."

"Just keep in mind that we're doing this for all staff, especially those who can barely pay the rent and feed their kids. Two single parents are already using food banks."

"As I said, I'll read everything over."

"Don't take too long," Marie said. "Walk me downstairs?"

Casey's jaw clenched. God, that woman was pathetic. Casey emerged from the kitchen as Marie was saying, "Unionization will happen, sooner or later, Lou. No doubt about it."

Casey was betting on later. It wasn't that she wouldn't welcome a higher wage and better benefits, but she believed Stan when he said that the company could go under if forced to suddenly pay significantly higher wages and benefits. Given that some of her father's assets, discovered only a couple of years ago, were still in legal limbo and the house she grew up in—and had inherited—hadn't yet sold, keeping any wage was essential. The last thing she wanted was for Mainland Public Transport to go under.

Before Lou followed Marie out the door, he glanced over his shoulder at Casey and shrugged.

By the time he returned, Casey was placing the chicken in the oven. "That took a while," she said. "Was Marie making a last desperate plea for the cause?"

"No. I saw Summer puttering around her kitchen and stopped to see how she was doing. I've hardly seen her the last few days."

"Neither have I. She wasn't in the kitchen when I came home."

Summer hadn't talked about their excursion Sunday night either. The homeless kids had laughed when they saw Casey's bloodied face, said she deserved it. That's when Summer told them to shut their mouths. A shouting match erupted, and Lou pulled Summer away before things got out of hand. Casey figured Summer needed time to process the teens' callousness and disrespect, never mind their living conditions.

"Is she okay?" Casey asked.

"She said she was fine, but she sounded annoyed. Probably still ticked about being grounded. Devon hasn't been around since Saturday, which has to be a record."

"I'd better go talk to her." She headed downstairs and found Summer poking something in a pot on the stove. Cheyenne was asleep in her bed. "What are you cooking?"

"Perogies." She didn't look up. "They should have risen to the top by now."

Casey peered into the barely boiling pot. "Did you boil the water before you put them in?"

"Oh." Summer plunked the fork on the counter and began emptying the dishwasher.

"How did things go at school today?"

"I did better on the math quiz."

"Excellent." She paused. "Everything else okay?"

Summer tossed cutlery into the drawer. "Is it ever?"

Meaning what? "Has Devon been bugging you to let him come over?"

"Yeah. I told him no."

Casey waited, but Summer didn't add anything. "If you want to talk, I'll be home all evening." She started out of the room.

"Casey?"

She turned around. "Yeah?"

Summer looked like she wanted to say something but then changed her mind. "Nothing." She put some plates away. "I might come up later."

Good. Maybe she was coming around. "Any time." Casey walked down the hall but only got as far as the staircase before her cell phone rang.

"Hey, girl. I'm on a break at juvie," Kendal said. "You won't believe what I learned."

Yesterday, Casey told Kendal that not everyone was upset about Mac's death, and asked her to keep her ears open for dirt. Had she learned something new?

"Is it about staff?"

"You bet. Residents said that Oksana and Mac were having problems, though no one seemed to know why, except that she's a lousy cook and a nasty human being."

"She must be one of the staff Mac planned to let go."

"Yep, and there'd also been friction between Amir and Mac. Word is that Amir didn't think Mac was running this place properly. Now, he and Winson are conspiring to keep Mia from getting the director's job permanently because they don't think she's competent either."

"Who told you that?"

"The girl with the dreadlocks, Roxanne."

"Given Amir's attitude about women in Fraserview, she's probably right."

"I also met that youth supervisor, Ruby, you mentioned, and she said that Mia's in the middle of a custody battle."

"You're kidding. I didn't know she had kids."

"Yeah, she has two. Six and eight years old. Apparently, Mia had some long-term virus that caused chronic fatigue to the point where she could barely function."

Kendal had a talent for getting information out of people, but for Ruby to discuss another employee's personal life was out of line. On the other hand, Ruby had obviously found a kindred soul in Kendal, who was a true lover of gossip.

"Did Ruby say why Mia's having trouble getting the kids back?" Casey asked.

"It's all the hours she works. Seems that Mia's an ambitious workaholic."

Was Ruby's word completely reliable, though? "I have news, too. Your shoplifters showed up today." After describing the boys' behavior,

Casey added, "Who besides the managers and loss prevention team know about me?"

"No one."

As far as Kendal knew. "Is it possible that an employee overheard something and tipped them off?"

"We've been careful, Casey. Maybe the boys recognized you or didn't like the way you were looking at them."

"I made a point of not looking at the boys." She'd worked in security for seven years and knew what she was doing, damn it. "I'm sorry, Kendal, but haven't you wondered how the kids have been so successful?"

"Of course. Don't you think I already checked staff out?"

"Sorry. I'm sure you did. I just need to make sure we've covered all our bases."

"I'll check again." A moment later, she hung up.

Kendal's abrupt, irritated tone was understandable. A loss prevention officer with five years of experience would resent the implication that she'd slipped up. At least Kendal had never been one to hold grudges. Still, the shoplifters' success had to be a sore spot for her. Even in high school, Kendal had taken a great deal of pride in her accomplishments. Who else but an insider could be making her look incompetent?

FOURTEEN

CASEY STEPPED INTO THE GIRLS' unit, noting familiar faces and a new resident. She hadn't looked forward to volunteering tonight, but she was hoping to confirm Kendal's info and see what else could be learned. The trick would be finding people willing to talk.

Mercedes emerged from the back hallway. "How'd you get that cut on your head?"

"I bumped into something a few days ago." Maybe getting rid of the bandage had been a mistake.

"Looks gross. Wanna play Scrabble till my uncle shows up?"

"Why do you always get time with volunteers?" Roxanne said, approaching. "I play better than you, so I should get a turn."

"Maybe she likes me better, *macha*."

"Don't call me that!"

"It doesn't mean anything bad." Mercedes rolled her eyes. "Go play your stupid game. I'll be busy soon anyway."

"I should see if the supervisor has anything planned for me first," Casey said. "Who's on duty?"

"Amir," Mercedes replied.

"Really? I thought he was in charge of Unit Three."

"Not tonight." Roxanne smirked. "Mia likes to play games too."

Bloody wonderful. Casey turned and saw Amir in the youth supervisor's office, his brow furrowed as he talked on the phone. As she drew nearer, she heard him say, "What's the big deal? The kid will be put in the Special Unit, so get Winson to process him. I'm too busy with this harem from hell."

Was Amir talking about Justin's return? Amy had called this morning to tell her that he and Tanya had been picked up, and that Justin could be sent back to Fraserview. Amy had asked Casey to see if he was all right. Still feeling bad about the rift between them, Casey agreed to try and check in on him. She'd confessed her attempt to bring Justin in Sunday night. Amy had thanked her for trying, but didn't ask for details. Maybe she wished Casey hadn't bothered.

Amir plunked the phone down.

"Roxanne wants to play Scrabble," Casey said from the doorway. "Is that okay?"

"Fine, but when Mercedes's visitor arrives, I want you to escort her to the visiting area. Make sure she doesn't take any detours." His dark eyes didn't blink. "Think you can manage that?"

"No problem." Asshole.

Roxanne had already set up the board. As she offered Casey the bag of tiles, Casey glimpsed the scars on her hand. Some were small round burns that looked like they could have been made with a cigarette. Others were cuts. One stretched across the back of her hand from thumb to pinky. While Roxanne chose her tiles, Mercedes browsed through the bookshelves near their table. Roxanne glared at her for a few moments before focusing on the tiles.

Casey made a point of keeping her voice low. "How are things with you?"

She shrugged. "I'm out of this shithole soon."

"Great."

Roxanne studied her tiles. "If you say so." She looked up. "You know Justin, right?"

Uh-oh. "Not really. I work with a relative of his and met him a couple of times when he was little. Why do you ask?"

Mercedes took a step toward the table.

Leaning forward, Roxanne whispered, "Tanya doesn't like you."

Casey's forehead twinged. "I know." The feeling was mutual. She moved her tiles around. "Did you know she was going to take off?"

Roxanne chewed her lower lip as she studied her letters. "No, and I'm pissed that she left me alone." She placed a word on the board. *Grinder.*

"Any idea how she slipped past staff?" Casey worked on her tiles.

"No." The answer came a little too quickly.

"Makes Mia look kind of bad, doesn't it?"

"Mia wasn't in the unit when Tanya left." She removed tiles from the bag. "She was supposedly trying to save Mac's life."

"Supposedly?"

Roxanne glared at Mercedes. "Why don't you stop making such a lame attempt to listen in?"

Mercedes spun around. "Like you have anything worth saying."

"We both know I do."

Interesting. Maybe this girl did know some things. Casey watched Mercedes stomp to a nearby table, then sit with her back to them.

Roxanne looked at Casey with smug satisfaction, and then her expression grew serious as she mumbled, "Mia's a two-headed snake you don't want to mess with."

Mac's words about rules and boundaries hovered in back of Casey's mind. She didn't want to get either of them in trouble, but the more she learned about Fraserview, the more she saw that residents weren't the only ones breaking rules and boundaries.

Casey placed the word *tour* on the board. "Why wouldn't I want to mess with Mia?"

"You shouldn't have used your *u*," Roxanne said. "If you get a *q* you're screwed."

"I'll take my chances." Casey fumbled in the bag for new tiles. "Do people think she might have caused Mac's death?"

Roxanne looked up from her tiles, her eyes sharp and wary. She then turned to look at Mercedes, who was still at the table, thumbing through a magazine. "Some do."

"Do you?"

She shrugged. "Dunno."

"I've heard that certain staff think Tanya and Justin had something to do with Mac's death."

"Yeah, right." Roxanne snorted. "People need to make others look bad so nobody looks too closely at them." Anger flashed across her face. "It's all about control and greed. Same old fucking story."

Roxanne grabbed the bag and seemed to be looking for specific letters. What the hell was she up to? As her search quickened, Casey worried that the girl was about to snap. Roxanne smacked tiles onto the board, separate from the other words. She stared at Casey and then nodded in Mercedes's direction. Casey read *Mias snitch*. It took a couple of seconds for her to realize that *Mias* needed an apostrophe. Was this why Mercedes stayed close by, or did Roxanne like badmouthing her enemies?

"I see," Casey murmured.

Roxanne swept the two words away as she murmured, "Outsiders need to know that Mac's death was no accident, but none of the kids did it."

Mercedes had offered a motive, and now Roxanne was confirming staff involvement. But hadn't the girl just said that people needed to make others look bad to divert suspicion? Juvie teens would be experts at this.

Amir's voice shattered the quiet. "Mercedes, your visitor's here. The volunteer will take you down." He directed a better-do-this-right look at Casey.

"Be back shortly," she said to Roxanne.

Once Casey and Mercedes were in the corridor, Mercedes said, "Don't believe anything Roxanne tells you. She's, like, the biggest liar here, and crazy. Attacks people for no reason."

And Mercedes was just a sweet, innocent angel. "Got it." Should she mention that Roxanne also believed Mac's death was no accident? Would it help or make things worse between them?

Mia was talking to Phyllis outside the first aid room. "There's still mud on the floor, and you dropped a banana peel while emptying the garbage. Get it right, Phyllis." She marched away.

Phyllis gave Casey a faint smile. "Frosty night, inside and out." She swished a mop in a bucket of dirty water.

Mercedes kept walking, but Casey hung back. "Bad night, huh?"

"For some more than others. Mind you, coming here's always a gamble."

"I suppose it is."

Cristano Cruz stepped out from the visitors' area. As Mercedes joined her uncle, Cruz gave Casey a brief nod. Returning the gesture, she watched the pair disappear inside.

"That's the bloke who helped you with Mac, isn't it?" Phyllis said.

"Yes. Mercedes's uncle, Cristano Cruz."

Phyllis's sweater fell from the cart's handle. As she bent down to pick it up, she said, "Wonder when the police will arrest him."

Casey was taken aback. "Why would they?"

"Well, it's common knowledge, isn't it? Mac died from too much medication, and Cruz hated him."

Geez, did everyone in Fraserview know about the meds? "What did Mac do to earn his hatred?"

"The uncle was here too much and upset the girl, so Mac restricted his visiting time. They had words about it." Phyllis shook her head. "Bloody foreigners."

"How could Cruz have messed with Mac's medication without someone seeing?"

Phyllis shrugged. "Visitors' room is opposite Mac's office. Mac didn't stay there much, but he always left his jacket behind. Granted, it was a gamble." She peered at Casey through her blue-framed glasses. "Lots of people take gambles. You meet all sorts on a Saturday night at the casinos."

Why was Phyllis bringing this up? "Like who?"

She winked and held her finger to her lips. "It's a secret, dearie." She picked up her mop and went back to work.

Why would Phyllis point the finger at Cruz for killing Mac? What an odd woman. Casey was debating whether to pursue this when two enormous sheriffs stepped into the building with a handcuffed Justin between them. It was hard to believe that exactly one week had passed since he and Tanya escaped. In the five nights since she had last seen him, it looked like Justin hadn't had an easy time of it. Dried mud caked his jeans and ski jacket. His blond hair was matted and greasy. He had dark circles under his eyes and his lower lip was swollen. Casey could almost feel his despair. Despite the fact that he'd brought a lot of this on himself, she still felt sorry for the kid.

The sheriffs stopped at reception, then headed for Mia's office. One of them went inside while the other stayed with Justin. Casey fought the urge to run up to him and ask if he was okay. The boy met her gaze. She saw the fear and the shame, then the struggle not to fall apart as he looked down at the floor in defeat.

FIFTEEN

AS SOON AS CASEY ENTERED Mainland Public Transport's security department, she felt the tension in the room. Where was the usual Monday morning chitchat? Why was everyone already working? At least Amy was behaving normally, but she rarely gossiped anyway. Her fingers danced over the keyboard as her gaze shifted from the computer screen to Stan's notes.

"Good morning," Amy said, still typing. "Justin wants to see me, thank heaven. I'm going to Fraserview tonight."

"That's great, Amy." Casey still wasn't sure if calling Amy after Justin's readmission had been a good move; however, she'd seemed grateful for the news and relieved that Justin was separated from Tanya. Casey didn't provide details about the boy's physical condition. Amy would learn more when she visited.

"Thanks for all you've tried to do for my grandson," Amy said. "Now that he's willing to see me, I'm quite sure his lawyer and I can help him."

Tried to do was accurate, yet it still bothered her. "He's lucky to have you both." The boy would need all the help he could get.

Amy checked her watch. "Stan should be ready for you."

Casey wasn't sure if she was ready for him. She'd told Stan that Kendal was checking out GenMart's staff, and Stan confirmed that he'd called the manager, but rather than elaborate, Stan had asked to see her. She figured he had news or a new strategy that involved Marie, both of which created more anxiety than she wanted to admit. Speaking of anxiety, Casey observed the accounting and human resources staff at the far end of the room.

"Why does everyone look so serious?" she murmured to Amy.

Amy scribbled on a notepad, which she handed to Casey.

Gwyn knows about union bid. Trouble coming!

Oh, crap. Had Lou signed Marie's documents? Casey handed the pad back to Amy, who ripped the note into little pieces. Casey had been waiting for Lou to tell her whether he'd officially endorsed the certification process. Time to find out. Although Labour Relations Board rules prevented employers from firing employees who wanted to unionize, Gwyn could use ongoing cutbacks as a handy excuse. Lou, who'd never been reprimanded, had a far better track record than Marie and Ingrid and was on his way to a supervisory role. Whether he still would be after this week was another matter.

Stan stepped out of his office. "You're here," he said to Casey. "Come in."

He took a few moments to survey the staff in the room, something Stan normally didn't do. Casey followed him inside and sat at her usual spot in front of his desk.

"The info you provided about that donair shop paid off." Stan settled into his chair. "It turns out the owner fences stolen goods. The kid you followed is his cousin."

"Excellent. Has the man been arrested?"

"Don't know, but we're to continue surveillance." He tapped a pencil on his desk. "The police want more on the other two boys, so Marie's now officially on the job."

Damn.

"No need for that hangdog look. You'll be there too, but as the decoy. Marie will exit when the boys do, and you'll stay put."

"Okay." At least she was still in the game. "Have you figured out how they learned about me?"

"No." Stan scratched his beard. "GenMart's manager is investigating employees."

"Kendal already did that and couldn't find anything, but she's trying again. She doesn't believe the leak's coming from the store."

"A second opinion wouldn't hurt." Stan leaned forward. "From now on, when you get the call from GenMart, you're to phone Marie, pronto."

Great. Just what she wanted to do while rushing out the door. "I take it she's already been briefed?"

"Yes." Stan began shuffling papers. A sure sign that the discussion was over. "Keep me posted."

"Will do."

As Casey left Stan's office, Amy looked up and said, "When's your next volunteer shift?"

"Friday night."

"Maybe I'll see you there."

"I'll look for you." Perhaps Amy wasn't trying to keep her at arm's length after all.

Casey hurried downstairs and out of the admin building. She waited until she was in her car before she phoned Lou.

"Gwyn knows who's behind the union bid and Amy thinks there will be trouble," she blurted. "Please tell me you didn't sign those papers Marie brought over."

No response. "Lou?"

"I did. Gave them to her on Friday."

"Crap! She should never have involved you in the first place." And he shouldn't have let her. "I just hope she hasn't left the papers on MPT property."

"Don't worry about it. There's not a lot Gwyn can do."

"He can come up with excuses to withhold promotions and cut back your hours even more."

"I guess so." He sounded too resigned.

"If Gwyn wants to see you, you'll stand up for yourself, won't you?" Casey asked. His silence worried her. "Lou?"

"You know what he's like." Lou's tone was subdued. "Maybe it's time to move on anyway."

"You can't quit! You've got tons of friends here, and the drivers think you'd make a great supervisor."

"You know as well as I do that what coworkers say and what they really think are often two different things."

"Not this time. Look, I understand why you're thinking about leaving. Gwyn's been a real ass lately, and you could probably get a better-paying job with Coast Mountain, if they're hiring. But isn't it easier to find a new job if you already have one? Don't give up, okay?"

"I'll think about it."

Would he? No way in hell would she let Lou quit under these cir-cumstances. She cursed Marie for stepping foot in their apartment.

SIXTEEN

CASEY JUMPED AT THE SOUND of the phone ringing. She'd been working on her school essay and trying not to worry about Lou's future with Mainland. Two attempts to contact Marie yesterday had gotten him nowhere, and as far as Casey knew, Marie still hadn't returned his voice mail.

"All three shoplifters just entered the store," GenMart's manager said with urgency.

If he was calling, then Kendal was either off duty or busy elsewhere. "On my way." She grabbed her coat and car keys, then dialed Marie's number. She answered on the fourth ring. "The suspects are in GenMart and I'm en route. Can you return Lou's calls later today? It's important."

"I just did. See you soon."

Damn it, she'd have to wait to learn what was said. On the main floor, Casey hurried into the kitchen, surprised to see Summer doing homework. She rarely started before supper.

"I've got to go to GenMart," Casey said, marching to the back door.

Summer looked up, her expression pensive. "For work?"

"Yeah. Lou should be home by suppertime. No friends over while I'm gone, okay? My cell phone's on if you need me."

"See ya." She returned to her textbook.

CASEY HADN'T BEEN at the M5 bus stop long before the blond shoplifter exited GenMart. He stepped up to the curb, apparently looking for the bus. He glanced at the other people standing around, but when he spotted Casey, his gaze lingered. She turned and strolled among the waiting passengers, sneaking a peek at the store's entrance. There was no sign of the others. The hint of a sunny break in the weather had vanished and rain was starting to fall again. Casey pulled up the hood of her coat.

The M5 approached and the other two shoplifters appeared. Freckles glanced at her. His cohorts ignored her. This was Tuesday, a school day. Strange that none of them were sporting backpacks. Casey stood well back from the passengers and boarded last. The bus was standing room only at this point. She exchanged a quick nod with Ingrid, who looked grumpier than usual. Maybe Gwyn had confronted her about the union issue. The boys nudged their way down the aisle, stopping near the center exit. Casey halted about a third of the way down.

As the bus merged into traffic, the boys fidgeted and whispered among themselves. They seemed to be checking out passengers, or perhaps looking for empty seats. When she caught the occasional glance directed at her, each boy quickly looked away. The contrast from last week's hostile stares was odd. Had they stolen something and were afraid she might bust them?

Casey popped a stick of gum in her mouth and chewed to ease the tension. She barely paid attention to the bumper-to-bumper traffic. When the M5 finally reached the next stop, passengers shuffled past her. She noticed that Stocky was staring at her. Since there was no point in pretending to be an innocent bystander, she returned the gesture until the kid backed down.

Another fifteen minutes went by before Ingrid pulled up to the stop where Marie was waiting. Her thick red curls were unmistakable beneath a purple wool hat with the pompom on top. A number of people prepared to exit. The boys stepped back just enough to give them room. Curiously, they didn't grab any of the vacated seats. Marie boarded behind a grisly guy who told Ingrid in raised voice that he'd put in too much money and wanted fifty cents back.

"We don't give change," Ingrid's booming voice replied. "Move down, please."

"I'm not going anywhere without my money!"

"Sir, if you don't move down, you'll have to leave."

"Make me, bitch."

"Get off the damn bus *now*!"

Casey cringed. Ingrid's manners had gotten her into trouble before. Apparently, the reprimands hadn't sunk in.

"Well then, let's see what's in your pocket." He grabbed Ingrid's arm and yanked her out of her chair.

Ingrid grunted and tried to pull her arm back, but he pulled harder. Casey wasn't surprised to see Ingrid's free hand punch him in the gut. Ingrid was a tall, husky woman more than capable of holding her own. The guy released her arm and stumbled backward, right into Marie. She grabbed the back of his jacket and started to drag him off the bus.

Casey took a step forward to help, but a kick to her lower back sent her careening into some passengers. She gripped the nearest seat while more kicks and punches bombarded her legs and back. "Shit!"

Shouts erupted and someone yelled, "Stop that!"

Casey drove her right elbow into the nearest body behind her and heard a loud gasp. Turning, she saw Blondie double over. Freckles swung at her, but she blocked his move and kicked him hard in the shin. As Stocky charged toward her, she spotted the knife in his hand. Casey ducked, dropping to her knees, but a sharp sting burned the top of her ear.

A woman shouted, "I've called the police!"

A middle-aged male passenger bashed Stocky's arm against the pole. The knife fell to the floor. Blondie jumped into the fray and punched the passenger repeatedly. The two boys were beating him down. The man fell backward. God, he needed help. Casey started to pull herself up when a fierce blow to her back knocked the air from her lungs. A second blow came, then another. She could scarcely breathe. Casey hunched down, pulled up her hood, and turtled her head as she gasped for air. Her hips, side, and shoulders were struck repeatedly until painful spots blended into one enormous, excruciating wound.

Casey spotted the blade just under a seat. If the boys saw it . . . Taking a breath, she shifted her weight and kicked Freckles's ankle so hard that he lost his balance and fell. Blondie and Stocky came charging toward her. Still on her knees, Casey raised her arm in self-defense. Heavy footsteps thundered down the aisle. Ingrid and Marie stormed past her and mowed the little bastards down.

Casey got to her feet and filled her lungs. Freckles jumped up and kicked Ingrid in the shin. Ingrid's face twisted with rage. She backhanded him and the kid collapsed on the floor. An older woman whacked Freckles's head with an umbrella.

Casey grabbed Freckles by the arm and together she and Ingrid hauled him to his feet. Casey handcuffed him to a pole while Ingrid went after Blondie. Freckles swore and spit at Casey but missed. Furious, she raised her hand but held back from slapping him. The kid wasn't worth the trouble it would bring. "Do that again and I'll make you clean the spit off the floor with your tongue."

"Get off me!" Stocky shouted. Casey turned and saw that Marie was sitting on Stocky.

Blondie wriggled away from Ingrid's grasp and scrambled to the exit, but Ingrid was fast, her strides long and quick. She caught up to him and pinned his arms behind his back. Passengers applauded; a few even cheered.

"Folks," Ingrid called out, "we aren't going anywhere until the police arrive. If you want to catch another bus go ahead, but we'd appreciate some witness statements."

"Or at least contact information," Marie added, removing her hat. Still sitting on Stocky, she waved the hat in front of her flushed face.

"What happened to the guy who wanted his money back?" Casey asked Ingrid.

"In handcuffs by the door."

"Are you okay?" Marie looked at Casey with concern.

Now that Marie brought it up, Casey could practically feel the swelling and bruising blossoming over numerous parts of her body. One side of her face was burning, and the upper part of her right ear hurt like hell. "Do I look that bad?"

"Don't you feel the blood running down your ear?"

She hadn't, until now. Touching her ear, Casey felt the warm trickle. She pulled a tissue from her pocket. "Stocky had a knife, but it went under a seat." Marie whipped out her phone and snapped a picture of Casey. "What the hell, Marie?"

"Evidence for court, if needed." When Stocky moved to get up, Marie clamped her hand on his shoulder. "Stay down and don't move!"

The kid muttered obscenities.

"I wouldn't be surprised if the jerk who scrapped with you two works with these punks," said Casey. Dabbing her ear, she turned to Ingrid. "The timing's a bit coincidental, don't you think?"

"Totally. Freakin' losers," Ingrid muttered. She tapped Stocky's leg with her boot. "What the hell did you think your lame-ass ambush would accomplish?"

"Don't touch me, bitch!"

"Oh, I'll be touching you all right, you little mother—"

"Ingrid," Casey interrupted. "We've got this, okay? Maybe you could take Blondie up to the front."

"Come on, loser." Ingrid hauled him away.

"You can't hold us," Stocky said to Marie. "We're minors."

"I sure as hell can. You'll be charged with assault causing bodily harm, sweetie pie, and I'm making a citizen's arrest." Marie pulled out a laminated card. "Under the Charter of Rights and Freedoms, you have the right—"

"I'll sue you, you fat bitch!"

The kid again tried to get up from the floor; however, Marie—although not as large as Ingrid—was no delicate petunia. She made sure he stayed put while she resumed reading him his rights.

Although most passengers left, a few stayed behind. Once the officers arrived, Casey moved to the front of the bus. The cops grinned at the handcuffed man.

"What've you gotten yourself into this time, Wayne?" one of them asked.

"Just a misunderstanding about the fare."

"And assaulting a driver," Ingrid said.

As the police heard from Casey, Marie, and Ingrid, Casey's pain worsened. The stinging in her ear escalated to a sharp burning sensation. Thanks to her ear and the boys' complaints of injuries, paramedics were called. While she waited, she wrote a detailed account of events in her notebook and fought the growing fatigue. The paramedics treated her ear and tried to persuade her to go to the hospital for stitches. Casey told them she'd head for a nearby clinic soon. First, she needed to call Stan. Seconds later, she almost wished she hadn't. As she described what had happened, he kept interrupting with questions.

When she finally finished, he said, "Are you sure you're all right?"

"I'm fine, really." Just embarrassed that she hadn't kept her guard up.

"Tell Marie and Ingrid that I expect full reports, pronto, and Gwyn wants to see them as soon as they get back."

Uh-oh. She might not like either woman, but she didn't feel great about them being in trouble for wanting to improve working conditions. Nor did she particularly want to be the messenger.

"Go see a doc right now," Stan added. "Have you called WorkSafe BC yet?"

"I will." But what she really wanted to do was take a nap.

Casey walked up to Marie and Ingrid, who were in an intense discussion. Marie was waving her hands and yapping at Ingrid.

"I just talked to Stan," Casey said. "He wants your reports quickly, and Gwyn wants to see you both as soon as you return to Mainland." She noticed the exchange of worried glances.

"What about?" Marie asked.

"Stan didn't say." She moved toward the door. "My car's at GenMart, so I'll catch an eastbound bus."

Casey stepped off the bus, wondering if those two would try to shift the blame elsewhere. Once she crossed the street, she phoned Marie. "I didn't want to say anything in front of Ingrid, but did you talk to Lou about destroying the document with his signature?"

"Hold on."

Was she consulting Ingrid or moving away from her?

Moments later, Marie said, "As I asked Lou, is there a reason I should?"

Was she bloody joking? "Futures are at stake here, Marie. Everyone knows Ingrid's behind the certification bid. Are you going to let her drag you and Lou down too? If her job's on the line, we both know she won't hesitate to put the blame elsewhere."

"I have all the documents."

"Does Ingrid have copies or access to copies?"

"No."

"Does she know that Lou signed?"

"Yes."

Great. Just great. "What are you going to do?"

"I don't know. She wants me to bring her everything before we see Gwyn, but that's not happening."

Marie and Ingrid may have had the same goal, but those two weren't friends. They'd only joined forces because of a common quest. They could easily turn on each other. Would Lou get trapped in the middle?

SEVENTEEN

CASEY STRUGGLED UP THE BACK steps and into the house, scarcely able to move. She'd stopped at a medical clinic, and after an hour-long wait, her ear was stitched up. It took another thirty minutes to find a pharmacist and have the prescription for a seriously needed painkiller filled. Cheyenne bounded up to her and took great interest in sniffing her coat and jeans. No doubt Casey had picked up plenty of new smells.

Summer was retrieving a can of pop from the fridge when she saw Casey. "Oh my god! What happened?"

"Just some work hassles, nothing major." Casey pulled off her gloves and unbuttoned her coat.

"What's wrong with your ear? Why are your knuckles scraped?"

Casey had no idea whether the damage to her knuckles was from the bus floor or the sole of someone's boot. "It's no big deal. I'm fine."

Summer's face paled. "You were in a fight."

"More of a scuffle, and we won."

"Who'd you beat?"

"The shoplifters I told you about. The police busted them, so it's all good."

Lou marched into the room. "Are you okay? I bumped into Marie as I was leaving Mainland and heard about the brawl."

Did he actually think she'd want to discuss this in front of Summer? "I'm fine. Did Marie meet with Gwyn?"

"Yeah." He looked her up and down. "How badly are you hurt?"

"Just a little sore." She saw the skepticism but felt too lousy to spend much energy reassuring him. "Did Marie say how the meeting went?"

Lou glanced at a pensive-looking Summer, then gazed at Casey. "I think you need to sit and rest. We can talk upstairs."

The truth was that she was about ready to collapse. Casey started out of the room, taking her time. "Tell me about Marie."

"Gwyn told her why he's been cutting back so much. Seems he's under pressure to comply with the GVRD's air-quality plan, which means he's supposed to replace all the older buses with newer ones. He's been scrambling to find ways to pay for it."

Given that the Greater Vancouver Regional District had been pushing livable, clean air policies for some time now, Casey was surprised that Gwyn had gotten away with an old fleet for so long.

"What about Ingrid?" Casey asked as she started to climb the staircase. "Did she see Gwyn?"

"Yeah. He canned her."

"What?" She stopped.

"Apparently, Ingrid started spewing the Labour Relations code in his face, so Gwyn pulled out a file full of complaints about her and the failed disciplinary measures. Seems there was so much documentation that she backed down."

"No doubt. Did Gwyn ask to see you?"

Lou nodded. "I got the same spiel about cutbacks. Then he said I should come to him first if I have concerns about the company."

"I'm just glad it's over." She started up the stairs again.

"It's not, though," Lou replied. "Marie wants to go ahead with certification."

"Is she out of her friggin' mind?"

"Probably. So, tell me where you're hurt, aside from the ear and hands."

"There are a couple of bruises."

"Uh-huh. You look like you can barely move."

"I'm fine, Lou, really. It's not that bad." She tried a quicker, more fluid motion and winced with the effort.

"I still don't get how those scumbags knew who you were," he said.

"Stan will find out." He wouldn't stop asking questions until he had answers.

When they finally entered their apartment, Lou said, "I thought we'd order a pizza."

Casey was about to suggest inviting Summer to join them when she heard shouting and pounding footsteps on the stairs.

Lou peeked out the still-open apartment door. "She's on the phone," he murmured to Casey.

"Don't lie to me!" Summer shouted.

A door slammed shut, muffling Summer's voice.

"I hope Devon's on the receiving end of that anger," Lou remarked. "She really needs to dump him."

"I'll talk to her after she's calmed down. Meanwhile, I need a hot bath." And Epsom salts. "Can you keep an eye on things? I don't want Devon in the house, and I don't want her sneaking out. I forgot to put the alarm on."

"Don't worry. I'll take care of it."

But she did worry. Summer rarely shouted like that without a good reason.

$$\rightarrow \quad \rightarrow \quad \rightarrow$$

BY THE TIME Casey finished in the tub, she could scarcely keep her eyes open. However, the pizza had arrived and she supposed she should eat.

"Summer's off the phone," Lou said. "I invited her up here, but she said she'd come up later."

"Was she okay?"

"Her eyes were red and she looked sad. Maybe it's finally over between her and Devon." Lou fetched two plates. "Oh, and Kendal called. She wants you to phone her. But have some food first." He helped himself to two large slices loaded with pepperoni, mushrooms, and back bacon. "Guess what a week from Thursday is?"

"An extra volunteer shift at Fraserview. I'm filling in for Kendal." When the corners of his mouth turned down, she realized this wasn't the answer he was looking for. "What?"

"It's Valentine's Day."

"Oh, no. Kendal asked if I could cover her shift, so she could take her mom out for dinner, but she didn't mention Valentine's."

"Because she was afraid you'd turn her down," he replied, frowning. "Think she could take her mom for lunch instead?"

"It depends on their work schedules, but I could find out." Casey paused. "You usually don't make a big deal out of Valentine's Day."

"Thought I'd make an effort this year and take you to a French restaurant."

An unusually romantic gesture. "Sounds lovely. Which one have you booked?"

"We'll wing it."

"Seriously?" Casey tried not to grin. "Valentine's Day is just over a week away. All the best restaurants are probably already booked."

He sighed. "Guess I better come up with a plan B." Lou munched his pizza, then added, "I want this to be the best Valentine's ever, to celebrate us living together and our future."

"Sounds wonderful." Okay, this was going to require giving him a really cool gift. Casey took a couple of bites, then pushed her plate away. Pain and fatigue weren't helping her appetite. "I should see if Summer wants to talk."

Lou wiped his hands on a napkin. "Can it wait? You need to relax, hon."

"I will after I see Summer and get some homework done."

Lou reached for her hand. "Casey, slow down. It's always full tilt with you. Don't you ever want to spend an evening at a pub, just relaxing?"

"It's not that easy right now."

"Yeah, well, did you ever stop to think that you're making it tough on yourself? You've become so distracted with Fraserview and Amy's problems that you're missing what's going on right here."

It had been two weeks since he chastised her for a lack of attention on the home front. She wasn't ready for another argument. "I'm here as much as I can be, Lou."

"Physically maybe. But half the time you're not here emotionally." He paused. "How about a little more *us* time? A date night once in a while. We could go to the Cultch to see a play or hear some music. I bet you've never even been there, and it's only a five-minute walk away."

She didn't appreciate being put on the defensive. "I know where the cultural center is, Lou, and I can tell you the name of every shop from here to Hastings Street."

"Because you've driven past them a million times. But how often have you stopped for coffee at one of the cafés?"

She sighed; he had her there. "Point taken." Casey's phone rang. "It's Kendal." She stood. "I need to talk to her about today." She hurried out of the apartment, keeping her back to him so he wouldn't see the pain she felt with every bloody step.

"I've got news, girlfriend," Kendal said.

"Where are you?"

"At juvie. I worked nine to three-thirty, grabbed some food, then came here. The kids are on a dinner break."

Her shift had ended fifteen minutes before the shoplifters entered the store.

"Justin's out of segregation," Kendal continued.

"Is he okay?"

"He's scared, Casey. The kid knows you and I are friends, so he confided that he and Tanya ran because they didn't feel safe in here."

Casey stopped at the second floor. "Aside from the hostility of juvie life, is something specific worrying him?"

"I asked, but all Justin would say is that it's about Mercedes and his stepbrother, and then he made me promise not to tell anyone in here."

"Interesting. What's the connection between Mercedes and Brady?"

"He wouldn't tell me that either. The kid kept looking around, afraid someone would overhear."

Would he tell Amy what it was? She'd have to wait and see. "Listen, we had an incident with the shoplifters today." Casey highlighted the afternoon's events, downplaying her injuries.

"I'm so sorry," Kendal said. "I've talked to the other LPOs, all of whom I trust, and none of us found evidence of any employee feeding these kids info. Most of the staff don't even know you exist."

Then how the hell had the boys learned about her? "Thanks for checking. It's all so weird, but now that the little bastards are in custody, Stan will get answers."

It was only after Casey had hung up the phone that she realized she'd forgotten to ask Kendal about switching on Valentine's.

Maybe Lou was right about her not paying enough attention to her personal life.

Slowly and painfully, Casey continued downstairs. Man, she'd be lucky if she could get out of bed tomorrow. When she finally entered the kitchen, she found Summer stirring something on the stove. Cheyenne was too busy scarfing down dog food to give Casey more than a glance. "Hi, Summer. There's plenty of pizza upstairs."

"I'm not that hungry."

"What are you making?"

"Hot chocolate."

Her favorite comfort beverage. "We couldn't help overhear you yelling on the phone earlier. Has something happened?"

Summer shook her head. "I'll tell you about it later. I need to think some stuff through."

Those thoughts likely centered on Devon. Whatever the butthead had done, Casey was grateful for the trouble he'd caused in their relationship.

EIGHTEEN

CASEY WAS HEADING TOWARD FRASERVIEW'S entrance when some-one dressed in dark clothing emerged from the trees to her left. Inhaling sharply, she stopped. When Casey spotted the red tip of a lit cigarette, she relaxed. "Phyllis?"

The cleaning woman moved closer and took a drag on the cigarette. She seemed to be the only employee who smoked far away from the building. Maybe she preferred solitude.

"It's good to see at least one friendly face here," Casey remarked.

"There aren't many, are there, luv?" Phyllis joined her. "Best dis-cover who your friends are on both sides of the door."

Riddles again? "I assume you mean at Fraserview?"

Phyllis peered at Casey through those big square lenses. "Everywhere. Those you depend on most are the worst, mark my words." She crushed the cigarette.

"I don't depend on anyone connected to Fraserview, except Kendal, and we usually don't volunteer together."

"No matter. It's all a gamble anyway, isn't it?" She started up the steps. "You never know who will drop by to play."

Another reference to gambling. What was Phyllis trying to tell her? "Do you like to gamble, Phyllis?"

"It's relaxing, it is. Never know who'll you meet."

Like someone from Fraserview, for instance? "Which casino do you go to?"

Phyllis gave her a name, then pressed the intercom button beside the door.

"Yes?" Rawan responded.

"It's Phyllis, and the volunteer."

The buzzer sounded and Casey opened the door. "Phyllis, have the police talked to you since Mac's death that night?"

She removed her wool hat and coat. "Why would they?"

"I heard rumors about there being too much medication in Mac's system, which might be true because the cops called yesterday and asked again how many pills I gave him." The officer wouldn't say much or even tell her if Mac's death was truly accidental or not. But they wouldn't have called if they weren't taking a closer look at things.

"Rumors are always flying." Phyllis headed toward her cleaning cart, which was parked outside the hallway entrance to the conference room.

Rawan, who was on her cell phone, flashed a tense smile as she took Casey's things. Had the police contacted her lately? Casey was tempted to ask, but now was not the right moment. Rawan had turned her back to Casey and was speaking a language she didn't recognize.

After signing in and picking up a visitor's badge, she headed for Mac's—now Mia's—office to learn where she'd be assigned. The lights were off. Casey studied the dim, empty corridor. The place felt even bleaker since Mac's death, and more ominous. If it weren't for the conversations coming from the visitors' area, she'd swear the building had been abandoned. She didn't really want to continue volunteering without Mac, but Mia had seemed desperate for help. Besides, she wanted to see how Justin was doing and learn a little more about the Special Unit for her term paper. If the youth supervisors gave her the info she needed, she wouldn't have to return.

Casey stood in the doorway to the visitors' lounge, happy to see Amy with Justin, until she saw the sadness on his face and Amy's pursed mouth. Amy spotted her and waved her over. Casey stepped inside, nodding to the correctional officer at the desk. He looked at her visitor's badge, then returned the nod.

"Hello, Casey," Amy said. "Justin has something to say to you."

Justin's face reddened as he looked up. His eyes widened with a mix of surprise and chagrin as he gaped at her wounds. "Sorry you got hurt on the trail," he murmured. "I told Tanya not to throw the rock, but . . ." He lowered his head.

"I know how strong-willed she is," Casey replied. "She only nicked my forehead. The ear injury is from something else."

"Some of the idiot staff think Justin and Tanya caused the director's death and are treating him like a leper," Amy said. "They're furious with them for making staff look incompetent, which is why I'm filing a complaint with the executive director of Youth Custody Services." She made her voice loud enough for the correctional officer to hear. The officer's bored expression didn't change.

"Are Amir and Winson causing you problems?" Casey asked Justin.

He shrugged, glancing at the guard.

Casey wouldn't be surprised if they were. She tried not to wince as she sat down. The bruises on the backs of her legs from her altercation three days ago were large and dark. Her hips and back had been aching all day. She'd tried to stay off painkillers, but had given in before coming here.

"Our lawyer's trying to have him transferred out of this cesspool," Amy added, "but we've been told it takes time. Far too much for my liking."

"Did you escape because Tanya didn't want to be transferred?" Casey asked Justin.

He hesitated. "Yeah."

"How did you pull it off?"

Justin peeked at the guard again. "With help."

"From whom?"

He looked around the room. "One of the visitors, but he's not here tonight."

"Who is he?" Casey asked.

"Mercedes's uncle. He comes here a lot."

"Cristano Cruz," Casey murmured. Based on what Ruby had said about him, she wasn't overly surprised. Cruz hung around Fraserview a lot and seemed to have an aversion to cops. She recalled the way he hurried out of the building when they arrived the night Mac died. "Why would Tanya accept his help?"

"She knew who he was, and figured he could get us out, as a favor."

"And how did she figure that?"

Justin fidgeted. "She knows Cruz is a criminal. Before Christmas break, Tanya saw him give Brady packets of drugs. Realized he was Brady's supplier."

Whoa. This explained the aversion to cops. "Where did the transaction happen?"

"At a strip mall near the high school," Justin answered, glancing at his frowning grandmother. "Lots of kids go there at lunch to buy pizza and stuff. Tanya, Brady, and Didi went to the same school."

"Didi is Brady's sister, right?" Amy had mentioned the name before.

Justin nodded. "Tanya and her are good friends." He bit his lower lip. "When Tanya found out she was being transferred, she got upset. Told Roxanne and Mercedes that she needed out of here. Next day, Mercedes promised that her uncle could get Tanya out fast."

"So, the escape was pre-arranged with Cruz's help?"

Justin nodded. "Tanya begged me to go with her, but I wasn't sure."

"Which was why she still wanted to talk to you so badly when I interrupted that night."

Another nod. "Later, Winson left the unit, and I saw Tanya hurrying down the hall. She waved me over, and I just kind of went."

"What did Cruz want in return for helping you?" Casey asked.

"For us to work for him. Gave us an address to go to." Justin paused. "But I didn't want to sell drugs, so now we're in deep shit."

Casey understood now why he'd told Amy that he couldn't repay a favor. At least Justin had sense enough to see that working for Cruz would be a no-win situation. She wanted to ask Justin how Cruz had pulled it off, but Mia was marching toward them.

"There you are," Mia called out to Casey. "I heard you'd arrived and have been looking for you."

"I asked her to join us," Amy replied.

Casey felt Amy's hostility, saw the steely resolve in her eyes.

Mia must have seen it too, because her own placid expression froze into something harsh and uncompromising. "I didn't realize you knew each other."

"We work together," Amy said.

"I see." Mia turned to Casey. "You should have told me."

"Mac knew, and Winson knows," she answered. "I thought you heard me talking about my relationship to Amy with the police that Friday night."

Mia shrugged. "It was a chaotic night. I don't remember half of what was said. Anyhow, I'm afraid you're needed elsewhere."

Casey gave Amy a reassuring nod before following Mia out of the room. Was she going to be lectured about fraternizing with Justin and his grandmother? Not that it really mattered. If all went well, she'd be done with volunteering after tonight.

"A new girl was brought in two hours ago and she's distraught," Mia said. "A sympathetic ear might calm her down."

Just then, a boy stepped out of the gym and walked toward them. The corridor's lousy lighting made it impossible to see his face, but Casey recognized the stocky build, short dark hair, and pigeon-toed gait right away. She should have known at least one of the shoplifters would end up here. When Stocky was only a few steps away from them, his expression first showed surprise, then transformed into a nasty sneer.

"Nice bandage," he remarked. "Any ear left?"

"Pardon me?" Mia said, staring at the kid. "We show respect in here, young man. Understand?"

Stocky ignored her as he glared at Casey, who threw it right back.

"I *said*, do you understand?" Mia stepped in front of him.

"Yeah, whatever."

Mia turned to Casey. "I want to talk to Jamal. You know where to find Ruby."

"There's something I need to tell you first. It's really important." She glanced at the kid. "Can we talk privately?"

Mia turned to Jamal. "Wait for me in your unit."

The kid's defiant stare made Casey wonder how far he'd go to challenge authority. She hoped it got him into a load of trouble. Finally, he turned on his heel and stomped into the unit.

Skipping as many details as she could about the assignment, Casey described the attack on the M5 bus. "Needless to say, the less Jamal knows about me and Kendal the better."

"He's the only boy who's been brought in this week," Mia replied. "Since you're in the girls' unit you won't cross paths, but I'll have a chat with him anyway."

Mia started to walk away when they heard the sound of raised voices coming from the gymnasium. Amir charged out the door, followed by Winson. Amir spun around and said something Casey couldn't hear. When he noticed Mia and Casey, he abruptly shut up.

"What's going on?" Mia asked as she approached.

The men frowned at each other. "Nothing you need to worry about," Amir answered, then marched toward the west wing.

Mia looked at Winson, who gave her a brief nod. He started to head inside the gym, but then stopped and stared down the corridor. Casey turned to see what he was looking at; it was just Phyllis mopping the floor outside the conference room. When Casey turned back, Winson had disappeared.

"That was bloody helpful," Mia muttered. "I'd better deal with Jamal."

Casey entered the girls' unit. Ruby was chatting with the residents but stopped when she spotted Casey. "Good lord, gal. What happened to you?"

"An altercation at work, but I'm fine."

"You sure about dat? You look all worn out." Ruby placed one of her big hands on Casey's left shoulder. It was one of the few body parts that wasn't bruised. "Come sit and rest for a bit."

Casey was tired, so she let Ruby escort her into her office. "Mia told me you have a new resident."

"Kids comin' and goin', and comin' back." Ruby shook her head. "Dat new gal's cryin' like the world just up and tore itself in two. Maybe you can calm her down."

"I'll try my best." She doubted that she would be much help, though. "The police called me about Mac a couple of days ago."

"Dey was here, askin' the same questions as before." She waved a dismissive hand in the air. "Bosses came by and asked stupid stuff too." Her expression became solemn. "Change is comin' fast. Place might be shut down sooner than expected."

No surprise there. "Roxanne was due to leave when I was last here. Has she gone?"

"For now, yeah."

Mercedes poked her head through the open door. "Hi, Casey. Are you seeing me tonight?"

She thought of Cristano Cruz. Would he show up and try to get to Justin? "Actually, I've been asked to spend some time with the new resident. No visitors tonight?"

Mercedes shook her head and gave a weak smile, but Casey wasn't sure if the girl was relieved about that or regretful.

"Mercedes is leaving tomorrow," Ruby said.

"Congratulations," Casey said, turning to her. "You must be happy."

"Can't wait." Mercedes's smile disappeared as she headed for the sofa.

"Where will she go when she's out?" Casey whispered to Ruby.

"With the uncle."

"Not a great arrangement."

"Best dat gal's got."

Cruz would no longer have his niece to visit. This was good news for Justin. Or was she kidding herself? Cruz was the type of man who trampled over rules and laws to get what he wanted. Had Mac known about Cruz's drug business? Was this the reason he'd died? She'd love to know if the police were looking at a connection between Cruz's visits and Mac's death.

THE NEW ARRIVAL hadn't wanted to talk to anyone, so Casey opted for a game of cards with Mercedes and two other girls. Forty minutes later, her bruised body began to rebel from all the sitting. The frequent bickering didn't help either, so she tried to distract the girls. "Did anyone ever find out who pulled the fire alarm the other night?"

It worked. The girls grew quiet until Mercedes said, "Some loser in Unit Three, for a joke."

Not a difficult stunt to pull off, since Amir had been with the police at the other end of the corridor. There might not have been enough staff to cover for him.

Yelling outside the girls' unit caught Casey's attention. Now what?

Those who heard the commotion scrambled to the door.

"Stay back," Ruby ordered, stepping outside.

Through the open door, Casey heard, "Your incompetence could have gotten someone hurt, or *worse*." It was Winson's voice. She poked her head out, startled to see a knife in Winson's hand as he scowled at the cook, Oksana.

Oksana pointed her finger at him. "I'm not the one who lets inmates roam the hall."

"No. You simply left a kitchen full of knives unlocked," Winson shot back. "I'll have to report this."

"Ruby, stay inside with the girls," Mia said as she rushed by, heading straight for Winson and Oksana.

Ruby complied, but Casey stayed in the doorway. Mac had been right. This truly was a dysfunctional place. As far as she was concerned, staff were a huge part of the problem.

"What's going on?" Mia asked.

"The new kid, Jamal, stole a knife while Oksana was out of the kitchen," Winson answered.

"I was gone just a few seconds to get more sugar," Oksana blurted. "And why are these delinquents wandering the halls alone? I see it every damn day."

Mia looked at Oksana. "How did you miss seeing the boy when the supply room's next door?"

Oksana's furious expression started to crumble.

"Well?" Mia crossed her arms.

"I was in the pool room."

"What for?"

"There's too much stock on delivery days, so Mac said I could have a couple of extra cupboards."

"You would have plenty of space if your organized your inventory and kitchen properly," Mia said. "The pool room is now off limits to all staff except the janitors."

Oksana's fat cheeks glowed red. Casey saw the barely contained fury in her eyes.

Mia turned to Winson. "Jamal's potential trouble for Casey and the other volunteer, Kendal. I'll explain why later."

Winson stared at Casey but said nothing.

"I talked to him a few minutes ago," Mia added, "then escorted him back to the gym. What happened after that?"

"He came in as two residents started fighting over the basketball. By the time I'd broken them up he'd disappeared. When he didn't come back, I went looking for him and found him heading toward Unit One with the weapon in his hand."

As everyone turned to her, Casey's skin prickled. Had that little puke planned to attack her? "I'd better get back inside." She just hoped to hell she got out of this place safely tonight.

BY THE END of her shift, Casey had managed to interview Ruby about the Special Unit and her time at Fraserview. Ruby had little to say about the altercation between Winson and Oksana, or about Mia's intervention, which seemed odd. Maybe she'd been warned about gossiping, or maybe she'd had enough for one day. Either way, Casey had now acquired the research material she'd come for.

She left the unit and started down the corridor. Visiting hours were over and all residents should have returned to their living units, but she wouldn't put it past Jamal to be lurking in the shadows, ready to strike again. Casey tiptoed past Unit Two's entrance. Glancing through the window in the door, she thought she saw a boy with short, dark hair. Casey picked up the pace, her senses alert.

Once she reached reception, she looked back down the dim, empty corridor. Phyllis was mopping the floor outside the gym.

Rawan put down the eyeliner she'd been applying. "How was your shift?"

"A little intense, but otherwise okay."

"I heard yelling." She handed Casey her coat and purse. "What happened?"

After Casey briefly described events, Rawan said, "Just between you and me, Oksana should have been fired ages ago. She's careless and rude. Mia will deal with her."

Casey tossed her visitor's badge into the basket on the reception counter. "Did the police talk to you recently about Mac's death?"

"Yes. You as well?"

"Uh-huh. The questions were pretty much the same, except for one." Casey put on her coat. "They wanted to know who else was nearby while Mac was having his attack. The only person I remember was Mercedes's uncle, Cristano Cruz, who helped me place Mac on the floor. Do you remember anyone else?"

"Just the corrections guy from the visitors' area. The idiot crossed the hall and stood in the doorway gawking while you and Cruz were with Mac. When Mia showed up he scurried back to his post." She picked up the eyeliner. "He should have been the one helping you instead of that creepy uncle."

Casey hadn't noticed the corrections officer. "I was a little surprised that Cruz involved himself."

"He's a nosy man."

"In what way?"

Rawan studied her eyes in a pocket mirror. "He talks to the other residents. Makes a point of knowing their business, which Mac didn't like, so he restricted Cruz's visits."

Phyllis had said as much last week, and Justin's revelation had provided a reason for the frequent visits. "Are his visits still restricted?"

"No. The guy shows up at least three times a week." Rawan wiped the old lipstick from her mouth, then prepared to put on a darker shade.

"Why does Mia allow it?"

Rawan shrugged. "She says it's to show gratitude for his trying to help Mac."

Or was there another reason? Casey watched Rawan apply the lipstick. "Hot date tonight?"

Rawan flashed a quick smile as she glanced at Casey. "I'm meeting someone for a drink."

"Good luck." Casey left the building and checked her phone

messages on the way to her car. There was only one, but it was from Stan. It was unusual for him to call at this time of night. She hit reply, and he answered on the first ring.

"Sorry to interrupt your evening," Stan said, "but I need to meet with you first thing tomorrow morning. It's about the shoplifters."

"You can't tell me over the phone?"

"We need to talk in person. Kendal's boss will brief her."

"Sounds serious." When he didn't respond she added, "Am I in trouble?"

"We'll talk tomorrow."

Oh, crap. Casey opened the car door. What the hell had happened? "Can you at least give me a hint?"

He paused. "Strictly between us, all right?"

"Sure."

"GenMart's manager and the police reviewed camera footage. It looks like Kendal could have caught these boys a hell of a lot sooner if she'd been paying attention."

Not good. "Maybe she was dealing with other issues at the time."

"Could be. Anyway, that's between her and the manager."

But it wasn't sufficient reason to need her there for a meeting. "Is there more?"

"Yes. Be here at 9:00 AM, sharp."

Casey rubbed her hands together while the car warmed up. She wished she could warn Kendal. A good friend would give Kendal a heads up, but Stan was also Casey's friend, as well as her supervisor.

Once the windshield had defrosted enough to drive, Casey pulled out of the parking lot. She was on the street and cruising through an intersection when she heard fire truck sirens. She glanced in her rearview mirror. Two trucks were heading her way fast. Casey cleared the intersection and pulled over, but the trucks didn't pass her. They turned into Fraserview.

NINETEEN

TWELVE HOURS LATER, CASEY WAS sitting in Stan's office on a quiet Saturday morning and wondering for the umpteenth time whether she should have followed those fire trucks into Fraserview. She'd been tempted to drive back and see what was happening, but it wasn't her place. Besides, what would her presence have changed? Winson Chen would have died anyway. Anaphylactic shock killed quickly.

Mia's phone call late last night had taken a while to sink in. Casey understood each word easily enough. "Winson's EpiPen was missing from his desk drawer. That's where he ate meals he brought from home." It was the meaning behind those words that Casey was still trying to process, the implication that his medication had been moved accidentally or—more likely—on purpose.

Her head began to spin. Where was Stan with that coffee?

Certainly, Mia had every right to ask if Casey had brought food into Fraserview, or if she'd seen anyone carrying food, which she hadn't. Had it been necessary, though, for her to sound so accusatory, or to order Casey not to say anything about Winson and Oksana's argument over the knife? "If you call Fraserview's reputation into question," Mia had said, "then don't come back." Casey had wanted to laugh. Wasn't Fraserview's reputation already in question? She should have replied that she didn't plan to go back anyway, but the news about Winson had thrown her off.

It wasn't long after Mia's call that the police contacted her. She would be providing a full statement later this morning.

Stan came in carrying two mugs. "Sorry I took so long. Had to make a fresh pot."

"Thanks." She'd been relieved to hear that Stan already knew about last night, thanks to Amy. The police had visited her in person. Amy had been angry and distraught enough to seek advice from Stan.

"I'm worried about Amy and Justin," Casey said. "Visiting hours were over when I left a few minutes after nine, so I didn't see her around. Did she say when she left?"

"About quarter to nine, before Winson had the reaction." Stan scratched his beard. "She doesn't think the police believe her about not bringing food into Fraserview." He sipped his coffee. "She's afraid Justin will become a scapegoat."

"How can that happen without proof?"

Stan put his mug down and began tapping a pencil. She was beginning to hate that gesture. Casey watched and waited until she couldn't take anymore. "What is it?"

"A half-eaten chocolate bar, loaded with peanuts, was found in Justin's locker."

"No way."

"It gets worse." He tossed the pencil down. "The bar was in a wrapper showing plain chocolate."

"Then it *was* murder, and someone set Justin up." It also meant that the cops might soon declare—if they hadn't already—Mac's death a homicide. The thought that someone had been arranging Winson's demise while she volunteered last night made the hair on the back of Casey's neck stand up. What really concerned her was Justin's safety. "I didn't see anyone with chocolate all night, but I saw Winson in heated discussions with the senior youth supervisor and the cook. Crazy as this sounds, the argument with the cook was about the kid who cut me on the M5."

After Casey highlighted events, Stan's already grim face darkened by a couple of shades. "Did you tell the police all this?"

"Yes, and I will again in a written statement this morning."

"I want a report on everything this Jamal kid said and did."

Terrific. More writing. She took a long sip of coffee. "Do people really think Justin would be dumb enough to leave evidence in his locker?"

"I agree it wouldn't make much sense, but Amy says he'd been in Winson's unit for over three weeks before he took off. Justin would know the supervisor's habits, which doesn't look good for him."

"Staff knew Winson's habits just as well. How hard would it have been for any of them to steal an EpiPen and plant a chocolate bar?" Casey stood and approached the window. She could see that the buses were all out, and there weren't many staff vehicles in the lot. Never was on a Saturday. "Whoever killed Winson also killed Mac."

"Why would anyone want the director dead?"

"Because Mac was apparently planning to fire more than one employee." Casey filled Stan in on what she'd learned.

"How many employees had motive and opportunity for both victims?" he asked.

"Five or six, I think." Casey returned to her chair. "The boys from Units Two and Three play basketball in the evening, so their quarters are empty a fair bit. The Unit Three supervisor didn't supervise the Friday night games, so god knows what he was up to while Winson was refereeing."

"Who would have access to locker combinations?"

"Supervisors, I suppose. There's probably a master list anyone could access from a computer in one of the supervisors' offices." Casey paused. "The gym bathroom's out of service, so boys are allowed to use their unit's bathroom, which is probably why I haven't noticed any unit being locked during visiting hours. Some of the kids head to the visitors' area alone, although I'm not sure they're supposed to. Any of them could have made a quick detour."

"So, Justin could have left his locker open by mistake and another resident slipped the bar in?"

"It's possible, although where would they get chocolate, unless it was smuggled in to them by a visitor?" Casey cupped her hands around her mug as she thought of Cristano Cruz. Was he there last night after all? But why kill Winson? And Cruz would have needed an accomplice.

"Much as I'd love to help Amy, this is out of our league, kiddo. The police will handle it." Stan began shuffling papers. "So, on to other matters."

Right. The reason he'd asked her here. Casey fidgeted.

"We know who triggered the fight on the bus, and why." He leaned back and clasped his hands over his belly. "One of the shoplifters has a cousin with shady connections. The cousin picked the fight with Ingrid to keep her busy so the kids could take you down. Obviously, they hadn't anticipated Marie's presence."

"I had a feeling the fight was planned."

Stan paused. "We know how the shoplifters found out about you."

Based on his solemn expression, Casey had a feeling she wouldn't like this.

"Did you tell Summer about your assignment?" he asked.

The question caught her by surprise, and it took her a few seconds to remember. "Indirectly. She overheard me and Lou talking about it, and I always let her know where I'll be when I'm going out. Why?"

Stan picked up a sheet of paper. "According to the constable I spoke with, two of the boys knew your name and about the assignment from someone named Devon Price, reportedly a family friend."

"Shit! Summer's boyfriend." Casey smacked the desktop. "I've never liked that little bugger."

"I take it the feeling's mutual."

Feeling hollow and numb, Casey slumped back in her chair. The last person she'd talked to before leaving for GenMart on Tuesday was Summer. Oh, god, had Summer fed Devon the info? Had she been so angry over the grounding that she wanted payback? Was she capable of this level of betrayal? On the other hand, Summer had been acting strange lately, and it seemed like she wanted to tell her something. After Casey came home with her ear bandaged on Tuesday, Summer had seemed upset. Then she'd been shouting at someone on the phone. Maybe Summer hadn't known what Devon had done until it was over, although she must have wondered. She'd probably confronted him.

"So, Summer told her boyfriend about the assignment?" Stan asked.

"Actually, Devon was there when Summer overheard me tell Lou about it. Our apartment door was open, and I had no idea they were listening outside until it was too late. That manipulative moron probably learned whatever else he needed to know from her." She was going to kill Devon.

"What's up with Summer?" Stan asked.

Casey didn't bother to hold back a sigh. "Our relationship's been strained since she hooked up with that disrespectful moron in December. Summer's lost herself in that piece of crap." Casey decided to stop venting before she completely lost it. "I'm sorry, Stan. I'll talk to Summer as soon as I get home."

"Good luck."

Luck, she didn't need. What she needed was patience.

→   →   →

AS USUAL, CASEY entered the house through the back door that led into the kitchen. There was no sign of Summer. She marched down the hall and peeked into the living room. Also empty. She started up the stairs and then paused, forcing herself to stop and think, to restrain the desire to barge into Summer's room and start yelling. She took a deep breath, then another, but the adrenaline rushed through her body so fast that her skin was hot and prickly. When she reached Summer's bedroom, she managed to knock quietly.

"Come in."

Summer was on the bed, playing an electronic game. Cheyenne rested on the mat beside her bed. The dog raised her head and wagged her tail a little before resuming her snooze.

"I just came from an interesting meeting with Stan," Casey said, walking up to the bed. "The police told him that the boys who attacked us on the bus learned about me and my assignment from Devon." Summer looked up, her face flushing red, eyes guilt-ridden and fearful. "Why, Summer?"

As she tossed the game on the comforter, her eyes glistened. "I didn't know he'd do that, I swear!" She moved to the edge of the bed and planted her feet on the floor.

Casey fetched a tissue from the box on the night table. "What *do* you know?"

Summer hesitated. As the tears began to spill, she took the tissue Casey handed her. "After we heard you talking about your job, Devon wanted to know more, so we followed you to the store on our bikes."

Crap. Casey wished she'd spotted them. "Go on."

"We were wet and freezing when we got there, so we snuck into the store while you were at the bus stop." Summer shredded the tissue. Small bits floated to the floor, some of them landing on the dog. "Devon ran into some guys he knew."

"Can you describe them?"

As she did so, Casey pinched her lips together to keep from swearing. Summer had just described the shoplifting trio. She sat next to Summer. "What did Devon say to them?"

"Dunno. He asked me to get him a chocolate bar." She paused. "When I got back, we left."

"How did Devon know his friends were the boys I was watching for?"

"After I got him the bar, they showed him how to hide it so he wouldn't have to pay. We figured they were the shoplifters you were waiting for." Summer choked back a sob. "Devon said I shouldn't tell you or the cops about him stealing the chocolate bar, because we'd get in trouble and maybe even get kicked out of school. I didn't like it, but I said okay."

Casey took another calming breath. "Then what happened?"

"He brought the bike he'd borrowed back here, then took off. I still felt bad about him stealing, so I phoned him and said we needed to talk. He told me to come to the rink."

"And then you brought him back here."

"We weren't finished talking when you called. So, I asked him to come with me; I told Devon I'd give him something to eat." More tears spilled down her cheeks. "But you freaked out and that made him mad, so he left."

And plotted revenge, the little bastard. "After that confrontation, he told the shoplifters about me?"

"I didn't know he'd do that!" Summer wiped her eyes. "When you came in all beaten up, I got a bad feeling about it and called him to find out if he'd talked to those guys, and he just *laughed*." She poked at bits of tissue with her toes. "Said it was your own fault. So I broke up with him." Collapsing against Casey, she began to sob.

"You did the right thing." She put her arms around Summer.

"I wanted to tell you that Devon knew those guys," Summer said between sobs. "But I knew you'd be really pissed."

Casey squeezed her tight. "Not with you, sweetie."

Summer sniffed and wiped her eyes. "Are you going to tell Mom?"

"No. You are."

Summer sat up. "She'll yell."

"Probably, but once she's had a chance to think things through, she'll be happy you dumped a guy who didn't deserve you." Rhonda would be disappointed, though, that Summer hadn't fessed up earlier. Casey had to admit she was disappointed too.

Her cell phone rang. When she saw Kendal's name on the screen, she cringed from guilt. "I need to take this call," Casey said and left Summer's room.

"This is one shitty day," Kendal grumbled. "The manager is blaming me for letting those boys rip us off so much. It will probably go in my file and blow my chance for a pay raise."

"I'm so sorry, Kendal." Casey headed upstairs to her suite. "I owe you a huge apology for suggesting GenMart staff were behind the leak." She closed the door. "I just found out that I was indirectly responsible."

After Casey explained everything, Kendal gave a low whistle. "Tell Summer not to feel bad. Choosing a loser boyfriend is practically a rite of passage. Can you get me a photo of this Devon jerk? If he comes into the store again, I'll want to know."

"Summer probably has one on her phone. I'll send it to you. And there's something else. Did you hear what happened at Fraserview last night?"

"No. What?"

The news of Winson's death prompted a "holy shit!" from Kendal. "We need to do some serious digging before Justin becomes the permanent scapegoat," she added.

"It won't be easy. Mia's not happy with me, so I doubt I can go back and start asking questions. Speaking of which, guess who Fraserview's latest resident is?" She told Kendal about Jamal's arrival.

"I'm not worried about that little shit," Kendal said, "and I want to learn more about Winson's death. The place is filled with gossips who'll bring me up to speed."

"I know a way to do some digging that'll be more fun," Casey said. "What are you doing tonight?"

"Nothing, why?"

"How would you like to go to a casino, incognito?"

TWENTY

"YOU TWO AREN'T GOING TO make trouble if you see someone from Fraserview, are you?" Lou asked as he pulled into the casino's parking lot. "I know all the high school stories."

"Not all of them," Kendal replied, winking at Casey.

Nestled between her two favorite people, Casey chuckled. "It does feel like old times."

"We're just older and wiser now." Kendal leaned forward and grinned at Lou. "Seriously."

Lou turned off the engine. "I'm already nervous."

Casey followed him out of the truck. "You'll be too busy reclaiming your former glory at the blackjack tables to worry about us."

Lou and his buddies used to hang out a fair bit at casinos, until grownup responsibilities consumed their time and money. With a self-imposed hundred-dollar limit, Lou was hardly a high roller these days, but he'd wanted to come along and had even offered to be designated driver. Summer was sleeping over at a friend's house, and Casey welcomed the chance for an evening out, even if they were on a mission. She knew that Lou truly was concerned about what might happen tonight. With two dead Fraserview staff members, maybe he had a good reason to be. Casey looked around the full parking lot but didn't see Phyllis's Smart car. Too bad she didn't know what types of vehicles the other staff drove.

"If you see Phyllis or any of the others we talked about, avoid them," Casey said to Kendal.

"Don't sweat it. No one will recognize us in these getups."

"How many others?" Lou asked.

"Six," Casey replied. "Amir, Rawan, Mia, Oksana, Cristano Cruz, and Ruby. Although Ruby wasn't working when Mac had his heart attack, and Cruz wasn't around when Winson died, as far as I know. But I think Phyllis mentioned the gambling thing because she knew

I'd recognize someone connected to Fraserview if I came here."

"What about the corrections officers?" Kendal asked. "I don't know their names but I'd recognize their faces."

"Same here," Casey replied. "Let's watch for them too."

The plan was to scour every inch of the casino for familiar faces. Kendal would scope out the poker rooms and, if possible, the VIP area. Casey would wander among the slot machines and gaming tables. The first one to spot a familiar face would call the other. Casey wasn't quite sure what this mission would accomplish, but given Phyllis's hints and the likelihood that a Fraserview employee, or Cruz, was a killer, checking into their backgrounds and off-duty activities seemed a more useful way to spend time than watching TV.

"What do you think of Casey as a redhead?" Kendal asked Lou. "Better than those old brown curls, right?"

"It's awesome," Lou replied, sweeping his hand down the long red wig.

Did he really like her better as a redhead? Casey felt like an idiot. Admittedly, the wig changed her appearance almost as much as Kendal's black one altered hers. The dark brown contact lenses and heavy makeup were a bit over the top, though.

"Rawan's been acting kind of strange," Kendal said, glancing at three couples who were approaching the casino's entrance. "I've caught her in two intense phone conversations, and both times she hung up the second she saw me. She also seemed kind of embarrassed. The chick is definitely hiding something."

"Maybe she knows more about what's really going on in Fraserview than she can say."

"We should talk to her away from the place," Kendal said. "Wouldn't it be cool if she was here tonight?"

"I thought we agreed that you two are just observing, not interrogating," Lou said.

"We are," Casey replied. "Right, Kendal?"

"Right," she said with less enthusiasm.

Judging from the look on Lou's face, concern had turned to worry.

Casey didn't blame him. In the old days, Kendal's willingness to confront people had nearly gotten them into bar brawls on more than one occasion. Hopefully, Kendal would keep her curiosity and boldness in check.

Lou opened the door for them and Casey followed Kendal into an enormous room decorated in red and gold. They faced a crush of bright lights and people. There was chatter, laughter, bells, whistles, and music—quite a contrast from the dark, quiet parking lot.

"Wow," Casey murmured. She'd been in casinos before, but the bombardment to her senses was always a shock.

Grinning, Kendal turned full circle. "Awesome."

"Can I buy you ladies a drink?" Lou asked.

"Just soda water for me," Casey replied.

"That's it?" Kendal asked.

"Want to stay sharp. Plus I have to get up early tomorrow."

"What for?"

"Tons of report and essay writing to catch up on."

After her conversation with Summer earlier, Casey had called Stan to let him know what she'd learned about Devon's involvement. He told her to document every detail and have her report ready first thing Monday morning. So far, she hadn't gotten around to it.

While Casey strolled past a bank of slot machines, bells rang loudly for a lucky senior with sprigs of purple hair on her balding scalp. The woman barely broke a smile, as if winning was routine. Somewhere in the middle of the room, cheers erupted. Casey slowed her pace and looked for Phyllis, but the slot machines faced different directions, making it impossible to see every patron. Worse, a disturbingly high number of players sported Phyllis's gray poodle curls. Some of them even wore the same style of blue-framed glasses.

Trailing Lou and Kendal, Casey tried to get her bearings, but the room was so large that she couldn't figure out where it ended. At the bar, Lou ordered drinks while she and Kendal people watched. By the time the drinks were ready, Kendal was antsy.

"I'm going to look for the poker room," she said and wandered off.

Lou leaned close to Casey. "What do you think of this place?"

"There are a lot of solemn faces."

"Who are counting on winning to pay down debt." Lou took Casey's hand and headed for the gaming tables.

When they reached the blackjack area, he stopped and watched the action. Casey glanced around the room. No sign of Phyllis.

They'd wandered past four tables when Lou stopped at a quiet table with only two other players. "I'll stay here," he said.

"Good luck."

Casey kissed him and then wandered toward another cluster of slot machines. Trying to be inconspicuous, she studied faces. It didn't take long before she realized she was lost and quite possibly strolling through ground she'd already covered. The bank of slot machines with the nautical theme looked familiar, as did the players with their blank stares and rounded shoulders, regardless of age. The mind-numbing, repetitive spin of symbols held these people captive, as if they were pinned to their seats by giant, invisible tacks. Casey's phone rang and a moment later she heard Kendal's exuberant voice.

"Guess who I just saw in the poker room?" Before Casey could reply, Kendal blurted, "Mia! And she's sitting at a five-hundred-buck-minimum table."

"Whoa. Given that she's in a custody battle and angling for the permanent director's job, she wasn't my first pick. Where are you now?"

"At a slot machine outside the room, but take your time. It looks like she'll be here a while. The woman has four stacks of chips in front of her, maybe more."

"Sounds like a hell of a lot of money," Casey said.

"It is. Our acting director's quite the player. But even if she knows what she's doing, you've got to wonder how long she can keep it up without completely crashing."

It did make Casey wonder. Mia's salary couldn't support a gambling habit.

She peered past the sea of bodies and machines. "Where's the poker room? I'm totally lost."

Casey tried to follow Kendal's directions but soon found herself back at the blackjack tables. Lou seemed fully absorbed in the game. With three stacks of chips in front of him, his eyes didn't waver from the dealer's cards.

A couple of old gals bumped Casey's bruised arm with their gigantic handbags. She winced and clamped her hand onto the sore spot while the ladies shuffled on, apparently oblivious to the incident. Despite the noise and other distractions, most patrons seemed oblivious to everything but the pursuit of winning. Sure, a few groups of people were socializing and having fun, but they were in the minority.

Finally, Casey found a sign with an arrow pointing in the right direction. Dodging and sidestepping the people constantly crossing her path, she managed to spot Kendal playing at a slot machine near the poker room's entrance.

"Are you winning?" Casey asked as she watched Kendal push a button.

"No, and it's boring as hell." She turned to Casey. "I'm going back in the room to get another drink and see how Mia's doing with the chips."

"Maybe I should go. If you show up too often, you could draw unwanted attention."

"Why don't we both go? It'll look like I was waiting for you."

Although Kendal's strategy wasn't bad, Casey would rather go alone. Surveillance often worked better without the distraction of conversation. "I don't know. Two hot chicks in the room will definitely draw attention. I'll just be a minute. Meanwhile, keep playing while I get you another Caesar."

Before Kendal could respond, Casey stepped into the long rectangular room, also draped in red and gold, and illuminated with enormous chandeliers. She liked this room. There were fewer people milling about, the music was quieter, and there was a definite absence of chatter. Still, the solemn concentration was more predominant here than in the rest of the casino.

Nearly every table was full, but Casey easily spotted Mia's short yellow spikes. Her black, sequined tank top showed off muscular arms and a rose tattoo on her right shoulder blade.

Casey ordered the Caesar and turned to face the room. From her spot at the bar, she could see Mia's downcast expression and only three stacks of chips in front of her. The quick, dramatic loss explained the strain on her face. Would Mia stay until she lost it all?

Casey paid for the drink and returned to Kendal. "She has only three stacks left and doesn't look happy."

"If she's addicted, she'll eventually lose her job, her home, and definitely her custody battle," Kendal remarked. "It makes you wonder who else, besides Phyllis, knows how Mia spends her free time."

"I wouldn't call it free," Casey remarked. "I suppose Phyllis could have told Mac about the gambling. She and Mia seem to have issues. Others might know, too."

"If Mac and Winson knew about the gambling," Kendal said, "then I wouldn't want to be Phyllis."

TWENTY-ONE

CASEY FOLLOWED MIA DOWN THE dim corridor toward the Special Unit, which separated troublesome residents from the others. Being in juvie again made Casey's stomach clench. The stench of mold oozing through the walls at this end of the corridor didn't help. After spotting Mia at the casino two nights ago, Casey felt more uneasy than ever around her. Mia's phone call hadn't been a surprise, though. In fact, she'd been expecting it after Amy's news.

Staff should never have discussed Tanya's suicide attempt within earshot of Justin. His distraught phone call to Amy had sent her on a tirade. Amy didn't become enraged easily, but when she did, it was memorable. Casey was delighted to hear that Amy had blasted Mia for Fraserview's lack of professionalism, and that she'd threatened to go to the media. Amy had been even more outraged when Mia refused to let her see Justin, claiming that Amy's emotional state wouldn't be good for him. Amy had insisted that Casey go in her place. Casey wasn't sure why Mia had agreed to the demand. Maybe she was afraid that Amy would follow through on her media threat. Knowing Amy, she would have, and still might.

As they walked past the gymnasium, Casey heard another basketball game.

"I'd like you to keep the visit short," Mia said. "Fifteen minutes at most."

"Why did Justin wind up in the Special Unit?"

"After he heard about Tanya, he asked staff to put him in touch with her," Mia answered. "Given their emotional states and that the trial's coming up, I didn't think it was a good idea. In fact, Mac shouldn't have let them communicate in here to begin with."

"He said that Justin was a calming influence on Tanya."

"Maybe, but things have changed since their escape. When Justin realized we weren't going to help him, he began pounding his fists into the wall and throwing things. He was going to hurt himself or someone else."

"Do you know if Tanya will be okay?"

"Physically, yes. She was found in time and is now in the hospital."

But would she be all right emotionally? "Which hospital is she in?"

Mia told her while she unclipped the key ring from her belt. She unlocked a heavy, metal door and stepped into a short hallway that was cooler than the rest of the stuffy building. One pathetic forty-watt bulb illuminated the area. Casey counted four cell doors. To her right, she saw a small kitchen.

"Normally, a youth supervisor would be with you, but she's needed elsewhere, so I'll have to lock you in."

"That's fine."

Mia stepped across the hall and looked through the small square of wire-meshed glass in one of the cell doors. She then unlocked the door.

"Casey's here. Come on out."

A pale, exhausted Justin emerged. Glancing at Casey, he shuffled toward the kitchen.

"If you need anything, use the radio I gave you," Mia said to Casey, turning on the kitchen light, "or press the button." She pointed to the button next to the light switch.

"Okay."

Neither of them spoke until Mia was gone. Justin slumped into a plastic orange chair that had been gouged in several places. She noticed he was trying not to look at the still visible wound on her forehead—a reminder of Tanya's violence. Casey waited until Mia had locked the outer door before she said, "Are you being treated okay?"

He shrugged. "They leave me alone."

Casey listened to the ancient refrigerator's labored hum. She glanced at the single plastic plate and cup in the dish rack. Leaning forward, she clasped her hands and rested them on the Formica table. Discussing Tanya would probably further upset him, so she decided to postpone it for a bit. Besides, other questions needed answering.

"Justin, can you tell me what really happened between you and Brady the night he fell down the stairs?"

He blinked at her, his eyes suspicious. "Why?"

"It's the reason you're here in the first place. Amy's convinced you're innocent, so if we can get it resolved, then maybe we can get you out of here."

Justin looked down. "Doubt it."

"Let's try, okay?" No response. "Humor me."

He rubbed his hands on his wrinkled pants. "Brady and me were fightin'."

"About what?"

"Him bringing drugs home. Could have got us all in deep shit. Me and Tanya and Didi had been trying to get him to stop but he wouldn't." Justin shifted in his chair. "But that night, he'd been drinkin', and he started bragging about his drug money, and it pissed me off."

The refrigerator clunked loudly, then resumed humming.

"I need to ask an important question. Whatever you answer stays between us, if you want it to." Casey paused. "Did you, or Tanya, push Brady down the stairs?"

"No!" Justin's right leg twitched rapidly. "Brady was wasted. He tripped over me, lost his balance, and fell. Hit his head on those stupid marble steps Carl put in."

"What did you do after that?"

"Told Tanya to call 911. Mom and Carl were out." Justin's face reddened. "Mom thinks Carl's so great because he buys her things, but it was Brady's dope that paid for everything."

"You mean Brady gave his dad money?"

"Hell, yeah. Brady told him some bullshit story about landing a union job at a warehouse. Carl didn't want to know the truth, and Mom wouldn't say anything against either of them." Justin's leg twitched faster. "I tried to tell her what Brady was doin', but she told me to shut up."

No wonder he hadn't sought his mother's help when he escaped. "Has Cristano Cruz tried to contact you?"

"Not yet. But he will."

She was afraid he was right. "I've been thinking about our last conversation. Is Cruz recruiting kids from here to sell drugs?"

Justin rolled his eyes. "What do you think?"

She didn't appreciate the sarcasm. "I need verbal confirmation for the police."

"They won't believe me."

"They'll believe me. I have friends on the force. Good friends. People I can trust."

Justin blinked at her a couple of times. "Mercedes finds girls to work for him."

That explained why she kept coming back to juvie. "Who else in here works for the uncle?"

He shrugged. "That girl with the dreadlocks, but I think she's out now."

Roxanne? That was interesting, given that she'd identified Mercedes as Mia's snitch and clearly didn't like the girl. "I doubt she's thrilled with the arrangement," Casey said.

"She hates Mercedes, Mia, and Cruz."

Casey again thought of Mia. "Justin, are any staff part of the drug ring?"

He glanced down the short, empty hallway. "How do you think Cruz got us out?"

"I don't quite understand."

He leaned forward and whispered, "Somebody gave him a key to the gate."

"So you didn't use those crates to climb over the fence?"

"Nah." He leaned back. "How could we have climbed over barbed wire?"

"I couldn't figure that out either. Listen, the last thing Mac said before he died was your and Tanya's name. But I don't think he was the one who gave Cruz the key."

Justin again looked down the hallway. "Tanya is pretty sure that Mia did it, though she never saw nothin'."

It made sense. Mia's gambling habit required a lot of cash, and who better to provide it than someone like Cristano Cruz? "Did you see Mac before he had his heart attack?"

Justin stared at the tabletop for a few moments before looking up. "Just before we left, I saw Mac leaning against the wall near his office. He was kind of hunched over."

"Was anyone else near him?"

"No."

"Anyone in the corridor?"

Justin shook his head. "Not that I remember."

Mia had relaxed the visiting rules for Cruz, rules that Mac had tightened to keep Cruz from talking to the kids. Mia had been on duty when both men died. Oh, god, had she killed Mac and Winson to protect her secrets? Or did other staff also hold secrets worth killing for? Was there some sort of conspiracy to hide illegal activity in Fraserview?

"You heard about Tanya?" Justin's voice was barely audible.

"Yes, and she's going to be fine."

"Who said?"

"Mia."

The boy's eyes blazed. "You can't trust what she says. You can't trust any of them!" He smacked the table.

"I know that." Casey sat up straighter, alert and wary. "Justin, listen to me. It's going to be all right."

"You don't get it!"

"What don't I get?"

Anguish twisted his mouth. "It's my fault she tried to kill herself!" He jumped out of his chair, knocking it to the floor.

"No, Justin. You can't control what other people think or do."

He swept his hand through his greasy blond hair. "I was glad she wasn't here, and she knew it." He paced the room. "Tanya never listens. Always has to have things her way. I wouldn't have run if she hadn't made me."

"I know."

He righted the chair and sat down. "I should have told her I'd stick with her, that I wouldn't dump her."

"You were planning to end the relationship?"

"Yes—No. I dunno." Elbows on the table, he clamped his hands on either side of his head. "Tanya's the only one who gets me. When I was fighting with Mom and Carl, she made things okay. She's been through family shit."

Given Tanya's assault record, Casey could only imagine how she had helped him deal with family trouble. "She was at the house a lot?"

"Yeah. She's good friends with Didi." He paused. "Could you go see if Tanya's okay?"

Oh, lord. "I don't think she'll want to see me."

"She will if you tell her you have a message from me." He hesitated. "Tell her I've still got her back."

Casey thought about this. "Because you think it's the right thing to do, or because it's true?"

He shrugged. "She just needs to hear it."

"Okay," Casey said. "I'll try to see her." But she wasn't looking forward to it.

A key turned in the lock to the main door. Justin grew rigid, his expression blank. Mia had apparently decided to cut their fifteen minutes short. Was she worried about what Justin would say? She was accompanied by a youth supervisor Casey didn't recognize.

"I know you're only here to visit," Mia said, "but I was wondering if you could do me a huge favor and help Ruby for a half hour? She's got her hands full with a new resident."

"Sure."

Justin's expression didn't change as the youth supervisor escorted him back to his cell. Casey and Mia returned to the main corridor.

"Maybe you could talk to the girl," Mia began. Then a call came in on her radio and she turned away from Casey.

Cold air wafted around Casey's shoulders. She turned to the south exit, but it was closed. She looked up at the flickering fluorescent lights, then at the pool room door. The door wasn't completely shut, and the air coming from the room increased the damp, moldy smell in the hall. Wasn't the door supposed to be kept locked? The small window in the door revealed darkness. Casey pulled open the door and was surprised to hear voices. She poked her head inside to find Phyllis murmuring to Oksana.

"What do you want?" Oksana asked, glaring at Casey.

"The door wasn't closed properly."

"You can leave now."

Why was this woman always so rude? Casey turned to Phyllis, who was wearing her cardigan and hugging herself in this chilly room. "How are things, Phyllis?"

"Middlin', dear. Middlin'."

Whatever that meant. Casey looked from one to the other. Obviously, they weren't about to continue their conversation in front of her. What had she interrupted? "Have a nice evening, ladies."

She started out of the room, when Mia pushed her way past Casey. "What are you two doing in here? I thought I said no storing supplies in the pool room."

"Just checking to make sure I got everything out," Oksana answered.

"Uh-huh." Mia turned to Phyllis. "And you?"

"Mopping the floor." She nodded toward the puddle near the deep end of the pool. "The leak's getting worse."

"Then shouldn't you get on with it?"

Both women gaped at her.

"Casey," Mia said, her tone even frostier than the room. "Will you excuse us?"

"No problem."

She didn't want to hear Mia lecture employees. Casey stepped outside. She hadn't gotten far when she spotted the shoplifter, Jamal, leaving the visitors' room with a taller man. Oh, crap, was that Jamal's relative? The man was too far away to see clearly, but he could be the guy from the donair shop. Both of them stopped and looked in her direction. Jamal said something to his visitor, who looked at her again. Even from where she stood she could see the scowl on his face. Casey's ear began to throb, as if she needed reminding not to tangle with them. Maintaining a casual pace, she lengthened her stride. Jamal started down the corridor with his pigeon-toed gait and hostile stare.

Casey slipped inside the girls' unit. The door closed. Three seconds later, a loud bang on the door startled her. She kept walking, ignoring the source. Why give the little shit any satisfaction?

"What was dat?" Ruby said, stepping out of her office.

"There's a boy named Jamal wandering down the corridor alone," Casey replied. "The kid hates me for busting him after he attacked me. He's the boy who cut my ear, and he just kicked the door, probably to try and intimidate me."

"We'll see about dat." Ruby charged into the corridor.

→   →   →

BY THE TIME Casey left the girls' unit forty minutes later, she was exhausted from the latest arrival's rant about how she wouldn't be here if her boyfriend hadn't screwed her over. The more she talked, the more riled up and aggressive she became. As a last resort, Ruby took her to the Special Unit, where Jamal was also now spending the night. Apparently, he hadn't shown Ruby proper respect either.

Casey hurried down the hot, smelly corridor. At reception, she found Rawan staring sullenly into space.

"You look a bit down," Casey said, tossing her visitor's badge in the basket. "Is everything all right?"

Rawan stood and adjusted her skirt. "I've got a lot on my mind."

"Understandable. Two employees have died over a short period of time. Kids are coming and going. I don't know how you survive the turmoil."

"Not sure I have a choice," Rawan mumbled, handing Casey her coat and purse.

Should she ask what that meant? Casey was still debating this when Rawan returned to her desk and began reading whatever was on her computer screen. Each time Casey came here, Rawan seemed less happy. Did she know about Cristano Cruz's drug business? Did she know that staff were involved? Hell, was she part of it? Maybe her background should be checked out.

Casey stepped out into the freezing night and put on her gloves. Gripping the railing, she descended the icy steps carefully. Her head down, she shuffled across the equally slippery parking lot. Casey almost reached her car when someone grabbed her arm and pulled her backward. She lost her balance, as did the person grabbing her. He fell on his side, letting go of her. Glimpsing the same man who'd been with Jamal, Casey grabbed the car door handle and shoved the key in the lock.

"Shit!" He struggled to stand.

Casey started to climb inside, but one leg was still out when he gripped the doorframe and reached for her. Casey screamed and kicked him hard. Down he went again.

"You stupid bitch!"

She slammed the door and locked it. "You testify against Jamal and you're dead!" he yelled.

It took two attempts before her shaking hand could insert the key in the ignition and start the engine. If that idiot came at her again, she'd honk the horn loud and long enough to raise the dead. Through the frosty passenger-side window she saw him slip-slide toward a vehicle. Without waiting for her windshield to fully defrost, she peeled out of the lot.

TWENTY-TWO

AS CASEY LISTENED TO A Michael Bublé CD, Lou placed a linen napkin—used only for special occasions—across her lap. She returned his smile, awestruck and grateful for the candlelit meal he'd prepared. The Cornish game hens looked baked to perfection, and he'd chosen a chardonnay, one of the few wines she liked. She was equally grateful that he hadn't bought chocolate for this special Valentine's meal. Lou had learned from harsh experience that chocolate drastically altered her mood, and not in a good way. At this moment, all was right with the world. Summer had been invited to dinner at a girlfriend's house and would be brought home later by the friend's parents. Casey could almost feel the tension of the last few days slip from her shoulders.

"I'm so amazed you did all this," she said.

"I should have been more help with the cooking, so I'm changing my ways, beginning with this dinner." He kissed her on the cheek. "Oh. Forgot the salt and pepper."

Casey pushed aside her worries about Justin and the disturbing events at Fraserview. She'd filed a police report about the attempted assault in the parking lot three nights ago, and had also briefed Mia and Kendal. If Mia kept her word, Jamal's visitor wouldn't be allowed on the premises, let alone in the building, ever again.

"I think we're all set," Lou said, setting her rarely used crystal salt and pepper shakers on the table.

Casey admired the colorful assortment of veggies around the hens. "This is fantastic." He'd even prepared shrimp cocktail. Granted, it wasn't the most challenging appetizer to make, but for Lou it was a milestone. "I had no idea you could cook a hen."

"Maybe you should taste it before you get too excited. Mom gave me the recipe and some tips, but I don't know if I did it right." He raised his wine glass. "Happy Valentine's."

"And to you."

After he kissed her and they sipped the wine, Lou lifted a hen onto her plate, then began serving carrots, beets, and broccoli.

"You're spoiling me," Casey said.

"This is just the start of what I hope will be many romantic evenings."

"It's perfect." She felt as if they were turning a corner. Habits and routines were becoming comfortable. A new sense of harmony was settling over the apartment like a velvet cloak.

"Thank Kendal for agreeing to volunteer after all," he said.

"She said it was no problem. Her mom preferred going to lunch instead of dinner anyway, and Fraserview desperately needs help tonight. Seems that Valentine's is a depressing night for some of the girls."

"Aren't they a little young for love affairs?" He paused. "Oh, wait. Summer's thirteen. Never mind."

"The residents are also hyper-emotional so it doesn't take much to set them off." Casey didn't add that Kendal also welcomed the chance to dig for more dirt on Mia and other staff.

Lou's gray eyes shone in the candlelight and his brown hair took on a coppery sheen. Those full sexy lips parted and he started to say something, but he then stopped.

Casey sensed his anticipation. "What is it?"

"I was going to bring this up after dinner, but I just realized I can't eat until I get this out."

It sounded serious. Lou wouldn't have gone to this much trouble just to dump bad news on her, would he? When he stood and turned the music down, she began to worry. Casey's phone rang. She glanced at the screen. "It's Kendal. She can wait."

Lou sat and fiddled with his napkin. "I don't know how to do this," he murmured.

Oh, god, this was bad. Had he decided to make some big, momentous change? Had he found another job?

"You know I loved you long before we got together, right?" he asked.

"Yes."

"And you know you mean the world to me."

Casey nodded. His news must be really bad.

"As far as I'm concerned, this arrangement between us is permanent," he said.

"Me too." She leaned back in her chair. Was he planning to take a job out of the city? "You're starting to scare me a little, though."

"Then I'm handling this badly." Lou took a quick sip of wine, then used his napkin to wipe his brow.

Good lord, he was starting to sweat, not something he did often. It couldn't be the wine, and the room wasn't that warm.

"There's no one else I'll ever want to be with," he blurted, rubbing his hands together. "But you have to understand that part of me likes tradition."

"I know."

"Okay, then. Good." He hesitated. "Then you won't be totally shocked by this." He removed a tiny, blue velvet box from under his napkin. "I want us to officially be a couple."

As her throat went dry, heat swooshed over her face. She focused on the gorgeous little blue box, and when Lou opened it, she gasped.

"Will you marry me?" he whispered, his face bright red and hopeful.

Casey gaped at three half-carat diamonds, set diagonally in a wide band with a delicate swirl engraved on either side. "Oh my god."

"It's platinum," he said. "A non-traditional band for a non-traditional woman."

She tried to speak but the words wouldn't come. Mesmerized, she watched Lou slip the ring on her finger. She touched the cool, smooth platinum, the diamonds, and grew lightheaded.

"A perfect fit. How did you know?"

"I snuck the only ring you own out of the jewelry box," he replied. "So, what do you say, aside from *oh my god*."

Lou's features blurred as her eyes began to glisten. "For real?"

He kissed her hand. "For real."

Casey leaned close to him until their foreheads touched. "Then yes. Absolutely, yes."

One kiss led to three, until Lou's stomach growled loudly. "Sorry. I haven't eaten all day."

If he hadn't eaten all day, then he must have been really nervous. "Were you afraid I'd say no?"

He nodded. "You were so down on marriage after Greg." He stroked her cheek. "But things change. People change their needs and wants."

"They certainly do." She kissed him again. "Let's eat before you faint, and then we can enjoy the rest of the evening in bed."

Lou grinned and then said, "I could use some water. How about you?"

"Please."

While he headed for the kitchen, Casey's phone pinged: a text message from Kendal. *Found dirt on Amir, Rawan, and others. Will call later.*

What had she learned? As Lou returned, Casey slipped the phone under her napkin and thoughts of Fraserview faded away.

$\rightarrow$ $\rightarrow$ $\rightarrow$

THREE HOURS LATER, she was nearly asleep after the best night of her life. The ringing phone shattered the silence. It had to be Kendal. Casey checked the time. Nearly midnight. Why was she calling so late? Lou snored lightly. He wouldn't notice if she took the call. Rubbing her eyes, she answered the phone.

"This is Deanne Winters. Sorry to call so late."

Kendal's mom? This couldn't be good. "What's wrong?"

"It's Kendal . . . There's been an accident."

"A car accident?"

"No."

Deanne's distraught tone sent fear surging through Casey. "What happened?"

"She had a bad fall at the detention center where she's been volunteering." Deanne's voice cracked. "She has broken bones and a head injury. The doctors don't know how serious it is, but there's a possibility . . ." Deanne started to sob.

Casey jumped out of bed. "Did she fall down some stairs?" She thought of the icy steps at the entrance to the building and the altercation in the parking lot.

"No." Deanne sniffed. "Into the deep end of the empty swimming pool."

"What?" That made no sense. What the hell would Kendal have been doing in the pool room? Had Phyllis and Oksana not closed the door properly last night, or had another employee gone inside?

"Kendal told me that you're also a volunteer," Deanne said. "So, I'm hoping you can find out how this happened. She told me about the suspicious deaths of two staff members. I need to know what's going on, Casey."

"I'll do my best. When can I go and see her?"

Deanne didn't answer right away. "They need to do some tests. I'll let you know."

Casey bit down on her lip. She put her hand on her stomach to calm the queasiness. "Kendal texted me earlier tonight and wanted to tell me something. It might have been important, so I need to talk to her."

"You don't understand." Deanne's voice quivered. "Kendal's in a coma. We don't know when, or if, she'll come out of it."

"Oh, no." Casey began to shiver. "Kendal's one of the toughest people I know. If anyone can pull through, she can."

"I believe that too." Deanne's voice was nearly a whisper. "I'll be in touch."

Casey put the phone on the night table and covered her face with her hands. She felt Lou stir, and then his hand on her shoulder. She tried to tell him what happened but kept stumbling over the words. By the time she finally finished, tears were sliding down her face.

"Two people dead and now this," she said, reaching for a tissue. "What if Kendal learned something she wasn't supposed to know?"

"The cops'll figure it out." He stroked her hair. "Let them do their job, Casey. They're your best hope for finding the truth."

Casey wasn't so sure.

TWENTY-THREE

CASEY TURNED OFF HER CAR'S ignition and took a deep calming breath. She looked out the windshield, side windows, and rearview mirror, checking for enemies in Fraserview's parking lot. She'd learned that Mia drove the silver Lexus SUV parked three stalls down, but there was no sign of Phyllis's Smart car. Other familiar vehicles were here, which was good. She needed to talk to the staff she knew.

Deanne Winters had called this afternoon to report no change in Kendal's condition. Her prognosis was still unknown. The police had no new information either, or at least nothing they were willing to share. The lack of answers surrounding the circumstances of Kendal's fall infuriated her. She'd bet a year's pay that it wasn't an accident.

Lou didn't support her plan to interview staff, yet he'd offered to go with her. She would have appreciated his company, but without security clearance he wouldn't be allowed inside. Besides, she didn't want Summer left alone.

Although Stan, not to mention the cops, frowned upon pepper spray, she was in no mood for an ambush. She fetched the can she kept under the passenger seat, then looked around once more before stepping out of the car. As Casey moved, she scanned the area, alert to noise and movement, daring some asshole to mess with her. At the top of the steps, Casey pressed the intercom and identified herself.

"We weren't expecting you," Rawan said.

"I won't be long." She shoved the can in her pocket. "I just need to talk to Mia about Kendal Winters's accident."

The buzzer sounded and Casey stepped inside. The corridor was as dim and empty as ever, as if nothing significant had occurred.

As Casey signed in, Rawan said, "What a gorgeous ring. I've never noticed it before."

"Thank you. I got engaged last night."

"On Valentine's? That's so romantic. Congratulations." Her expression became wistful. "Have you set a date?"

"No." She'd been too upset about Kendal to let the reality of her engagement sink in.

"If you were volunteering, I'd say leave it in your purse," Rawan said. "But since you're only here to see Mia, I suppose it's all right."

Casey had no intention of telling Rawan that she planned to speak to others as well. "Where is Mia?"

"No idea." Rawan placed Casey's coat and purse in a locker. "I can call her on the radio."

"Don't bother. She won't be hard to find." Casey signed in, then picked up a visitor's badge. "Were you working last night?"

"Yes." Rawan paused. "It's so awful. Thank god the ambulance arrived quickly."

Awful didn't begin to cover it. Casey hadn't forgotten Kendal's text message about finding dirt on Rawan. "Any idea how she wound up in a room that was supposed to be locked?" Casey waited for an explanation. All she got was a small shrug. "Come on, Rawan. You must have heard something."

"Supervisors don't share much with me." Rawan adjusted the elastic holding her dark, blond-streaked ponytail. "Ask Mia."

Casey looked down the corridor. A corrections officer was strolling toward the south end. "I take it Phyllis isn't working tonight? I didn't see her car."

"It's her night off."

Damn. "How about Oksana?"

"She's here."

"Was she working last night?"

Rawan frowned. "Why are you asking all these questions about staff?"

"Why do you think?"

Rawan crossed her arms. "You have no right to suspect employees. It was just an accident."

"Really?" Casey removed her phone from her jeans pocket, then located Kendal's message. She held the phone in front of Rawan. "Read the text Kendal sent last night." As Rawan did so, her mouth parted and those dark eyes filled with trepidation. "What did she find out about you, Rawan?"

"I've nothing to say." She held out her hand. "You have to leave the phone here."

"Like hell. No one touches this phone until the police see the message." Casey let her anger rise. "It's evidence in what could be attempted murder. So, start talking or I take this to Mia's boss and the police right now."

Rawan gaped at her. "No. You're wrong!"

"Bull. Kendal is an award-winning athlete and trained security officer." She glanced at Mia's dark office. "I've known her nearly twenty years and I've never seen her trip over anything in her life. And with two suspicious deaths in this dump, surely you must have wondered. Now, do you want to tell me what Kendal learned about you, or should I call the authorities right now?"

Rawan's face paled. "I didn't have anything to do with what happened to her, I swear."

"Good to know. What's the text about?"

Rawan propped her elbows on the counter and covered her face with her hands for a moment. "This has to stay between us. It's nothing illegal."

"Okay, but you've been secretive and distracted lately. What's going on?"

Rawan cleared her throat and whispered, "Kendal caught Amir kissing me."

Good lord. What did Rawan see in that rude, macho idiot? "So?"

"We've been involved for about three months. He has a wife and kids."

"Oh." Casey paused. "How did he take it when he realized Kendal saw you two?"

"He was upset. Told Kendal not to say anything or he'd make sure that . . ." Rawan gripped the edge of the counter. "Look, I know that Amir can be abrupt, but he's not violent. He wouldn't hurt anyone."

Right. Sure. "Is he here tonight?"

She shook her head. "I've been trying to break it off, but he won't." Despair swept over her face. "It's not just that he's married. My family's from Lebanon, but we're Christian. He's Muslim. If his wife's family learned about me . . . No one must know."

Which meant that Amir might do anything to keep their secret. And how far would Rawan go to protect herself? "Did Winson or Mac know about you two?"

She looked away. "I don't think so."

"Rawan, I saw Winson and Amir in a heated discussion a few nights ago. Was it about the two of you?"

Despair turned to fear. "Amir never said anything to me. And it was common knowledge that Winson didn't like Amir's no-nonsense, militaristic style with the kids. They'd argued about it before."

Was *that* why Amir hadn't been appointed acting director? Had Winson badmouthed him to the executive director? If Winson knew about the affair, he might have mentioned that too.

"The night Mac died, Mia said something to you about the wife always being the last to know," Casey remarked. "I think she has a pretty good idea about you and Amir."

"She can't prove anything, and she has her own secrets to protect."

Did Rawan know about the gambling? Given that Kendal had caught Rawan and Amir kissing, how discreet were they? "Any idea where Mia was when Kendal fell into the pool?"

"No." Rawan leaned over the counter and peeked down the corridor. "But it wouldn't surprise me if she'd been nearby."

"Why?"

"That paranoid, power-tripping bitch is always lurking about, eavesdropping." Rawan kept her voice low. "She'll do whatever it takes to get what she wants." She leaned closer to Casey and whispered, "We both saw Mia working on Mac during the heart attack. I've been wondering if she was helping him, or making things worse."

"You honestly believe she'd go that far to get his job when the facility's closing in a few months anyway?"

Rawan shrugged. "She's nasty and ambitious, and even a short period as acting director would improve her résumé. Maybe you should ask where she was when Winson died." She looked at Casey's phone. "You won't tell anyone about us, will you?"

"No." Unless there was sufficient reason to let the police know. "I'd better go find your acting director."

Casey started down the corridor, glancing into the visitors' area. Damn. Mercedes and Cristano Cruz were there. Mercedes had been released only six days ago, so how had she wound up back here so quickly? Had Cruz told her to break the law so she'd be brought back? After all, he had a score to settle with Justin.

"Casey?" Mia said, stepping out of the conference room. "What are you doing here?"

"I came to see you about Kendal. Her mother wants to know what happened."

Mia scratched the back of her head. Her short, spiky hair looked like it needed washing. "I've been trying to find that out myself, but no one saw anything. I can't begin to fathom what Kendal was doing in the pool room in the first place. The lighting is poor and Kendal was found at the far end, where the leak is worse. The tiles there are really slippery."

"The pool room door's supposed to be locked, right?" Casey asked. "Who would have opened it?"

"Phyllis is supposed to check the floor every time it rains." Mia frowned. "She won't admit it, but I'm sure she didn't close the door properly. She doesn't half the time."

"Someone, or something, must have drawn Kendal down there," Casey said.

Mia hesitated. "Jamal left the gym to use Unit Two's bathroom and didn't return right away."

Oh, crap. "Did you question him?"

"Of course. He denied heading in that direction, and no one can place him by the pool room."

"But the pool's next to the gym."

"There are simply no eye witness accounts, Casey."

"What about CCTV cameras?"

"The one at the south end's still not functioning. Fixing things isn't a priority here."

If Jamal truly was involved, how had he figured out who Kendal was? Had he recalled seeing her in GenMart?

"Listen," Mia said. "I know it seems suspicious, but sometimes coincidences are just that. And sometimes accidents really are accidents."

Not in this place. "Who found Kendal?"

"Amir. He called the code at 8:05 PM."

Damn. The bastard could have pushed Kendal in, then called for help. Even if he were innocent, he'd be the last person to share information with a volunteer.

Casey glanced at the visitors' room. "When did Mercedes come back?"

"Yesterday. Why?"

Given that she might be mixed up with Cruz, Mia mustn't know Casey had her suspicions about him. If he'd been here, would he have ventured to the far end of the building? Why would he hurt Kendal, though?

"She was out only about a week," Casey answered. "I've gotten to know her and she seems like a good kid."

"Mercedes has her problems."

If Mia was working with Cruz, had she given him access to the Special Unit? Had he gotten to Justin? Casey began to sweat from the smelly, overheated air.

"Justin's grandmother told me that Justin's still separated from the others," Casey said.

"He insists on staying there until he's transferred. The boy does seem more emotionally stable on his own. Still, it would be better if he rejoined the others. I simply don't have enough staff to keep someone down there. There's no room at another facility, and nothing I can do about that."

"May I see him a moment?"

Mia didn't answer right away. Then she said, "Only if you try to persuade him to rejoin his unit."

"All right."

They walked down the dim corridor, the air made even more oppressive by the silence. Usually, the boys would be playing basketball in the gym, but not tonight.

"Would you be interested in staying on with us?" Mia asked. "I realize I haven't helped make things easy for you, and I apologize for that, but we could certainly use an extra pair of hands."

Considering their strained conversation, Mia's request surprised Casey. She wanted to say no, but she had to find out how Kendal wound up in an empty swimming pool. Besides, as long as Justin was stuck in this place, he wasn't safe. Amy needed another pair of eyes watching out for the boy.

"I'll work another shift, then see how it goes." As they passed the girls' unit, Casey asked, "Is Ruby on duty?"

"Yes. She was working last night too and is still shaken by the accident. Probably won't stop talking about it for weeks."

"I assume that Roxanne's still out."

"Yes." Mia's eyes narrowed as she tilted her head slightly. "Were you two friendly?"

"We played Scrabble once," Casey replied. "Got along pretty well."

As they neared the pool room, Casey noticed the lack of crime scene tape across the door; that was discouraging. After two questionable deaths, did the police honestly think Kendal's fall was an accident? Still, without solid evidence, what could they do?

Inside the Special Unit, Mia unlocked Justin's cell. "Casey's popped by to say hello."

Justin stepped out and gave Casey a brief nod as he made his way to the kitchen. The boy looked more exhausted and paler than he had the last time she saw him.

"Buzz if you need anything. I'll be back shortly," Mia said, locking Casey in.

Peering through the outer door's window, Casey could see the pool room's entrance. She looked at the window in Justin's cell door. It lined up with the other windows.

"Did you see Tanya?" he asked.

"I'm sorry, I haven't had time. I promise I'll go tomorrow night." She felt guilty for putting off the visit, but she had no desire to see the girl who'd beaned her with a rock.

Justin slumped into a chair, his expression blank.

"I guess you heard about the volunteer's accident last night," Casey said.

"Yeah."

"Kendal's a close friend. It was my idea that she volunteer here."

Justin looked up. "Will she be okay?"

"We don't know yet," Casey replied. "I noticed that you can see the pool room door from your cell. Did you happen to see or hear anything last night?"

He shifted in his chair. "I saw Amir go in."

Good. "Do you remember what time it was?"

"Just after eight. He let me out so I could watch TV."

Casey glanced at the small TV perched on a table. "What happened after that?"

"I'd just switched on the TV when I heard shouting. I went and looked out the window. Supervisors were running into the pool room, but that's all I saw. At least no one can blame me for her getting hurt." He paused. "When you see Tanya, ask her to tell you the truth about what happened to Brady."

"Okay." But would Tanya cooperate? Would her word even mean much? "Listen, Mia only allowed me in here because I agreed to try to persuade you to return to your unit." Justin looked up, his gaze suddenly sharp. "Has Cruz approached you, or threatened you?"

"No."

"Then why won't you go back?"

He shrugged. "I'm tired of being treated like scum for what happened to Mac and Winson."

"Mercedes returned to Fraserview yesterday and Cruz is with her now," Casey said. "With Mia's help, he could get at you in here and no one would see what was happening."

"Shit."

"You need to return to your unit."

"Think I'll be safer there?"

"As long as you're not left alone." Casey heard keys jangling and the door opening. Mia stepped inside. "That was fast," Casey remarked.

"Sorry, but this is an unscheduled visit and all the time I can give you." She turned to Justin. "Has Casey talked to you about rejoining the others?"

He hesitated, then nodded. "I'll go."

"Thanks." She managed a quick smile. "Get your things and I'll have you escorted back to your unit in a few minutes."

Justin looked at Casey with what she interpreted as both gratitude and trepidation. After Mia locked the unit's outer door behind them, she and Casey started down the corridor. Casey nearly bumped into Oksana as she emerged from the kitchen. The cook glowered at both of them before stomping down the hall with quick, determined strides.

"Why does that woman look so miserable all the time?" Casey whispered.

"My guess is exhaustion and frustration, thanks to a deadbeat husband, five kids, and a boat load of debt. She has another job stocking store shelves. I suppose I should cut Oksana some slack, but she sure makes it tough."

"What did she have to say about last night's accident?"

"Claims she saw nothing, which is what I'd expect from her."

Oksana worked at this end of the building. She could have seen something, but she wouldn't want to cooperate with Mia. Casey needed an excuse to stay in the building a bit longer. She needed to talk to Oksana. "Can I pop in to say hi to Ruby and the girls?"

"I'm not sure that's a good idea. Talking about Kendal will upset Ruby even more," Mia replied. "Two deaths and a serious accident have made everyone edgy."

"I understand, and I promise to keep it short and upbeat."

Someone called for Mia on the radio. Mia gave Casey a quick nod and continued down the hall. Casey entered the girls' unit and found Ruby talking to a couple of girls who were making greeting cards. Two more sat on the sofa, watching TV.

Ruby looked up. "Hey der, gal. Didn't know I had a volunteer tonight."

"I'm not on the schedule. Just came by to see Mia and thought I'd pop in to say hi." The girls on the sofa turned around. All were familiar. "I see that Mercedes is back."

Ruby clicked her tongue. "Dat girl never learns."

"Was her uncle here last night as well?"

"He was supposed to be. I caught her standing in da hallway waitin' for him, but he never showed."

Or maybe he had. Had Cruz gone into the pool room? Was Mercedes the lookout? But what would Cruz have against Kendal?

Ruby grasped Casey's hands. "So sorry about Kendal." She ushered Casey into her office and closed the door. "She okay?"

"She's in a coma." Casey watched Ruby ease her bulky frame into the chair. "The doctors don't know when she'll come out of it."

"Dat girl is strong," Ruby said. "I'll pray for her. You should talk to her. Dat would help."

Casey felt her cheeks coloring. The pathetic truth was that she'd been too afraid to go to the hospital. Could barely admit how terrified she was to see Kendal so vulnerable. "Did you see anyone near the pool room last night? I know Amir was the one who found her."

Ruby seemed to think this over. "I'll tell you what I told the police." She peered at Casey. "Miss high and mighty was in der."

Casey frowned. "Mia? She didn't mention that to me."

"Why would she? Got to keep her fancy job. Don't want no one blamin' her for anyting."

"Was she in the pool room before or after Amir?"

"Before," Ruby replied. "She went in der about seven-thirty. I found Mercedes in the hallway just as Mia was goin' in the pool room."

Interesting that Mia hadn't ordered Mercedes back into her unit, but if the girl—already accused of being Mia's snitch—had been the lookout, then of course Mia wouldn't have said anything. "Did either of them look nervous or guilty about anything?"

"Dey looked the same as ever." Ruby gazed past Casey's shoulder toward the common area. "Here comes the she-devil now."

Mia appeared in the doorway. "Hate to break this up, but you said you'd keep it short."

"True. Bye, Ruby."

Casey left the unit alone, glad that Mia was staying behind. Casey started down the corridor and nearly bumped into Oksana, who was leaving a storage room. She blinked bloodshot eyes at Casey and her mouth tightened into a disapproving pout.

"Hello, Oksana. Did you see the volunteer Kendal in the pool room last night?"

"What's it got to do with you?"

Enough of the damn rudeness. "First of all, she's a good friend of mine. Secondly, her mother asked me to find out what really happened. Is that all right with you, or should I tell the police that you're hiding something?" Had Kendal found some dirt on this woman?

Her apple cheeks darkened into an unflattering fuchsia tone. "I've got nothing to hide, and don't you *dare* talk to me like that."

Time to push this witch's buttons. "You're withholding information, aren't you? I can see it in your eyes."

Oksana shifted the paper bag she was carrying. "What was the girl doing in the pool room in the first place? Volunteers got no business in there."

Not the explosive denial Casey had anticipated. "Kendal wouldn't have gone in without a reason."

"I didn't see nothin'." She looked away.

"I think you did." Oksana pushed past Casey and marched toward the kitchen, muttering something Casey couldn't hear. "I won't stop till I find the truth, Oksana. My cop friends will take a close look at each and every employee until all the secrets are exposed!"

Oksana's body fat jiggled as she practically jogged into the kitchen.

Casey headed in the opposite direction. She spotted Jamal glaring at her through the small window in Unit Two's door. The kid gave her the finger. Fuming, Casey returned the gesture and continued toward reception.

Did that little shithead have something to do with Kendal's injuries? Or did Rawan, Amir, Mia, or Oksana? They'd all been here last night *and* the nights that Winson and Mac were killed. Casey glanced into the visitors' area again. Cruz, perhaps the most dangerous of them all, was still there. The answers were within these walls, yet all she had were bits and pieces and the start of a timeline. Key questions still needed answering. The biggest one was what, or who, had drawn Kendal into the pool room to begin with?

TWENTY-FOUR

VISITING TANYA WOULD BE EASIER than Casey thought. Justin's beloved wasn't in the hospital's psychiatric area, but in the children's medical ward. Still, Casey had to acquire permission from Tanya and hospital staff. Even then, the visit would have to be short, which was fine. Chatting with the girl who'd pelted a rock at her forehead wasn't Casey's idea of a good time.

As she walked down the hall, she suspected that Tanya's room was close to the security guard sitting with his chair against the wall. Casey remembered working patient-watch shifts after completing basic security training. She spent two of the most boring weeks of her life observing patients who were flight risks or suicidal. When the site she was finally assigned to turned out to be just as boring, she'd jumped at the chance to take bus driver training with MPT, until that horrible night when she was attacked by a passenger with a knife. She didn't regret transferring to MPT's security department. She'd learned a lot from Stan and still enjoyed helping drivers and passengers, although she didn't picture herself doing the same job for the next thirty years.

Casey nodded to the seventysomething guard, who observed her with curiosity and caution. She figured a guard had been posted to Tanya because she was both suicidal and a flight risk.

"Are you here to see Miss North?" the guard asked.

The nurse must have given him a heads-up. "Yes. Is she allowed to leave her room?"

"Uh-huh. But not the ward. There's a TV room at the end of the hall, if you want to go there."

"Thanks."

Casey stepped into a semi-private room that smelled faintly of bleach. Tanya's bed was nearest the door. The other bed was empty, but the blankets were rumpled. Next to the bed, a bouquet of flowers sat on the windowsill surrounded by cards. Tanya's area had no flowers or cards. Her head was lowered and her hair covered much of her face as she searched what was probably music on her phone. Had Tanya's parents brought the girl her belongings, or had the items been transferred directly from Fraserview?

"Hello, Tanya."

Tanya looked up, her face clouding over. When Tanya raised her arms and removed her earphones, the white gauze around her wrists made the unsettling reality of her desperation and despondency clear. Although Casey didn't like the girl, she sure in hell didn't want her to take her own life.

"Have you seen Justin?" Tanya asked.

"Yes. He asked me to come here."

The girl's eyes lit up. "Really? Is he okay?"

"He's fine, but he's worried about you."

The light dimmed. "How'd he find out?"

"Justin overheard staff talking."

"Fucking morons. Guess he got sent back to that shithole."

"Yeah, his lawyer's trying to get him transferred."

"He hasn't been hurt, has he?"

"No. Is there a reason he would be?" She wanted Tanya to raise the topic of Cristano Cruz.

"You know what a hellhole it is."

Tanya looked so sad that Casey felt sorry for her. She pulled up a chair and sat down. "Justin wanted me to tell you that he still has your back."

Tanya's mouth quivered and she burst into tears. Casey glanced at the doorway, concerned that the sobs would draw a nurse's attention. She handed Tanya a tissue from the box on the side table.

"I'm sorry," Casey said. "I didn't mean to upset you."

"I'm just glad he doesn't hate me." She blew her nose. "Wish I could see him."

"That could happen." Casey paused. "If there was proof that Justin didn't kill his stepbrother, then he'd be free to see you."

Guilt flickered over Tanya's face. She turned toward the window.

"Would you like to go for a walk down the hall?" Casey asked.

"You could probably use a change of scenery."

Tanya kept her gaze on the window for a few more seconds, then slowly swung her legs over the side of the bed. It took her a minute to put on her robe and slippers, but once ready, she gripped her IV pole and shuffled toward the door. Casey followed, nodding to the guard, who seemed surprised that his charge was on the move. The old guy stood awkwardly. Luckily, Tanya wasn't moving fast.

As they made their way down the hall, Tanya said, "Did Justin say anything else about me?"

Thoughts of his initial relief over their separation flashed through Casey's mind. "He's sad that you're here."

Tanya turned away. "It's not his fault."

True. Casey tried not to look in the rooms. Few things in life were more disconcerting than a hospitalized child. For the most part, the ward was quiet, almost subdued.

"I miss him so much," Tanya mumbled. "But when he's free, his grandmother will turn him against me."

"What makes you say that?"

"Wouldn't you, if your son brought home a girl like me?"

"A girl like you?"

"With a juvie record."

And, based on that record, serious anger management issues. "Amy respects Justin's wants and needs. As long as you don't hurt him, I doubt she would try to keep you two apart."

"As if she could."

Great. The snarky attitude was back. Casey was about to say something when she saw Tanya tearing up again.

"I have hurt him," she mumbled.

This was unexpected. "In what way?" Tanya didn't respond. What was she hiding? "If you tell me, maybe I can help."

Tanya stopped moving and glared at her. "Why should I trust you?"

"Because Justin does. He wouldn't have sent me here otherwise. And he wouldn't have asked me to persuade you to tell the truth about what really happened to Brady."

"He said that?"

"He did. Ask him yourself."

Tanya glanced at the guard who was trailing behind them. Furrowing her brow, she seemed to be thinking things over. "It was an accident."

"I know. Justin told me," Casey replied. "What, exactly, happened?" Tanya continued down the hall. If she and Justin were innocent, why the reluctance to talk? "I understand why you threatened to tell the police that Justin pushed Brady down the stairs. It was to keep him with you." The predictable behavior of an insecure manipulator.

Tanya stopped again. "I can't believe he told you that!"

Casey sighed, her patience fading. "As I said, he trusts me."

"Whatever." Tanya continued on. "Anyway, wouldn't you do the same if he was all you had?"

"Maybe." If she was fifteen, insecure, and alone. Tanya had parents, though. If she felt unloved and unsupported, had she helped create the situation?

They entered a room with a birch table and chairs, a wall-mounted TV, and two sofas. Thankfully, no one else was here. She needed Tanya to talk freely. Tanya collapsed into the nearest chair and rested her chin on her hands. Casey sat across from her. The guard, looking like he could use a chair too, leaned against the wall and stared straight ahead. If Tanya decided to run away, that poor old man had no hope of catching her.

"Justin and Brady were fighting that night," Tanya said.

"So I heard." Casey leaned forward. "What happened just before Brady fell?"

"They were screaming at each other outside the bedrooms." Tanya gripped the edge of the table. "Brady swung at Justin and missed. He then went and kicked him right in the knee, and Justin fell." She took a breath. "Brady went after him again, only he tripped over Justin's foot . . . Lost his balance and tumbled backward all the way down to the bottom. The stupid cops didn't believe me."

"I can see where proving it will be a problem."

Tanya picked at her chipped nail polish. "Maybe not."

THE DEEP END   169

"What do you mean?"

"Didi saw it happen."

Brady's sister? "Do the police know?"

"No one does. I made her promise not to tell anyone and not to delete the footage."

"Footage?"

"On her phone."

Holy crap. "How did Didi come to be there?"

"She wasn't feeling good that night, so she stayed home. She was in her room, on the phone, until the fight got loud." Tanya's narrow shoulders hunched. "She came out, saw how bad it was, and started recording everything."

Oh, god. "And she didn't tell the police because of a promise to you?"

Tanya paused. "It's more than that. She was afraid of what her dad would do if she told the cops it was Brady's own fault. Brady's dad hates me and Justin. Wants to see us in jail forever."

Damn. This needed following up. "I'm guessing that Justin was too busy brawling to notice what Didi was doing?"

"He didn't even know she came out of her room. At least, he never mentioned her." Tanya hesitated. "After Brady fell, Justin ran down the stairs to check on him. Didi was so freaked out that she ran back to her room. Told everyone she was listening to music and didn't hear anything."

Clever girl. Tanya's arrangement with Didi allowed her to control Justin and make juvie bearable for a while. She'd probably planned to escape with him all along. Casey didn't bother to hide her irritation. "You should have told Justin."

Tears filled her eyes. "I wanted to, but the longer I waited the more pissed off he'd be."

And the less control she would have. "Do you think Didi still has the footage?"

Sniffling, she nodded. "Didi doesn't break promises . . . Unless her dad found it. When they stuck me in that other juvie, I wanted to call her, but they wouldn't let me have a phone." She wiped her eyes. "That's when I . . ." She looked at her wrists.

Had Tanya manipulated Didi as cleverly as she had Justin? "Have you tried contacting Didi from here?"

"Yeah." She lifted her phone. "Got this back and called a few times, but it always goes to voice mail. I've left messages but . . ." She shrugged. "We haven't talked much since that night. I don't even know if we're still friends. Didi's always been a little messed up."

"In what way?"

"She hated Brady for treating her like shit. And Didi's afraid of her dad, but he's family. She's probably confused about loyalty between them and me." Tanya fiddled with the tips of her hair. "If Didi still has the recording, she needs to turn it in now. Justin and me need to be together. But what if she won't talk to me or still won't do anything 'cause of her dad?" She started to sway and gripped the IV pole.

"We won't know until you and she can communicate."

"They won't let me out of here." Tanya fidgeted. "Will you talk to Didi for me?"

Part of Casey wanted to say no, but another part of her wanted to see that recording. "Would she talk to me?"

Tanya looked at Casey, then sighed. "Tell her that Princess has a message for Pixie. That you're friend, not foe, and that the last promise she made can now be broken."

Casey raised an eyebrow. "Princess? Pixie?"

"I know it's kid stuff, but it's what Didi understands." Tanya paused. "She's not retarded, but she's a little slow, and she's scared of a lot of things. We've played a lot of make believe over the years. It makes her feel better when things are bad."

So, Tanya had a compassionate side after all. "I have to ask, is her dad abusive?"

"He doesn't hit her or anything, but he yells and threatens a lot." Tanya glanced around the room. "When we were little, kids picked on her pretty bad at school, so I stood up for her. We've been friends ever since. Or we were."

"I guess it wouldn't be a good idea to meet Didi at her home."

"Hell no," Tanya replied. "This is Saturday, right? Didi always hangs out at the Brentwood Mall food court on Saturdays because a boy she likes works for the sandwich place."

"How will I know her?"

Tanya removed her phone from her pocket and quickly sorted through her photos. She then handed the phone to Casey. Pixie was right. The girl in the picture standing next to Tanya was several inches shorter than her, with short dark hair and large round eyes in an oval face.

"She usually doesn't show up till after three 'cause she has to do chores and homework first."

Casey checked her watch. Just enough time to get there.

"Tell Didi that it's okay to give the cops the recording now," Tanya added. "If she doesn't believe you, then get her to call me."

"Think she'll cooperate?"

"Didi's the most loyal person on the whole stupid planet. Big on doing the right thing." She flashed a derisive smile. "I'm amazed she stuck with me as long as she did."

Still, it was a long shot. The incident with Brady happened a couple months back. And it wasn't Justin's only problem. "Didi's footage could get the attempted murder charge dropped, but what about the drugs? I heard that the police found heroin on Justin."

"Brady planted it." Tanya rested her elbows on the table. "Justin was pissed at him for bringing drugs into the house, and threatened to call the cops. We figure Brady stuck some in Justin's pocket at the party. Probably planned to call the cops on Justin himself, but then realized we were heading home early. I wouldn't be surprised if his friends saw him try to set Justin up, or if Brady bragged about it. Bet none of those losers fessed up."

"Now that Brady's dead, maybe they will." Casey leaned back in her chair. "It's time to put things right, Tanya, which means talking with the police."

She shook her head. "They won't believe me."

"They won't have to if Didi still has the recording."

"What if she doesn't have it?"

"She can still give a statement, away from her dad." Understandably,

Tanya still looked skeptical. "There's another problem, though." Time to push the issue. Casey leaned forward. "Justin told me that Mercedes's uncle, Cristano Cruz, was Brady's supplier, and that the uncle helped you escape from Fraserview."

Tanya turned and glanced over her shoulder. "I've been scared that Cruz will come here. That old security fart can't protect me."

"The police can."

Her mouth twisted into a sneer. "How many times do I have to tell you that they hate me?"

"They don't hate kids who are trying to do the right thing." Casey understood, though, why this girl would try their patience. "Some Fraserview residents, including Roxanne and Mercedes, work for Cruz, don't they?"

Tanya's blue eyes became suspicious. "Who told you that?"

"Justin."

Tanya slid further down the chair. "He shouldn't have said anything. It could get us both in deep shit."

"Listen, the more I learn about Cruz, the more I can help protect you and Justin. But you have to work with me, okay?"

Tanya glanced nervously around the room, as if expecting Cruz to materialize. "I dunno."

"Please, Tanya. This is your chance to put things right and do something good for you and Justin."

Tanya studied her, as if trying to gauge her sincerity. A woman pushing a girl in a wheelchair entered the room and made their way to the far end.

"Roxy started working for Cruz a couple months back. He promised her a nice house to stay in and tons of food and cash," Tanya murmured. "Turned out not to be a great deal. Roxy wants out, but Cruz says he'll hurt her if she doesn't do what he wants."

Casey believed her. "Roxanne's out of Fraserview now. Are you keeping in touch?"

"No. They monitor all her calls. They know where she is and who she's talking to every minute. It's like living in a ginormous cage nearly as bad as juvie."

"Any idea how I can find her?"

"Just follow Mia or Cruz. Mia works for him too."

Casey nodded. "I gather that Roxanne hates Mercedes because she spies for Mia?"

"Totally. The last time Roxy was due to get out of juvie, she was gonna run away from Cruz. Mercedes found out and told Mia, who told Cruz. He threatened her the night you first showed up."

"I remember the fight and a missing twenty-dollar bill."

"The money was from Cruz to buy her off. Mercedes was the one who actually gave it to her, but then it went missing. Roxy figured Mercedes stole it back for Cruz, but it was one of the other girls."

Casey said, "Are any other staff involved with Cruz?"

"Dunno." Tanya's expression hardened. "But it wouldn't be a shocker if there were." She glanced at the other patient, then whispered, "I think Mac's dead because he found out what was going on."

Casey leaned closer. "Do you think Mia or Cruz killed Mac?"

"Maybe."

"Do you know what Mia does for Cruz?"

"It's her house the kids stay at. She keeps everyone in line for him." Tanya's eyelids were starting to droop. "I should go back to my room." Casey stood while Tanya used the IV pole to pull herself up. "Tell Justin I love him and that I'm really sorry, okay?"

"I will."

"He needs to get out of juvie fast. If Mia finds out how much he knows, he could get hurt too."

"Agreed."

Returning to Fraserview would be riskier than ever, but she needed more corroboration about Cruz and Mia, preferably from an adult, one who wasn't trapped in one of Cruz's schemes. Only one staff member came to mind; however, that would have to wait. "I'll go see Didi now."

"Be nice to her, okay? And don't force her to talk 'cause that'll only scare her."

"Right." Be gentle with the Pixie.

TWENTY-FIVE

CASEY DIDN'T MIND MALL FOOD courts. Some of her favorite foods lived here, which was also the problem: so many sweet, fatty flavors and not one salad bar to be found. Oh, well. She lined up for a burger, mainly because this vendor gave her a clear view of Didi.

The girl sat at a table in front of the sandwich vendor, her adoring gaze fixed on a boy with large green eyes and dimples. The boy had the body of a gymnast and a smile that revealed large white teeth.

Didi wore a minimal amount of makeup, but her bling and bright cashmere sweater were definite attention grabbers. The boy flashed a smile at Didi, who blushed bright red as she beamed right back at him. Apparently, the girl didn't know how to play it cool.

Casey carried her burger and fries to Didi's table and sat down, smiling at Didi's shocked expression. "Hi, Didi. My name's Casey. I'm a friend of Justin and Tanya."

The girl blinked at her. "How do you know them?"

"I work with Justin's grandmother, and I've known Justin since he was a little boy." She unwrapped the cheeseburger. "Amy used to bring him to work sometimes. His picture's always on her desk."

Didi glanced at the sandwich boy, who was busy with another customer. "I don't know Justin's grandmother."

Tanya had said the girl was slow. She'd have to tread carefully. "No, I guess you wouldn't. Have some fries. There's too many for me."

"I can't take food from strangers, or talk to them." Didi glanced over her shoulder, as if afraid of being caught breaking the rules.

"I have a message from Tanya." Casey leaned forward. "The Princess says to tell the Pixie that I'm friend, not foe."

The girl's eyes bugged out and her mouth fell open. "Really?"

"Totally."

"Well . . . Okay then." Didi glanced at her phone with the pink rabbit ears protruding from the top, then sipped what remained of a chocolate milkshake. "I miss her."

A good sign. "Tanya's been calling and leaving messages. She's afraid you're mad at her."

"No! I'm not." She shook her head vehemently. "I just don't know what to say."

"I understand." Casey nibbled the cheeseburger and chewed slowly as she prepared for her next comment. "Tanya told me what happened with Justin and Brady the night Brady fell, and that you recorded their fight on your phone." She noticed Didi's pensive expression and the fading color in her cheeks. "Do you still have the video recording?"

Didi glanced around the food court. "I never play it."

"Then you still have it?" As the girl gave a tentative nod, Casey wanted to jump up and shout halleluiah. "I'd like to see it."

Didi said, "It's bad."

"That's all right." She needed to know if Didi had actually recorded Brady tripping over Justin's foot. "Please, help yourself to some fries," Casey said. "Can I buy you something to eat?"

Didi looked at her beloved, evidently longing to be served by him. Casey drummed her fingers on the table, hoping this wouldn't drag out too long. "How about a sandwich?"

"You mean up there?"

"Yeah."

"I can't do that!"

Casey sighed. This was going to take some patience. Casey turned and looked at Sandwich Boy, who was giving Didi a small smile. The kid seemed infatuated with her too. She turned back to Didi. "Does that guy go to your school?"

Didi's face was now turning candy apple red but without the glossy shine. She looked everywhere but at Casey or the boy. Tanya's warning to be gentle with the Pixie was easier said than done.

"I'm sorry," Casey said. "I didn't mean to invade your privacy. I was just trying to make conversation."

Didi slowly turned to her. The girl's scrutiny went on for several long seconds before she finally slid the phone toward Casey.

Casey let out a long sigh. "Thank you."

She picked up the phone, found the footage, and began to watch the altercation between Justin and Brady. By the time the recording started, their fight was already intense. Brady had been a big, pudgy kid, who—perhaps because he was drunk—punched recklessly, missing Justin far more than he connected. His kicks weren't much better. The kid staggered a bit and then tripped over Justin's foot, exactly as Tanya had said. Brady's arms pinwheeled in an effort to regain his balance, but he was already so off balance that it was too late to prevent what would happen, and down he went.

The footage didn't reveal every second of the fall, but clearly Brady had fallen backward. It was also clear that Justin was still picking himself up off the floor when it happened. The footage became haphazard for a moment, as if Didi was running. The next clear shot was of a motionless Brady at the bottom of the staircase, his limbs twisted at unnatural angles. Justin ran down the stairs, shouting at a screaming Tanya to call 911. He seemed oblivious to the fact that Didi was watching all this. Suddenly there were brief fragmented images of the floor and hallway, and then nothing.

Casey put the phone down and observed Didi's downcast expression. "Justin told the truth. It was an accident."

"Brady was wearing socks. Socks are slippery on the stairs. I've fallen before."

Casey nodded. "Tanya wants the police to see the footage now."

Didi shook her head. "My dad wouldn't like that."

"I understand, but is it right that two innocent people remain in jail?" Didi's mouth pinched closed. Man, this girl could be stubborn. "The police really do need to see this right away." The girl remained frustratingly still. What would it take to get through to her? Unless . . . Casey leaned forward. "There was a second part to Tanya's message."

Didi perked up, her expression hopeful. "For me?"

"Absolutely." Casey paused. "Her message is that the last promise you made to her can now be broken." More silence and downcast eyes. Casey kept a gentle tone of voice. "Listen, you don't have to say anything to your dad. If the police download this footage, then the truth will come from them."

"Really? So I wouldn't have to tell him?"

"No, you wouldn't. Remember, I'm the one who came to you. You didn't come looking for me, and I'll be the one who tells the police about it."

Didi's wispy brows furrowed together. She appeared to be thinking this through, deciding if this would be enough to keep her out of trouble with her dad. "Maybe."

"Since this is your phone, we should probably go to the police together. I could drive you there right now."

"I can't leave!" She tossed a worried look at her beloved.

Casey stifled a groan. Good god, would she ever get this girl away from Sandwich Boy? "Is the guy behind the counter expecting you to stay?"

"What? No! He doesn't know me."

Sure. Right. "Would you like me to introduce you?"

Didi's mouth dropped open. "You know Chad?"

Casey gritted her teeth. Patience. Just a bit more persuasion. "No, but what matters is that you two get to know each other. Should we go up to the counter?"

"No! I couldn't!"

She sure in hell could. "Let's be courageous knights, okay?"

Without waiting for a response, Casey stood up from the table, took Didi by the hand, and led her toward the sandwich counter. Mercifully, Didi wasn't struggling. Casey ordered a pop from Chad and then introduced her to Didi, who hid behind her.

"You go to my school," Chad said, flashing a perfect smile. "I've seen you around."

Didi stepped out from behind Casey, clasping white-knuckled hands in front of her. She smiled through a deep red blush. "Seen you too."

As stimulating as this conversation was, Casey needed to get going. "Maybe you two could get something to eat after your shift next week, Chad."

He hesitated, but then shrugged. "Cool."

"Good," Casey said. "We have to take off, but I'm sure Didi will remember next Saturday."

Didi's mouth again fell open, as if she couldn't believe what she was hearing.

"Okay." He smiled a perfect smile at Didi. "See ya."

"See ya too."

Casey led a dazed Didi back to their table so the girl could collect her coat.

"Chad seems nice."

The dreamy eyes became panicked. "Oh my god, oh my god! What will I talk about?"

"Your teachers, kids at school, movies, plans for the future. Lots of stuff. Anyway, you have a whole week to think about it."

"That's not enough time!"

Be gentle with the Pixie, be gentle with the Pixie. This would be her mantra until she got that damn phone in the hands of police. "I'll help you with ideas on the way to the police station."

"I can't go now. I have to be home soon."

Oh, crap. "You know this is important, right?"

A woman approached them, her face suspicious as she looked from Didi to Casey. "Didi? Who's this?"

"She's Casey."

Double crap. "I'm a friend of Justin Sparrow's grandmother," Casey said. "Justin is a friend of Tanya North's, who is a friend of Didi's."

The suspicion deepened. The woman's entire face began to resemble a gnarly tree knot whose many lines were broken only by eyes, nose, and mouth. "Justin is my son, and Didi's my stepdaughter. What do you want with her?"

Now the attitude made sense. "You must be Kirsten," Casey replied, noting the woman's trepidation. "I'm Casey Holland. I work with Amy

Sparrow and I volunteer at Fraserview Youth Custody Services, which is how I know Justin."

"Oh. I see."

"Tanya asked me to tell Didi that she and Justin are doing okay, but that she really misses Didi."

Kirsten scratched the back of her head, ruffling the thin brown hair. "That's hard to believe, when Tanya's been so busy glomming on to my son and getting him in trouble."

If Kirsten cared that much, why wasn't she doing more to help him? "They're separated right now, and not likely to be reunited anytime soon."

"Good." Kirsten turned to Didi. "As I've said before, you're better off without her, sweetie. Tanya's bad news."

Didi looked down. The girl probably never argued with her stepmother, or any adult.

"Ready to go home?" Kirsten asked Didi.

Didi glanced with uncertainty at Casey. "I, uh, should . . ."

"Should what?" Kirtsen asked.

Casey jumped in before the girl said too much. "She wanted some tips about how to talk to boys."

"From you?" Kirsten turned to Didi. "You should come to me, not strangers."

"Casey's nice," Didi said. "She wants to help."

Casey held her breath.

"Nobody can help you better than me." Kirsten's piercing gaze zeroed in on Casey.

"She's right. Moms have a way of knowing these things." Casey plastered on a friendly expression for Kirsten. "Which reminds me, have you been able to see Justin lately?"

As Casey hoped, the woman seemed taken aback. "He's a teenaged boy," she snapped. "He doesn't want his parents showing up and embarrassing him."

"Really." Casey's gaze hardened. "Is that what you tell yourself? Because I think Justin desperately needs a mom who's got his back."

"I don't have to take this shit."

Kirsten grabbed Didi by the arm, then stopped. When she turned around, Casey saw not only anger but also shame in her eyes. "You have no idea how complicated things are," Kirsten began. "Carl believes that tough love makes kids strong." She stroked Didi's hair. "Which leaves me with difficult choices to make." She bit down on her lip. "But don't think for one minute that I don't love my son. I know in my heart that Justin will be released and that he wouldn't deliberately hurt anyone." Her eyes glistened. "But I can't tell Carl that, understand?"

"I do." But she wasn't about to let Kirsten's need for a harmonious marriage block Justin's chance at freedom.

"Come on, Didi," Kirsten said. "Your dad wants dinner early."

Didi looked at Casey, then at the phone she'd left on the table. The phone was partially hidden behind the container of fries. Didi looked back up at Casey, gave a brief nod, then followed Kirsten out of the food court.

Casey slipped Didi's phone into her pocket. The girl might be a little slow, but she also had moments of brilliance. Once the footage came to light, all Didi would have to say was that Casey must have taken her phone, which she'd forgotten at the food court. And that she'd snooped through the phone and decided to take some old, forgotten footage to the cops, hoping for a reward or something.

Casey smiled. Time to put things right.

TWENTY-SIX

CASEY PARKED IN THE STRIP mall opposite Fraserview's entrance. She'd arrived just in time. A quick call to reception earlier had confirmed that Phyllis was working tonight and that her shift ended at 11:00 PM. It would be interesting to see if the old gal headed straight home or to a casino. Either way, Casey intended to question her.

Approaching Phyllis in Fraserview's parking lot would have saved time, but Casey didn't want to be seen on the premises this late at night. Given the woman's hints about the casino and the fact that she'd put Casey onto Mia, it was a safe bet that Phyllis wasn't a fan or part of the drug ring. She was observant, though; probably knew more than she'd said about Mia's relationship with Cruz and her home for aspiring drug dealers.

Part of Casey wondered if she should have gone inside tonight. She hadn't yet given Tanya's message to Justin or told him about the footage. Truth was, the thought of contacting anyone in Fraserview, even to get Justin on the phone, made her nervous.

After her meeting with Didi, she'd asked the police to meet her at the hospital. Once they finally arrived and saw the footage, then took Tanya's statement, Casey contacted Amy.

An emotional Amy had thanked her profusely. "They'll have to release him right away, won't they?"

Casey had no idea. She hadn't wanted to worry Amy further with revelations about the drug ring inside juvie. She'd confided that info only to the police, along with what she knew about Cruz, Mia, and the recruits. The problem was that Justin's earlier escape could keep him inside long enough for Cruz to punish him for breaking their agreement. Based on the way the officers exchanged glances when she mentioned Cruz's name, they knew the guy. If they'd already been investigating his connection to Fraserview, they hadn't told her.

Casey wasn't sure Phyllis had told the police everything she knew either, but it would be good to find out. They needed to pool information. Once Phyllis learned that Mia and Cruz were on the cops' radar, maybe she'd be more forthcoming.

By the time Phyllis drove out of the parking lot, Casey was cold and tired, and relieved to finally be moving. Following Phyllis was easier than expected. Traffic was light as they headed north on Boundary Road, and Phyllis stuck to the speed limit in the slow lane.

It would be great if she lived nearby. Lou was waiting up because he wasn't thrilled about tonight's mission. It took time to convince him that she had to do her part to ensure the corruption inside Fraserview was stopped, and whoever tried to kill Kendal was caught. The bottom line, she'd told him, was that if Phyllis did know more than she'd said, she could be in danger as well.

Phyllis turned right onto Lougheed Highway and headed east. After fifteen minutes of this, Casey began to wonder just how far away the woman lived. Finally, the Smart car turned left onto Gaglardi Way, a wide stretch of road that led up to Burnaby Mountain. God, they weren't going all the way up there, were they? There were some residences at the top, adjacent to Simon Fraser University.

At the base of the mountain, Phyllis made a right turn. Casey followed her into Coquitlam, and then Port Moody. Maybe this wasn't such a good plan after all. What if Phyllis realized she was being tailed and had decided to take Casey for a joy ride? She knew the make of Casey's car. Even if Casey managed to talk to her, Phyllis could take offense at being followed and refuse to say a damn thing. Still, there was no backing out now.

Casey followed her in the slow lane down St. Johns Street in Port Moody, alert for signals or sudden turns. Phyllis moved into the fast lane, yet didn't increase her speed. A pickup drove past Casey on the left, preventing her from also changing lanes. When she pulled in behind the pickup, she lost sight of Phyllis, until the Smart car wound up in one of two left-hand-turn lanes for Ioco Road.

The light changed to green and Phyllis started to make her turn. Good lord, Zambonis turned faster than this. They crawled down the street, through two more sets of stoplights. As Phyllis approached the third light, she moved into the curb lane, then turned right into a condo and commercial complex. Phyllis started up the short road, made another right turn, and then stopped in front of a closed fish market. She probably lived in one of the condos above the shops. Casey pulled in beside her and saw Phyllis lean over and open the passenger-side door. So, she knew she'd been followed. Was this why Phyllis hadn't taken a more direct route home? Had she been playing some sort of game to see if Casey stuck with her?

As Casey slid in, she said, "When did you realize it was me?"

"A while back."

She didn't sound upset or even annoyed. Casey scanned the shops. The complex appeared to be one large square of ground-level shops with condos above. Just beyond the complex were high-rise structures. In the courtyard directly behind her, a building housed a bakery and a deli.

"I gather you live in this complex?" Casey asked.

Phyllis nodded as she lit a cigarette. "It's a long drive to work, but I like Newport Village. It's close to the library and parks." She rolled down the window. "What's this about then?"

"I needed to talk to you away from Fraserview about how my friend Kendal wound up in an empty swimming pool."

Phyllis lowered her head. "Tragic, that. Will she be all right?"

"The doctors don't know. There's brain damage. She's in a coma."

Phyllis blew out a puff of smoke. "So much darkness. No light in sight."

Casey ignored the odd remark. "I've learned some disturbing things about Fraserview staff and a couple of residents, and I was wondering what you've heard, and what you saw the night Kendal fell."

"Not my place to say."

That attitude wasn't going to cut it. "If anything immoral or criminal is going on in there, then it sure in hell is your place."

Phyllis blinked at Casey through those big lenses. "Criminal?"

"I don't believe that Mac and Winson's deaths were accidents,"

Casey replied. "I know that Mercedes's uncle, Cristano Cruz, has been recruiting Fraserview residents to sell drugs after they're released, and that certain staff are involved. Now I'm wondering if Mac found out and died before he could do something about it."

"It's likely, all right. Some of those poor girls don't stand a chance. Horrible."

"You've known about Cruz's arrangement?"

"Had my suspicions."

"Then maybe you could help me stop it," Casey replied.

"Enemies everywhere," Phyllis mumbled. "Nothing can be done."

"Yes, there *is*," Casey insisted. She was far too tired to put up with resistance. "Kendal might have seen or heard something about this drug business that she shouldn't have, and someone tried to kill her because of it." She shivered and rubbed her hands together. "I know that Amir found Kendal. I was also told that Mia was in the pool room before it happened, and that she had you mop the floor."

Phyllis looked at her. "I made sure that door was closed and locked after I left. Someone else opened it. Amir and Mia have keys."

"I'm sure they do." Casey paused. "Why did you want me to know that Mia is a gambler?"

Phyllis turned to her. "You don't work at Fraserview. She can't make your life hell for telling the executive director. He needs to know."

"Why would he listen to me?"

"You have no agenda or history with Fraserview. And you're clever enough to get proof." Phyllis tapped her cigarette out the window. "Evil lurks in juvie walls. Those walls know everything and whisper to those who listen."

"And what have they whispered to you, Phyllis?"

Phyllis didn't respond right away. "Mac wanted Mia to get help, and she didn't like that. Tore right into him, she did. Said she didn't have a problem and that he should mind his own business."

Interesting. "Did they argue about anything else?"

"That's all I heard." Phyllis stared out the windshield. "Desperation and addiction cause insanity. My Frank was an ugly drunk. Used his fists and his belt, he did. But I found hiding places, learned how to stay out of sight until he'd slept it off."

A frightening way to live. "So, Mia's had a gambling addiction for a while?"

"Must have." Phyllis took another drag on her cigarette. "She gets calls. I've heard the excuses, her assuring people that she'll get their money." Phyllis inhaled deeply on the cigarette. As she blew the smoke out, she said, "Trying to make people happy can drive you crazy." Phyllis looked out the windshield, her eyes unblinking. "Mia's a bottomless well that can't be filled. Forced her to turn to nasty folks."

"Like Cristano Cruz."

Phyllis tossed the cigarette out the window. "Some people aren't meant to be in charge, are they? They live to control others . . . Order them about."

"I've been trying to locate Mia's address but can't find anything under her name," Casey said. "There's probably an address in her personnel file, but you're the only person I can trust to search for it. Can you do that for me?"

Phyllis nodded. "I traded shifts with someone and will be in before noon tomorrow."

"Thank you. I appreciate it." Casey removed a business card from her purse and wrote her cell number on it. She'd been counting on Phyllis's help, especially if it meant getting the acting director removed from her position before she could fire employees. "Now, about Kendal. Did you see Amir go in the pool room?"

"Can't say I did."

"What do you know about his personal life?"

Phyllis gave a little laugh. "Which one?"

Just as she thought. Rawan's secret wasn't as well kept as she hoped. How many other staff knew about him and Rawan? "Did Winson and Mac know about Amir's dual life?"

Phyllis gave Casey a long look. "The walls whispered to Mac too."

And what he heard might have gotten him killed. "Was Oksana in the pool room the night Kendal fell?"

"Ask her, luv."

"You know she won't tell me anything. I'm sure she's hiding something." Casey fixed her gaze on Phyllis. "Is she?"

Phyllis stared at her. "If you must know, Oksana kept extra food in the pool room. Snuck it home when she thought it was safe. Can't blame her, really. She barely earns enough to support her family."

If anyone had spotted Oksana stealing, it would have been Kendal. She caught thieves for a living, for crying out loud. She knew all the tricks, would have recognized the signs. Damn.

"Did Mac know she was stealing?"

"I expect so."

"And Winson?"

Phyllis shrugged. "Possibly."

"Please call my cell as soon as you have Mia's address."

Although the police were probably in full investigation mode where Mia was concerned, a little recon mission could definitely help the cause. Besides, she wanted to see firsthand if Mia really did house former Fraserview residents.

TWENTY-SEVEN

CASEY STOPPED POUNDING THE KEYS on her laptop when Lou stepped out of their bedroom and tucked his clean uniform shirt into his pants. She loved that he didn't mind doing the laundry or ironing, including her things. He'd even learned to stop throwing her underwear in with his work pants.

"Will you be home when I get back?" he asked, with a touch of caution.

"Yeah. I need to finish an essay." But that wasn't what had her typing so frantically. She didn't want to tell Lou that she was compiling a suspect list. He hadn't been thrilled to hear how far she'd had to drive to question Phyllis last night. Lou made it clear he didn't want her traipsing after people alone at night anymore. If she hadn't been tailing a senior puttering along in a Smart car, his point would have been more valid.

This morning, Lou had been cordial as he busied himself with the laundry and other chores, but she could tell he was still a little ticked. A new rift had fractured their harmony and she didn't know how to fix it, at least not until Justin was safe and a killer in jail. Why make things worse by sharing her suspect list with him or revealing that she intended to scope out Mia's place?

"What else have you got planned for today?" he asked.

Staring at her computer screen, Casey scrambled for something to say. "A trip to the grocery store."

"We're pretty well stocked."

"I know, but I was thinking of cooking a roast beef and Yorkshire pudding dinner. I haven't cooked a traditional Sunday dinner in ages."

"Cool." He started to leave the room, then stopped. "Think you'll visit Kendal soon?"

Lou had asked her before, but she'd put him off. She still couldn't express how depressing and frightening it would be, how she just wasn't ready to face the tubes and needles and machines binding her friend to a bed.

"If I get this essay finished, I'll go."

"Good." Lou headed for the kitchen. "I was thinking we could talk tonight about setting a wedding date."

"Sure." With all that had happened over the last couple of days, she'd barely had time for his proposal to sink in. And why was he bringing this up now when they'd had all morning to discuss it? Had he been that angry?

"How does a mid-August ceremony on the beach sound?"

"Wonderful."

"Mom will have something to say about skipping a church wedding, even though she's already married off two kids that way." He picked up the bagged lunch he'd made. "I'm pretty sure I can talk her into this."

Possible conflict already? "Have you told her the big news yet?"

"No. She'll insist on a family celebration and you've got enough on your plate."

"Thanks." Lou might not approve of her quest for answers, but at least he respected her commitment to helping find those accountable. It was one of many reasons she was marrying him. "I'll check out the calendar." August was six months away. Plenty of time to arrange a simple, romantic wedding.

"Great. I should be home at six. Thank god for the short shift." Lou kissed her and left.

Did his sudden cheerfulness mean things were back to normal between them, or was she deluding herself? Either way, she had a lot to do before he came home.

Casey resumed work on her suspect list, describing every incident and event since her first shift at Fraserview. It wasn't hard. She'd kept detailed notes. This morning, she'd created a spreadsheet listing the four primary suspects in Mac's and Winson's deaths and Kendal's hospitalization: Mia, Oksana, Amir, and Cristano Cruz. She'd also come up with a secondary list: Rawan, Mercedes, and that little delinquent

Jamal. Casey typed possible means and motives beside each name on her primary list, yet she was missing something—aside from solid evidence—that she hoped to obtain shortly.

Summer entered the apartment, her face flushed and frowning. Cheyenne jogged into the room behind her and headed for the guinea pig's cage.

"What's wrong?" Casey asked.

"Devon's talkin' shit about me." She plunked into the rocking chair. "Everyone's texting about it."

"I know it's irritating, but what he or others think doesn't matter. You know that, right?"

"I guess." She began rocking. "Worse things were said about me after Mom went to prison, so I can handle it. Just wish I didn't have to. By the way, Mom called last night."

"Glad to hear it. How's she doing?"

"She's stoked that I dumped Devon." Summer shrugged and attempted a smile. "She wants to see me. Can we go out there soon?"

"Of course." The women's correctional facility was one of Casey's least favorite places in the world, but the visits meant a lot to Summer and her mother.

"I hope you don't mind, but I told her you were engaged. Thought she could use more good news."

"No problem. Was she pleased?"

"Are you kidding? It was the happiest I'd heard her in a long time." Summer giggled. "She made as much noise as I did, though she wanted to know why you didn't call her right away. So, I told her about Kendal and that you've been having work problems."

When Casey told Summer about the engagement, she'd screamed with joy so loudly that she'd had to be reminded about disturbing the tenants. Rhonda probably felt sad about missing the wedding. She'd wanted Lou and Casey to become a couple and was thrilled when they finally got together. That Rhonda was incarcerated over a crime of passion regarding her own thwarted dream of marriage exposed a bitter irony that none of them would want to dwell on.

"Do you want to have supper with us tonight?" Casey asked. "I'm making roast beef and Yorkshire pudding."

"Sure." Summer noticed Cheyenne whimpering by the door. "I'd better take her for a walk."

"I'm going to pop out too, so take your key."

Casey returned to her notes. By the time she'd finished typing, tension had stiffened her neck and shoulders. She'd been debating whether to call Amy as well to see if Justin had been released. Twenty-four hours had passed since the police picked up Didi's cell phone and Casey hadn't heard a word since.

Her phone rang. She grabbed it, noting that the call came from Fraserview.

"I've got what you wanted," Phyllis said and then recited the address.

After Casey jotted it down, she said, "Do you know if Justin is still inside?"

"Haven't seen him, but the police questioned one of the boys this morning. Thought I heard the pool room mentioned."

Casey held her breath. "Which boy?"

"He has some Arab name. I gather they're moving him out of here soon."

"Was the name Jamal?"

"That's it, yes."

A chill ran through Casey. "Thanks for your help." She threw her phone onto the sofa.

Had the little bastard hurt Kendal? Maybe her injuries had nothing to do with drugs and corrupt staff, but with a nasty punk out for revenge. Pacing the room, Casey's mind swirled with her own desire for revenge. She told herself to calm down and think. Secondhand information didn't prove anything. Jamal could simply be a witness. She needed to shove the negative stuff back. Her pacing slowed. She was tempted to call her police contacts for more info, but first things first. She grabbed her purse and car keys.

TWENTY-EIGHT

CASEY LOWERED THE BINOCULARS IN frustration. She'd been watching Mia's large three-story home for forty-five minutes and there'd been no sign of activity, at least from this vantage point. Casey hadn't parked on Mia's street, but at the nearest intersecting road, behind a Camry just back from the stop sign. Looking to her left, she could see the front of the house and part of one side. Although Mia's was the largest home in this older, middle-class neighborhood, it was also in the worst shape. The house needed power washing and a nicer fence than the high chain-link monstrosity imprisoning the property.

The taxes and mortgage on a house that size would be hefty. Since she couldn't find documentation listing Mia as the owner, Casey had tried Cruz's name as well, but she wouldn't be surprised if he owned it under a company name. Just how deeply indebted to him was Mia anyway?

Casey checked the time: nearly 1:00 PM. If teenagers lived there, they probably weren't early risers, but wouldn't somebody have left the house by now? Maybe Tanya had been wrong about kids living there.

Casey poured coffee from her thermos into the little cup and then scanned the streets, looking for another place to park. She couldn't stay in this spot much longer without attracting the attention of nosy neighbors.

Sipping the coffee, she checked for phone messages. Nothing. She was hoping Deanne Winters would call with good news about Kendal. Casey had been thinking a lot about Kendal—how dynamic and funny and full of energy she'd been since high school, and how they'd always had each other's backs. Kendal had been at the funerals for both of Casey's parents. After Casey's marriage fell apart, Kendal took her away for a weekend of skiing, drinking, and pampering at Whistler. "Where better to start healing," Kendal had said, "than at a world-class resort?"

God, she really should go to the hospital. Cowardice was no excuse.

Neither was guilt. And the guilt wouldn't disappear until she'd asked Kendal's forgiveness for involving her with Fraserview in the first place.

Mia's front gate opened and someone stepped onto the sidewalk. Still holding the coffee cup in one hand, Casey lifted the binoculars. Familiar blond dreadlocks made it easy to identify Roxanne. Excellent. The girl was alone and strolling at a leisurely pace.

Casey turned the binoculars on the house in search of more signs of life. Still quiet. She was trying to zero in on Roxanne again when a sharp rap on the driver's window made her jump. Coffee sloshed onto her hand. "Damn it!" Wincing, she dropped the binoculars at about the same time she noticed Mia's withering stare. Crap!

"Why are you watching my house?"

There was no point in denying it. Stalling for time, Casey wiped her hand on her jeans and poured the remaining coffee back into the thermos. She rolled down the window just enough to speak.

"I heard a rumor that former Fraserview residents are living with you, and wanted to see if it was true."

"A rumor from whom?"

"It doesn't matter."

"It sure in hell does. If someone's slandering my reputation, then I want that person's name."

This could be going better. "What really matters, Mia, is that the rumor appears to be true. I just saw Roxanne leave your house."

"What are you talking about? She wasn't there."

Casey lifted the binoculars. "Her hair is quite distinctive."

Mia looked about ready to implode. "She is *not* living with me. She was just visiting, and I resent the invasion of privacy." The steely glint in her eye was unnerving. "If I was you, I'd tread carefully."

"Tread carefully?" Casey's voice rose. "When one of my closest friends is in a coma because of what happened in the facility you're responsible for?"

The glint faded. Mia straightened up and looked around, as if concerned about being watched. She leaned over again until her eyes were level with Casey's. "I wasn't anywhere near Kendal when it happened."

"Phyllis told me about Jamal."

"Phyllis?" Her mouth tightened. "What did she say about him?"

"That he's been questioned by police about the incident."

Mia rolled her eyes. "She's so far off base it's almost laughable."

"What does that mean?"

"I already told you that no one could place Jamal near the pool room that night."

"Phyllis sees more than you might realize."

"Phyllis lies more than *you* know," Mia shot back. "She's a seventy-year-old eccentric who Mac only hired because he felt sorry for her. Her husband died leaving her with debt and all she knew how to do was clean, and she's not even good at that."

"Why would Phyllis make up a story about a kid she doesn't know?"

"Because she's a lonely, bored nut job, which is why I'm going to follow through on what Mac intended to do and sack her *and* that pathetic cook." Mia's stare bore into Casey. "Don't come back to Fraserview." She marched toward her house.

Was Mia trying to make Phyllis a scapegoat? God knows Mia had a lot to hide. On the other hand, Phyllis was a couple of steps beyond eccentric, and she did seem to want to stir things up. Had Mac truly planned to let her go? If Phyllis believed that Mia was planning to fire her, it explained why she wanted to expose Mia's secrets. So, which woman was the bigger liar, and how far would either of them go to save her job?

Casey started her car and drove straight ahead, avoiding Mia's street. The woman was likely still watching her, but Casey needed to talk to Roxanne. She turned left at the next block, then took another left. Soon, she was back on Mia's street, but farther north.

Casey didn't see Roxanne. She must have made it to East Hastings, which meant she'd be harder to find. This busy, commercial part of Hastings was usually too congested with vehicles and pedestrians to easily spot someone, let alone pull over to chat. If Roxanne hopped on a bus before Casey saw her, she could lose what might be her one chance to talk to the girl. Once Mia told Cristano Cruz about their encounter—and she could be doing so right now—he could move Roxanne to another location. Worse, Cruz could come after Casey. Thanks to their little encounter, Mia knew the make of her car. She also had access to her address on the volunteer application.

Casey made a right turn onto Hastings and stayed in the curb lane. She stopped for a vehicle attempting to parallel park. As the driver made a second attempt, Casey scanned the sidewalks on both sides of the street, but there was no sign of Roxanne. When the driver finally managed to tuck his vehicle in, Casey eased forward. She didn't have much time. Mia would probably try to round up Roxanne. Tension rippled across her shoulders.

Casey passed two more blocks before she spotted the familiar dreadlocks. Roxanne was walking into the parking lot of a supermarket. Her heart pounding, Casey turned into the lot and parked between two large SUVs. She stepped out of her car and ambled toward Roxanne, hoping she wouldn't spook the girl. The last thing she needed was a chase. With any luck, Roxanne's hatred for Mercedes and Mia was strong enough to make her want to help shut down the drug ring. Casey's heart pounded, not from trepidation about Roxanne but from fear that Mia or Cruz would show up. If Roxanne had told Mia where she was going they could both be in danger.

"Roxanne?" she called out and then smiled.

Roxanne slowed her pace, her expression wary. "What are you doing here?"

"I came to see you . . . To see if you're all right."

Roxanne studied the ground. "Was I ever?" Her phone rang. She pulled it out of her shabby wool coat.

"If that's Mia, please don't answer," Casey blurted. "I've got to tell you something important about her first, and she won't want me talking to you."

"If I don't answer, she'll send Cruz's goons after me. They can track me with this thing." Roxanne waved the phone in the air.

"Then don't tell Mia you've seen me. Our safety depends on it."

Roxanne kept her eyes on Casey as she answered the phone. "Hey,

Mia. What's up?" Her pensive expression became worried. "I haven't seen no juvie volunteer. Wouldn't want to."

Casey held her breath as Roxanne listened to whatever Mia was saying.

"I'm on my way to the store, like you told me to," Roxanne said.

Casey cringed.

"Okay, sure," Roxanne said smoothly. "If I see her, I'll call. Bye."

Casey sighed in relief. "Thank you."

"No problem." She shoved the phone in her pocket. "She said you want to cause trouble."

"For her and Cruz, yeah. I want those two in jail."

Roxanne tilted her head and hugged herself from the cold or fear. Casey didn't know. "For what?"

"Aside from recruiting minors to sell drugs and possibly killing Mac, I don't know. I was hoping you could fill me in."

"Are you serious? You think they really killed Mac?"

"And Winson, yes. It's highly likely, but I need evidence."

Roxanne snorted. "Good luck with that." She shoved her hands into her coat pockets and looked around the lot. "If Mia finds out I lied about seeing you, I'm in deep shit."

"Then we'll have to make sure she doesn't."

The girl grimaced. "It's not that easy."

"I have friends in the police force who'll make sure nothing happens to either of us."

"Cops, huh?" She glanced around the parking lot again. "Like that'll help."

"They will, especially if I ask them to." Casey understood the girl's skeptical frown. "More and more people are learning about Mia and Cruz's activities. I know that former residents live with her, and that it's arranged by Cruz."

Roxanne looked over her shoulder, studying faces. She seemed nervous, probably afraid that the longer they spoke the more dangerous things could become.

"Let's talk in my car," Casey said. "It's warmer and we'll be less noticeable."

The girl shrugged and followed her to the car. Once inside, she shifted in her seat, so she was facing Casey. "Mia must have seen you watching her place."

"She did, and we had words." Casey paused. "You live at Mia's place, right?"

Roxanne nodded. "From one prison to another."

"How did you become involved with Cruz?"

"He saw me in juvie. Said he could give me a place to crash, and food and money. Of course I knew there was a catch but as long as it wasn't sex I was cool with it . . . Until I realized that once you're in you can't leave."

How had Cruz arranged accommodation for a minor he wasn't related to? Either he and Mia were well connected or Cruz spent big bucks on bribes. "How many kids live there?"

"Six."

"What happens if you try to leave?"

"You get beaten by Cruz's goons." Roxanne answered, looking straight ahead. "Got the bruises to prove it."

So, the kids were essentially slaves in exchange for food, shelter, and a little spending money. Cruz wouldn't want them dead, just scared to death. "Then you're definitely not going back. There are other options."

Roxanne gave a short laugh. "Must be nice living on *planet delusional.*"

Casey didn't have time to debate this. "How large a quantity of drugs does he make you sell?"

"None. I do the smurfing."

Casey had read about this . . . Kids being used to buy allergy and cold medicine or weight loss pills containing pseudoephedrine and ephedrine. They were ingredients used to make crystal meth. "Since the stores only let you buy a small amount, I imagine you have to go to a lot of places."

"Yep. Cruz has been teaching me how to cook."

Unbelievable. "Sounds risky."

"It's not, really. You just crush the pills and cook them with—"

"It's okay." Casey raised her hand. "I don't need the recipe."

"It's not hard."

"Do you keep ending up in juvie because you're making the stuff?"

"No." Roxanne looked around. "I steal other shit to get caught. Mia thinks I'm a klepto, which is what I want. I figure if they put me in another juvie, I could get away. But I always end up back at Fraserview. I'm sure Cruz arranges it."

If his network was that extensive, did he have connections inside the police department? She'd have to be careful. "You really want out?"

"Yeah, I do." Roxanne looked at Casey. "Why do you want to help? And don't tell me you got no angle 'cause everyone does."

"I do, but it's about the other volunteer, Kendal. She's a good friend of mine." Casey paused. "Did you hear about her accident?"

Roxanne shook her head, but her pensive expression suggested that she knew whatever Casey had to say wouldn't be good. By the time Casey had finished telling her everything, Roxanne's expression was solemn.

"She was cool," Roxanne mumbled. "But if she found something that could be used against Mia and Cruz, then it's no wonder she wound up in the pool."

"I can't be completely sure they're responsible. There are other people I'm looking at as well. But whether your handlers are involved or not, they should still be in jail for other crimes."

Roxanne rubbed her face and groaned. "If Cruz controls the cops, we're both dead. You know that, right?"

"Yep, but I have a pretty solid connection inside VPD. I'll make sure he's aware of that possibility." Seeing the girl's glum face, Casey added, "I know we can bring them down with enough evidence."

Roxanne glanced around the lot. "I dunno."

"Please?" Casey asked. "This is your chance at freedom. By giving a statement to the police, you could make a *huge* difference for a lot of kids."

Roxanne shook her head. "Some of them like the arrangement. Others are too afraid to go against them."

"What about what you want? Wouldn't you like to see Mia and Cruz in prison?"

Roxanne's blank face didn't give anything away. Finally, she said, "What the hell? I'd rather die trying to do something good than have the crap beat out of me all the time. If I have to keep making dope for a living, I might as well be dead anyway."

The resignation bothered Casey. "Your life matters, Roxanne."

She shrugged. "Don't worry about it." Roxanne looked over her shoulder. "Shit! Mia just drove into the lot. I can't be seen with you!"

"She knows my car." Casey opened the door. "Get out and stay down. I'll let her see me enter the store, then find a way to lose her. Meet me in the Dairy Queen in five minutes." She nodded toward the separate building at the front of the parking lot.

"I'll ditch my phone," Roxanne said.

"Good. Now, *go*."

As Casey walked toward the store, she dialed 911. "I've just help free a girl who's been held captive in a drug dealer's house, and now they're after us!"

As the dispatcher asked questions, Casey saw Mia step out of the car and head her way. Casey hurried inside and headed for the other side of the store. "I have to go. The woman chasing me knows where I live and could send someone to my house. I have a thirteen-year-old at home and need to call her right now."

"What's your address, ma'am?"

While Casey recited it, she cringed at the sight of Mia charging inside the store.

TWENTY-NINE

SUMMER WAS STANDING NEAR THE book return counter when Casey ushered Roxanne inside the library. The escape plan had worked. From the Dairy Queen, they'd crossed Hastings Street just as a westbound bus arrived. Meeting up with Summer in their own neighborhood was the best way to protect both girls before Mia or Cristano Cruz found them.

Casey hadn't seen any police cruisers in the area. There weren't any officers in here either. The dispatcher had assured her the police wouldn't be long. As far as Casey was concerned, every passing minute made their situation more precarious. She doubted Cruz would find them in a library. Still, there were no guarantees. She'd left a message with Lou, explaining where she was and why he shouldn't go home after work until he'd called her first. Lord, there would be hell to pay once Lou heard the details. Mercifully, both tenants were away for the weekend.

Casey gave Summer a hug. She'd been confident that Summer would get out before Cruz and Mia found the house. And since neither of them knew Summer existed, she could have walked right past them on the street without drawing attention.

"Any trouble on the way here?" Casey asked.

"No. I left right away like you said to. No one followed me here." Summer hesitated. "You think Cheyenne will be okay?"

"I'm sure she'll be fine."

As Summer removed her backpack, she looked at Roxanne, who fidgeted and stole furtive glances at library staff, as if half expecting to be kicked out.

"This is Roxanne," Casey said. "Roxanne, this is Summer."

Summer gave a quick nod. "Hi."

Roxanne barely looked at her before mumbling, "Hey."

Casey hoped they would get along. The last thing she needed was an argument in here, and, based on what she'd seen, Roxanne's behavior was unpredictable. Casey led the girls to a cluster of tables not far from the entrance.

"What took you so long anyway?" Summer asked.

"The bus was slow and we had to transfer at Commercial." A risky but necessary venture. "Thanks for staying calm and doing exactly as I asked without too many questions."

Trepidation passed over Summer's face. "You wouldn't have told me to get out of there if it wasn't serious."

Something she'd learned from harsh experience. Summer wouldn't have forgotten the incident nearly eighteen months ago, when Casey had her stay with Lou's mom, thanks to a killer's threat.

"I asked Summer to bring you clothes to change your appearance," Casey told Roxanne. "You're both about the same size, and it might be a while before you can return to Mia's place to collect your things."

Roxanne scowled. "I'm not stayin' in some shithole foster home again."

Casey didn't blame her. "Do you have family outside the Lower Mainland?"

"An aunt and uncle in Winnipeg, I think. But they could be dead for all I know." She shrugged. "I was a little kid the last time I saw them."

"Take the pack to the washroom," Casey said, nodding toward the door just a few feet away. She had used the bathroom before. There was only one entrance to the windowless room. Although Roxanne wasn't likely to escape, she couldn't be completely trusted either.

"Try on whatever you want." Summer placed the pack by Roxanne's feet. "I had to hurry, so I grabbed as much matching stuff as I could."

Roxanne hesitated a few moments, then lifted the backpack and headed for the ladies' room.

Summer leaned toward Casey and whispered, "She has a lot of scars on her hands. Is she a junkie?"

"I don't think so, and those scars aren't from needles," Casey replied. "Volunteers aren't told much about residents, but I think she's had a rough time."

Summer looked at the bathroom door, her face solemn. "What will happen to her?"

"She might be sent away to live with relatives. If that's not possible, she could wind up in foster care."

"Can she stay with us for a while?"

Casey hadn't seen Summer's compassionate side in a long time. She'd shown a lot of empathy when she was young, but Rhonda's incarceration had hardened Summer in some ways. Perhaps Summer sensed a fellow outcast who wasn't high on the popularity list either and for whom friendships had come and gone. The problem was that Summer saw only scars and fear on a vulnerable face. She hadn't seen Roxanne's volatility, how she lashed out at people and made issues over stupid things like the TV remote.

"The truth is I'm not sure where we're staying tonight," Casey said.

"A hotel would be awesome."

Casey looked around the library. Where were the damn cops?

Five minutes later, Roxanne emerged looking pleased with her choice of black jeans, olive T-shirt, black-and-white hoodie, and a navy coat. It was better than her torn jeans and red coat. Her dreadlocks were inside the hoodie, so when she pulled up the hood her hair wouldn't be visible. She'd also put on a pair of purple-tinted glasses.

"You look great," Summer said.

Roxanne sat down. "Got any makeup?"

"Yep." Summer unzipped a small pocket in the pack and pulled out the bag of cosmetics she used for special occasions. As the girls discussed shades and skin tone, Casey noticed the way Roxanne seemed to hang on every bit of advice from Summer.

Casey checked the time. She'd called a cop friend at VPD, who assured her that Cruz hadn't made any friends on the force. In fact, everyone wanted to nail this guy big time. Had they caught up with Mia? If so, Casey doubted that she'd admit to any involvement with Cristano Cruz. Mia was a fighter with far too much to lose. But she wasn't the only fighter. Thoughts of Kendal, Justin, Mac, and Winson only strengthened Casey's resolve to make sure the guilty parties were punished.

After Summer left for the washroom, Casey said, "Roxanne, did you ever hear Mia talk about Mac's death outside of Fraserview?"

"No." Roxanne put the lipstick down. "They act like it never happened."

Roxanne was out of Fraserview when Winson died. "What about Winson?" Casey asked. "Has his name cropped up at the house?"

"Not from Mia." She sat back and looked at Casey. "I heard kids talk and it freaked me out, how he died like that. Everyone knew how paranoid Winson was about his food." She removed the glasses and tossed them on the table.

"Cruz wouldn't have been allowed in any of the units, unless Mia looked the other way," Casey said. "Even then, one of the staff could have seen him. It would have been a huge risk."

"Cruz takes big risks," Roxanne replied. "Anyone on his payroll could have planted somethin' in Winson's food," she said. "Cruz was the one who got Tanya and Justin out of juvie."

"So I heard. But he would have needed help, and I'm assuming it was Mia?"

"Of course." Roxanne picked up another lipstick tube. "It wouldn't surprise me if Winson found out, so the bitch planted bits of peanut in his food."

Kids and adults glanced at them from the next table. Casey gave them a reassuring smile and leaned closer to Roxanne. "We need to keep it down."

"Whatever." She tossed the tube on the table. "Wish I could see Tanya. Heard she was separated from Justin."

She didn't know the latest then? "Yes."

Roxanne peered at her. "Is Tanya okay?"

There was nothing like female intuition. "She's fine."

"You got a funny look on your face." Roxanne studied her. "She's not fine."

"She is." Casey paused. "But Tanya's in the hospital. I went to see her."

Roxanne's eyes narrowed. "She tried to kill herself, didn't she?"

Casey was caught off guard. "How did you know?"

"She swore she'd do it if she lost Justin."

Summer returned and looked back and forth between Casey and Roxanne. Casey noticed the way she sat quietly and kept her gaze lowered. She must have sensed that the conversation had become serious.

"Everybody thinks about suicide in juvie, sooner or later," Roxanne said. "No more pain, disappointment, or trouble. Some days it seems almost too good to pass up."

Summer made a point of looking everywhere but at Casey. Maybe the topic was depressing or even shocking to her. Or maybe it wasn't. Were Summer's cheeks coloring because Roxanne's remarks were hitting close to home? A disturbing thought.

"I wanna see Tanya," Roxanne said.

"Good idea," Casey replied. "I think she could use a friend."

"Being alone sucks," Roxanne mumbled. "I used to think that staying at Mia's with other kids would be better, but there's no real friends there either. At least I had Tanya in juvie."

Which reminded Casey, "Did you see anyone near Mac's office before his heart attack? I remember him sending you back to your unit when we were all in the corridor, but I'm wondering if you went out again."

"For a sec. I only saw that chick at reception and that weird old cleaning lady."

Casey smiled. "Phyllis is a little eccentric."

"She wouldn't be so bad if she didn't always go on about how evil men are, and how girls have to look after themselves and shit."

"I didn't know Phyllis talked to residents," Casey said, even though she had heard Phyllis make sympathetic remarks about the girls the other night.

"Only when staff aren't watching." Roxanne examined another shade of lipstick. "Sometimes she used the computer in the supervisor's office. Don't know what she did on it. Probably just liked snooping."

Casey sat back in her chair. She'd assumed that Phyllis simply peeked at a file in a drawer to find Mia's address; Casey hadn't realized she knew her way around a computer. Mac had kept his computer password protected, but had Phyllis somehow learned of his plan to let her go?

As Casey replayed the events of the night Mac died, an uneasy feeling niggled at her. Phyllis had been cleaning the conference room earlier that the evening. She could have slipped into his office through the adjoining door. She also likely knew that Mac kept his pills in his jacket pocket, and that he often left his jacket draped over the chair. What if she'd stolen one or two pills at a time over several evenings, then mashed them into a powder and stirred the powder in Mac's coffee thermos? Casey remembered the spilling thermos when she found him vomiting.

But why would Phyllis go to so much trouble to save a job that ended in a few months anyway? It didn't make sense. At her age, she qualified for government pensions. On the other hand, she did like playing the slots, and how much of her husband's debt was she still paying off? Even if Phyllis had killed Mac—and that was a big if—wouldn't she have gone after Mia by now? Surely, she knew that Mia intended to fire her as well. Was Mia's life in jeopardy? Not that Mia was an easy target, seeing as how she didn't like or trust Phyllis.

"Are you all right?" Summer said, looking at Casey with concern.

"Yeah. Just thinking."

Watching people enter and leave the library, Casey remembered how Winson had left the unit to talk to Mac that night. When he returned he seemed disturbed, which was probably due to the way Mac must have looked just before he went into cardiac arrest. Winson might have spotted Phyllis near Mac's office, but he wouldn't have thought anything of it at the time. Once everyone had learned about the over-dose of Mac's medication, Winson might have started rethinking what he'd seen that night. And Phyllis might have started to worry.

THIRTY

"CASEY?"

"Yes." The voice was familiar, but Casey couldn't place it.

"This is Rawan Faysal, from Fraserview."

Rawan? Why was she calling at 9:00 PM on Sunday night? Did she know that Mia had been picked up by the police today? Casey had gotten the call just before five, and Roxanne was now in the care of people Casey's police contacts trusted. Refusing to be chased out of her house by a thug, Casey had returned home after dropping Summer off at a friend's for the night.

"What can I do for you, Rawan?"

"I'm sorry to bother you, but we need you at Fraserview right away. Justin Sparrow has a knife and is threatening to hurt himself unless he can see you. Please come."

Adrenaline catapulted Casey out of her chair. Lou, who was stretched out on the sofa watching a hockey game, sat up.

"Who's in charge tonight?" she asked.

"Amir. He asked me to call you. Can you come right away?" Rawan sounded almost desperate.

"Why is Justin so upset?" she asked.

"Something about still being stuck in Fraserview and afraid of staff. There've been some developments, something to do with Mia, but I don't know the details."

How would Justin know what happened today? Or had he discovered that there were other staff to worry about? "He didn't ask for his grandmother?"

"Apparently, he doesn't want to worry her."

As of two hours ago, Cristano Cruz was still on the run, but Casey wasn't overly worried about her safety. The house alarm and extra police patrols would likely keep Cruz away. Justin, however, was another matter. She glanced at Lou who was watching her, his expression pensive. She smiled and headed for the bedroom, certain that the rest of this conversation should take place out of earshot of him.

"Shouldn't Justin's lawyer and the police be called?" she asked, shutting the bedroom door.

"They have been and they're on their way, but you're the one he wants to talk to first."

"And Amir supports this?"

"Under the circumstances, yes."

Casey thought about it. "Can you put Justin on the phone?"

"It won't help. Justin insists that you come here."

No. This wasn't right. "What's really going on, Rawan?"

"I told you. Lives are at stake here, Casey. Please come quickly."

"Lives? As in more than one? What are you talking about?"

"Please, just get here."

It wasn't a stretch to believe that Cruz had taken Fraserview hostage. Since he couldn't get to her, it appeared that Cruz had chosen a quick way to make Casey come to him. She had no idea what the hell this would accomplish. The police knew what was going on and she had no access to Roxanne now. Still, if Rawan was as frightened as she sounded, then Cruz was calling the shots. Everyone inside was in danger. Damn, what was she supposed to do?

"Casey? Are you there?"

"Yes. I'll leave shortly."

"Thank you." Rawan hung up.

As Casey returned to the living room, Lou said, "What's going on?"

Oh, boy. He wasn't going to like this. "Justin supposedly has a knife and is threatening to hurt himself unless he can see me in person."

Lou crossed his arms. "Do you know how sketchy that sounds?"

"Yep, which is why I'm calling the police."

"That's all you've got planned, right?"

Casey glanced at him. "I'll do whatever the cops want me to do."

She phoned the officer who'd left his number with her this afternoon, and explained the situation. Five minutes later, he called her back and confirmed her suspicion. The police hadn't been dispatched to Fraserview and there'd been no report of a disturbance. Cruz hadn't been located either.

"I'll send patrol cars to Fraserview right now," the officer said. "If Cruz is there, we'll find him."

"Won't he spot the cars a mile away?"

"I wouldn't worry about it, Miss Holland."

But she did worry. "Cruz probably knows what I drive. If he doesn't see my vehicle pulling up he'll be suspicious. Maybe I should go."

"We can't risk that. The guy could shoot a bullet through your head before you even turn off the engine."

"If I don't go, Justin Sparrow could take the bullet, and god knows who else. Cruz could be inside Fraserview with a gun pointed at Rawan's head."

"What if Miss Faysal works for him?"

Casey's stomach churned. "All the more reason to get Justin out of there now."

"We'll handle this, Miss Holland. Just stay away from Fraserview."

"Look, shouldn't my car be seen from a distance at least? There's a strip mall I could park at across the street from the place." She spotted the worry on Lou's face and heard the officer swear under his breath. "Please, I've been involved with police operations before, which Constable Denver Davies can vouch for."

The officer let out a long sigh. "I'll have an unmarked vehicle go to your address. The officer will follow you. Stop two blocks before Fraserview. If we feel it's necessary, the officer will drive your vehicle onto Fraserview's premises, but you'll stay behind, understand?"

"Got it."

"Wait for the officer before you leave your home."

Casey rolled her eyes. "Wouldn't it save resources if I just met up with the police?"

"Are you a hundred percent sure Cristano Cruz or his men will wait until you reach Fraserview to strike?"

She paused. "I guess not."

"Cruz won't hesitate to shoot you while you're behind the wheel."

Casey gave him her address. "I'm parked off the lane in back." After providing the make of her vehicle and her plate number, she said, "How soon will a car be here?"

"In about five minutes."

"Fine." Casey shoved her phone in her pocket, then fetched her coat.

"What's happening?" Lou asked.

"I'm driving to Fraserview without actually going on the property." He stared at her. "Why?"

"Because Justin's in danger. I think Cruz is holding the place hostage. The police believe he expects me to show up and will be watching for my car. They're going to drive it onto the property."

"I thought you told me that Cruz helped you with Mac. He knows your face."

"Yep, but it's dark and if they use a female officer, it could work." Lou crossed his arms. "I don't like this."

"Neither do I."

"I should go with you," he said. "Since you're not driving onto the property, I don't need security clearance."

"But you do need police permission, and they won't want to be responsible for another civilian, trust me."

"Screw that."

Casey was afraid this would happen. "If Cruz happens to catch up with me before I get to Fraserview and sees two people in the car, we could both be in danger. I couldn't live with that, and Summer shouldn't have to."

"What I couldn't live with is losing you."

"You won't."

His gray eyes sparked with anger. "Do I get a guarantee?"

How was she supposed to answer that? Casey picked up her purse. "I'll keep you posted."

Scowling, Lou turned back to the TV. Casey doubted he was paying attention to the game. It was going to take a lot of heat to defrost this atmosphere.

Heading downstairs, her heart beat faster. She checked her watch.

The police would be here any minute. She peeked through the back door window and saw what looked like a thick frost—probably hiding a layer of ice—covering her windshield. Damn. Might as well start scraping.

Casey activated the house alarm and stepped outside. Grimacing in the frosty air, she took the slippery wooden steps slowly, then crossed the lawn. As she inserted her key in the car door lock, a gloved hand clamped over her mouth.

Her arms flailed and her purse dropped to the ground. Huge, shadowy figures surrounded her. Oh, god! What was happening? Casey was pulled backward, lost her footing, and started to fall. Somebody caught her and yanked her upright. The hand was on her face again. She couldn't call out. Couldn't move. Large, firm hands gripped both of her arms. She inhaled the smell of leather.

"Make any noise," Cristano Cruz said, appearing in front of her, "and you're dead."

The hand left her face, but the men on either side of her kept their grips on her arms. Casey prayed the cops got here fast. Eyeing Cruz, she took a deep breath and felt the chilly air cool her flushed face. Beneath layers of clothing, sweat trickled down her body.

"You know me, yes?" Cruz asked.

"Yes." She'd know Cruz's accent anywhere. "Does Rawan Faysal work with you?"

"Who?"

"The administration clerk at Fraserview. The one who called me."

"Ah, yes. The young lady who has secrets to keep." Cruz moved closer. "You've been interfering in my business."

Her thoughts swirled. "Not on purpose. I just want to find out who nearly killed a close friend of mine inside Fraserview."

"Which friend is that?"

"The volunteer, Kendal Winters."

He stared. "What does she have to do with Roxanne?"

"Nothing. But Roxanne is a lead to Mia, and she's the one I'm after."

Cruz's dark eyes didn't blink. "What for?"

"She had motive and opportunity." Casey's arms hurt. "Would you mind telling your guys to loosen their grip? I have no intention of running away."

"Mia has hurt no one at Fraserview," he said. "My niece likes you very much, which is why I'm being nice. But I warn you, stay out of my—"

The arrival of an unmarked police cruiser cut the conversation short.

THIRTY-ONE

"KENDAL OPENED HER EYES AND spoke to me," Deanne Winters said as she held her daughter's hand. "She knew who I was, but doesn't remember what happened."

Casey stood next to Deanne and observed the sleeping Kendal. At first glance, she seemed almost part machine as tubes and needles linked her body to beeping equipment. Her complexion didn't have much more color than the bandage around her head. Her frailness and vulnerability was upsetting. She wished Kendal would open her eyes, sit up, and free herself of this sterile nightmare. She also wished that Kendal's prognosis wasn't so vague. But head injuries like this were complicated, unpredictable, terrifying. It had taken nearly every bit of courage Casey had to come here today.

Casey replied, "That's a good sign."

"It is." Deanne kept her gaze on her daughter.

Casey couldn't imagine how alone Deanne felt. She'd been a widow for as long as Casey had known her, and Kendal was her only child. "Was Kendal able to remember going to the pool room?"

"No, and I didn't want to overwhelm her with questions."

Casey looked around the dimly lit private room, wondering if Deanne had acquired privacy through luck or good insurance. Kendal was still vulnerable here, even though the room was close to the nurses' station.

"Deanne, I don't want to alarm you, but based on what I've learned over the past twenty-four hours, I'm pretty sure that Kendal's fall was no accident," Casey said. "I think she needs police protection."

Deanne's stark, exhausted face became wary. "What's going on?"

Casey described the tumultuous staff relationships at Fraserview and Mia's connection to Cristano Cruz. "Cruz came to my home and threatened me last night, but the police arrested him before he got away. It looks like his drug ring's about to be demolished."

"Oh, Casey." Deanne gave her arm a light squeeze. "Do you think he tried to kill my baby?"

"Quite possibly. But as I said, there are a lot of people with secrets and serious anger issues in Fraserview. Until the police have found enough evidence to charge Mia or Cruz or someone else with murder and the attempted murder of Kendal, I don't want to take any chances."

Deanne rubbed her forehead. "When Kendal and I had lunch on Valentine's, she said two staff members died under suspicious circumstances. Then later that night, this happened."

"I'm just glad the police are re-investigating both deaths."

"When I called you about Kendal that night, you said she sent you a text and wanted to tell you something," Deanne said. "Any idea what it was?"

"No, but it looks like Kendal learned too much about one of the staff that night." Casey paused.

Deanne looked around the room, as if searching for danger in every corner. She ran her hands through her short straight hair, which was a couple of shades darker than Kendal's. "I need to talk to hospital staff. I'll get security to keep watch, and tell them I don't want anyone from Fraserview near her." She hurried to the door. "Stay here, okay?"

"Absolutely." Casey sank into the chair and took a deep, calming breath until the smell of antiseptic and other unpleasant things made her queasy. She spotted Kendal's fingers twitching.

"Kendal?" Casey jumped up. "It's me, Casey."

Kendal's eyelids flickered open.

"Hi." Casey smiled with relief. "It's so good to see you. How are you feeling?" Kendal stared but didn't respond. "Are you in pain? Should I get a nurse?" The lack of acknowledgment made Casey uneasy. "You must be tired." Still no response. Deanne was probably right about not pushing her, but if Kendal knew something incriminating about Fraserview staff, then this whole thing could soon be resolved. "Kendal, do you remember the night you fell into the empty swimming pool? Do you remember texting me? You said you had info about Amir, Rawan, and others. I think that what you wanted to tell me was important."

Kendal's expression remained blank. "W-who are you?"

Casey inhaled sharply. Was she joking or just groggy? "I'm Casey, your best friend since high school. You and I have been volunteering at Fraserview Youth Custody Center. You were at Fraserview the night of your accident." Judging by the lack of change in Kendal's face, she had no clue what Casey was talking about. "Do you remember where you work?"

Kendal blinked at her a couple of times. "No."

"Do you know what you do for a living?"

A small frown emerged. "No."

This was bad. Casey didn't know what to say.

"I'm tired," Kendal murmured. She closed her eyes and turned her head away.

Feeling useless, Casey retreated to the chair. Maybe coming here had been a mistake. Kendal wasn't ready for visitors. Her memory couldn't be permanently gone, could it? It was just the trauma. Once she had healed a little more, the memories would come back. Casey sat still, willing Kendal to turn to her, to remember something . . . anything.

Deanne reappeared. Casey fought the urge to run out the door and not come back until her friend was well again.

"Security says it sounds like a police matter and that I should call them," Deanne said. "They'll send someone here now and step up patrols when they can. But if they're called to an emergency, Kendal will be left alone." She shook her head. "That's not good enough. What should I do?"

"Hire private security," Casey suggested. "I can recommend a couple of companies."

"Okay. Meanwhile, I'll stay here all night if I have to."

Casey stood. "Kendal woke up and we spoke for a minute, but she . . . Well, she doesn't remember me, or even what she does for a living."

Concern clouded Deanne's face as she looked at her daughter. "She remembers me." Deanne moved around the bed and peered at Kendal's face. She leaned over the bed rail and stroked Kendal's long hair. "Honey, it's Mom." She touched Kendal's shoulder and said, "You remember, Casey, don't you? You two have been friends a long time."

Casey held her breath.

"No." Kendal's voice was weak.

"You used to hang out every day. You babysat together, trained in security work at the same time. Went on many camping trips."

As the silence grew longer, the fading hope on Deanne's face was painfully clear. She patted Kendal's shoulder, then returned to Casey.

"I'm sorry, sweetie," she whispered. "I was told this could happen, but I never thought she'd forget people she's known for so long. Maybe it's because she's associating you with Fraserview."

"I understand." Casey squeezed her hand. "I know her memory will come back."

"Of course it will. Kendal's been strong-willed from the day she was born." The tears in Deanne's eyes betrayed her upbeat tone.

Time to leave. An elephant had trounced into the room and no one wanted to acknowledge the unthinkable: that Kendal's memory might never be restored. Even if it was, would she be the person she was before the fall? How much brain damage had she sustained? Hard as she tried, Casey couldn't hold back her own tears.

Deanne embraced her with a comfort and warmth that made her sob harder. "Trust me," Deanne murmured. "She'll be fine. The healing's begun. There'll be no stopping her now."

"I know." Casey couldn't escape the knowledge, though, that if she'd never mentioned Fraserview her friend wouldn't be here now.

Deanne moved to the door and poked her head out. "No sign of security. They said they'd send someone over right away. Can you stay here a minute while I go light a fire under their butts?"

"Sure." Wiping her eyes, Casey slumped into the chair. Kendal hadn't moved since she'd turned away. Was she sleeping again, or did she not want to deal with the stranger in her room? "I don't know where to go from here, Kendal," she mumbled, more to herself than her friend. "Guess I have to wait for the cops to figure things out."

Casey fiddled with the sparkling diamond ring on her hand. "I got engaged." She stood. "Lou proposed on Valentine's."

Kendal didn't move.

"Congratulations," Deanne said, stepping back into the room. She gave Casey a hug. "Kendal will be thrilled."

"I hope so."

"I bumped into the security guy and he'll be here shortly. You should head home. I'll keep you posted about developments."

Although she wanted to go, it didn't feel right. "Make sure they understand that she shouldn't be left alone."

"Definitely. I called my brother, and he and my sister-in-law will spend the evening with her."

"Good."

Casey took a last look at Kendal before stepping into a corridor that was busy with nurses and visitors. The dinner cart had also shown up and the smell of chicken and potatoes filled the air. She prayed that Kendal would soon be well enough to complain about the food, to reminisce about the past and look forward to the future. Yet, her friend probably faced enormous hurdles. Recovery would take weeks, if not months, or longer.

Stepping into the elevator, Casey's thoughts turned to Phyllis and Mia. Which one of them had lied about Jamal's involvement in Kendal's fall? If Kendal had come across evidence implicating someone in Mac or Winson's deaths, she might have tried to learn more. Confrontation was part of her job; Kendal relished it. So, what the hell had she discovered that night?

THIRTY-TWO

AS AMY PRESSED THE INTERCOM buzzer, Casey scanned Fraserview's parking lot. She'd called Amy at dinnertime to ask about Justin. Amy had confirmed that he was still inside, and since she planned to visit tonight, Casey had asked to meet her outside Fraserview. Now that Cruz had been arrested and Mia was officially on "personal" leave, Justin was much safer, as was she.

Mia and Cruz were probably involved with both deaths and Kendal's fall. Yet, Casey needed confirmation, and that required a talk with Mercedes. Since the girl had been in the corridor when Mia entered the pool room that horrible night, it was time to learn exactly what she had seen.

Gaining clearance had been easier than anticipated, especially when Casey clarified that her purpose was to accompany Amy while she visited Justin. The fact that Rawan and Amir weren't on duty this evening definitely helped.

Amy identified herself, and the buzzer sounded. Casey's shoulders tensed as she followed Amy inside this foreboding and overly warm cesspool. After she signed in and picked up a visitor's badge, she told Amy that she'd meet up with her in the visitors' room shortly.

"I hope the lawyer's correct about this being Justin's last night here," Amy muttered.

Casey hoped so too. It was a relief to learn that several partygoers had—now that Brady was dead—admitted to seeing the kid plant drugs on Justin. One by one, the charges against Justin had dissolved. Apparently, the only reason left for keeping him here was added punishment for his escape. But given that Mia's actions had made the escape possible, the authorities could hardly justify keeping him locked up.

Before she went to see Kendal, Casey had managed to reach Justin by phone and pass along Tanya's message. His lukewarm response hadn't surprised her. Casey knew that Amy and the lawyer must have told Justin that his beloved had kept vital info from him. "I'm glad she's okay," he'd said, and that was it. The kid had to be furious, though.

Hurrying down the corridor, her senses alert, Casey spotted Phyllis's familiar black sweater draped over the janitor's cart through the open conference room door. For a brief moment, she considered asking Phyllis the truth about Jamal's alleged role in Kendal's accident, then decided against it. If Phyllis had lied, she'd probably continue to do so. Mercedes was the priority, and she needed to talk to her before staff realized she wasn't in the visitors' area. Afraid that she would be turned down, she hadn't asked to speak to Mercedes directly, and she definitely wasn't supposed to be wandering through the building.

Judging from the yells and squeaking runners, a basketball game was underway. Casey reached the girls' unit and stepped inside, recognizing Mercedes's short black hair instantly. The girl sat with her back to the door and was watching a music video. Casey entered Ruby's office, where Ruby was reading a file.

"Well hello der, gal." She pushed her chair back. "Didn't know you'd be here tonight."

"I'm not officially; just thought I'd pop by to say hi," Casey replied. "Have you seen Mia lately?"

Ruby grinned. "Don't think I will for a long time. Seems our acting director's steppin' down. Personal problems of a legal nature, dey say."

Casey smiled, but she didn't want to discuss those problems with Ruby, not when there was a more important task at hand. The music video ended. Casey turned and saw Mercedes staring at her with an unreadable expression.

"How is Kendal?" Ruby asked.

"She's out of her coma, but there's some amnesia. She doesn't remember being in the pool room, among other things."

Ruby clicked her tongue and shook her head. "Dat girl has a strong spirit. She'll be better."

"I hope so." Casey turned around again. A couple of residents were playing a board game. Mercedes was still watching her. "It looks quiet tonight. Can I speak with Mercedes a minute?"

Ruby's gaze drifted toward the girl. "She might not be up for talkin'. Been real quiet lately." She gave Casey a knowing look. "Her uncle's got legal trouble too, but you can try."

"Thanks." Casey entered the common room. "Hi, Mercedes."

"*Señorita*," Mercedes replied, keeping her gaze on the TV.

Casey stood behind the sofa. Even sitting down, the girl was nearly her height. "Can we chat a minute?"

"I'm not supposed to talk to you," Mercedes answered.

Cruz's order, no doubt. "I understand, but all I want to know is if you saw my friend Kendal, or anyone else, go in or leave the pool room the night Kendal was injured."

Mercedes turned and sneered. "Why should I help you?"

"Because you're a good person who wants to do the right thing."

"Like you?"

Right. How to play this? Hash out events or gloss over what happened? "I guess you're pretty mad at me."

Mercedes's gaze drifted to the table. "You made things worse. My next stop is probably foster homes."

"That wasn't my intention, and I'm truly sorry."

Mercedes shook her head and muttered something in Spanish. Casey wasn't sure she'd get anything out of her, but she had to try. "You were in the corridor that night. Any idea who went near the pool room between 7:30 and 8:10 PM?" Mercedes gave her a cold stare. "Please, I really need your help, for Kendal's sake, not mine."

"She was nice," Mercedes answered and then sighed. "Mia went in, then came out after a minute, looking pissed. She told that crazy cleaning lady to go in and mop the floor."

Casey recalled Mia mentioning that. "Did you see Phyllis go in?"

Mercedes nodded. "She started to push her cart through the door, but her stupid sweater fell and got caught under a wheel. She pulled it out, then went inside. Ruby called me back into the unit after that."

"So, you didn't see Kendal enter the pool room or Phyllis leave?"

"No."

"Was anyone else in the corridor at the same time you were?"

"Just that hag of a cook."

Oksana? "What was she doing?"

"Carrying one of those stupid pails. Who cares?"

Casey did. That bloody cook probably did know more than she'd said. "Thanks."

After a quick goodbye to Ruby, Casey left the unit and looked up and down the corridor. Phyllis's cart was now outside Mac's office, and no one else was in sight. Good. Casey marched toward the kitchen, not caring how nasty Oksana would be. She was going to get some bloody answers. Peeking through the small window in the door, she spotted the woman mixing something in a large bowl. Casey pushed the door open.

Oksana looked over her shoulder and scowled. "You can't come in here."

"This won't take a minute."

"Get out!"

"You either talk to me, or I call the police to tell them about the supplies you've been stealing."

The woman spun around so fast she nearly swept the bowl off the table. "How dare you say that to me!"

"Hey, I'm only repeating what I've been told by staff."

"Who?"

"Does it matter?"

"They're all liars!"

"Really, Oksana? Come on." Casey stayed near the door, should the woman come after her. "I just need to know who you saw entering and leaving the pool room the night the volunteer was injured."

"I don't have to tell you *nothin'*."

"Mac was planning to let you go, wasn't he?" Casey said. "He probably caught you stealing, which would be grounds for dismissal." Oksana's worried expression told Casey she was on the right track. "All I want is the truth about what you really saw that night, and I won't go to the authorities. Before you deny anything, one person has confirmed that you were in the corridor when Phyllis went in the pool room, so don't waste my time."

Oksana grunted as she returned to the mixing bowl. "No one minds their own business."

"Did you see Kendal go in the pool room?"

"Yes. Happy now?"

"Did she go in before or after Phyllis?"

"After."

"How long after?"

Oksana gave an impatient sigh. "How should I know? I wasn't timing her."

"Can you think of any reason why Kendal would go in there?"

"Probably returning something to Phyllis."

Casey frowned. "So, Kendal and Phyllis were in the pool room together?"

"Yeah."

Why hadn't Phyllis mentioned this? "What would Kendal be returning to Phyllis?"

Oksana shrugged. "The girl picked something off the floor, then went inside. End of story."

"And you didn't see what she picked up?"

"I already said no."

Mercedes said that Phyllis's sweater had caught under the wheel of the cart. By pulling it out, she could have lost a button. Maybe Kendal picked it up, noticed Phyllis in the pool room, and went inside to see if it belonged to her.

"Stupid girl had no business going in that room. It's out of bounds for a reason, you know. Tiles are slippery."

"So I heard." Casey's thoughts swirled as she left the kitchen and headed back down the corridor, her gaze on the janitorial cart.

Phyllis was emptying the trash basket when Casey stopped in the doorway. "Hi, Phyllis. Got a question for you." She stepped inside Mac's office, feeling uneasy about being back in this room. "I've just had confirmation that Kendal went into the pool room while you were there. Why didn't you tell me?"

Phyllis stared at Casey, and then her shoulders sagged. "Didn't want you jumping to the wrong conclusion, did I? Word would get out. Give Mia another reason to twist everything into a chain of knots to strangle me. They say these kids are bad seeds, but that piece of work leads the bloody pack."

"Fair enough. What did Kendal want to see you about?"

"I lost a button. She returned it, started to walk away, but then skidded on the wet tiles. I tried to grab her, but she was moving too fast."

"You should have told me."

"I know, and I'm very sorry." Phyllis's knuckles turned white as she gripped her mop.

"Why did you point the finger at Jamal?"

"He's a mean one. Doesn't belong here."

Quite the assessment. "You know you'll have to tell the police the truth."

Phyllis shrugged. "I will. Now that Mia's probably gone for good, I won't have to worry."

"Can you give the police a statement tomorrow? Her mother's frantic with worry that a killer's after her daughter. Things need to be set straight as soon as possible."

"All right." She swished the mop in a bucket of water. "How is Kendal doing?"

"She woke up but doesn't remember much, not even being in the pool room."

"I feel terrible about what happened. Have hardly slept a wink. If I hadn't lost that button, she wouldn't be in hospital. Would it be all right if I paid my respects?"

If Phyllis was the last person Kendal saw before she fell, then a visit could trigger Kendal's memory. But a good memory or a bad one?

"She's being watched twenty-four-seven, so you'll need her mother's permission," Casey said.

Phyllis nodded and went back to work.

THIRTY-THREE

"HAS SECURITY BEEN AROUND?" CASEY asked Deanne while they watched Kendal sleep.

"A guard was here five minutes ago, but there was some sort of incident in emergency," Deanne whispered. "They've been good about trying to keep a guard posted outside the door. Between the hospital security staff and my family, she hasn't been left alone."

"Have any visitors from Fraserview come by?"

"Not that I'm aware of."

"What about the cleaning woman I mentioned?"

"Haven't heard from her," Deanne replied. "Despite those two arrests, I still don't feel comfortable leaving Kendal alone. And I don't completely trust the cleaning lady either. She was there when Kendal fell. She should have done the right thing and said something."

"Agreed."

Clearly, Phyllis was odd, and she was also a liar. Had she told the truth about Kendal's fall? But why would Phyllis push her into the pool? What threat had Kendal been to her?

Something niggled at the back of Casey's thoughts. Memories of every incident in recent weeks bounced around. She tried to slow her thoughts and concentrate, but the answer wouldn't come.

"Phyllis was supposed to give the police a statement today," Casey said. "I wonder if she did."

Deanne yawned and closed her eyes for a moment. "You could check, couldn't you?"

"Yes, and I will," Casey replied. "Deanne, you look exhausted. Why don't you take a break while I stay with Kendal."

"I could use a coffee. Are you sure you don't mind?"

"Not at all. If Kendal wakes up, I brought a book to read to her." Casey removed a copy of *Rebecca* from her purse. "A few years back, we were camping on a long weekend and it started to rain. Kendal didn't want to go home, so we stayed in the tent and I read this out loud because she hadn't brought anything to do."

"She never was big on reading," Deanne said.

"True, but after one chapter she was hooked." Casey hoped that reading it again would jog Kendal's memory. "We read the whole book that weekend. She loved the story."

"Thank you," Deanne said. "I really appreciate this."

"It's the least I can do."

Deanne stepped closer to Kendal, lightly brushed her hair, then left. Casey sat down, clutching the old copy of *Rebecca*. She didn't own many books, but this one she treasured.

Watching her friend, she murmured, "What happened that night, Kendal?"

A security guard stepped into the room. "I just saw Mrs. Winters. She says you're staying for a bit?"

"Yeah."

"Okay. I'll come back in a few minutes."

"Thanks."

Kendal stirred. Her eyelids flickered and closed again. Casey pulled the chair closer to the bed and tried to ignore her discomfort at being alone with a best friend who no longer remembered her. This dim little room only added to the discomfort. Hospitals had a different feel after dark: quieter and more subdued. Desolate.

"I brought our favorite book," Casey said. "You probably don't remember that god-awful weekend in Manning Park. I wanted to pack it in and go home, but you insisted that the weather would break. So, I read to you." She opened the cover. "Time for an encore."

Casey was about to start reading when her cell phone rang.

"This is Phyllis. I'm in my car, here at the hospital."

"Oh." Strange that she hadn't arranged a visit with Deanne.

"I just spotted that Latino man, Mercedes's uncle," Phyllis said. "I think he's seen me."

Cristano Cruz was out of jail? Casey jumped out of her chair. "Which parking lot are you in?"

"Outside of emergency. I'm nervous that Cruz is here. I know you work in security. Can you come down, or have one of the guards escort me in? I don't have their number."

"Stay there and don't do anything until you hear from me."

Casey hung up. Phyllis and Cruz were both here? What was going on? And how did Phyllis know Casey was here? Had she seen her Tercel? Whatever Phyllis's and Cruz's motives were, security help was a good idea.

Casey left the book in the chair and stepped into the hallway. She spotted a nurse down the hall, then glanced back at Kendal's room. As long as she kept an eye on the entrance, it would be fine.

Casey hurried toward the nurses' station, arriving just as the nurse answered the phone. Damn. The plan was to request her help. As Casey waited, she looked around the station for security's number but didn't see it. She scanned the corridor for a public phone, which usually posted security's contact info nearby, but couldn't see one of those either.

As she watched Kendal's door, Casey grew impatient. Taking a deep, calming breath, she gazed at a tray of pills by the phone and tried to stay calm. If Cruz got too close to Phyllis and if she really was afraid of him, she could always blast the car horn to draw attention. Gazing at the pills again, Casey tried to sort things out. An idea sprang to mind, then another until the thing that had been niggling at the back of her brain emerged in the form of a tiny white pill.

Even though Phyllis's sweater had gotten caught under the cart's wheel, she would have needed to put it on in the chilly pool room. No woman would put on a sweater that had been trapped under a dirty wheel on a dirty floor without giving it a good shake. Oksana hadn't seen the object Kendal picked off the floor because it was too small. Kendal could have seen Phyllis shake out her sweater. Maybe she'd headed down there to talk to Phyllis and spotted a bright pill on the dull floor. Kendal would have assumed the pill belonged to Phyllis and tried to return it. Except the medication had been Mac's.

The nurse hung up.

"Get security to Kendal Winters's room!" Casey shouted.

Holding her breath, Casey dashed down the hallway, regretting that she hadn't kept a closer watch on Kendal's room. She bolted inside, horrified to see Phyllis about to inject something into Kendal, who was still sleeping.

"Get away from her!" Casey ran around the bed.

Phyllis turned as Casey grabbed her arm and pulled. Clutching the syringe, Phyllis tried to yank her arm free, then pushed her weight into Casey. Casey stumbled backward.

"Help!" Casey shouted, still gripping Phyllis's arm. "Somebody help!"

Phyllis tried to wriggle free but Casey kept a firm grip.

Kendal had awakened and was trying to sit up. "What?" She stared at Phyllis. "Do I know you?"

"No. Nobody pays attention to me." Phyllis tried to drag Casey toward Kendal.

"Stop it!" Casey yelled. "She doesn't remember!" She could feel Phyllis weakening.

A nurse charged into the room, saw what was happening, and froze. She hurried back to the doorway and shouted for help.

"Protect Kendal!" Casey shouted at the nurse. "And where's the guard?"

"Don't know. He must have left the floor."

"Enemies everywhere," Phyllis mumbled. "Nothing you can do."

Casey reached for Phyllis's hand and pulled her thumb back until Phyllis yelped and dropped the syringe on the bed. The nurse grabbed the syringe as a second nurse appeared. The first nurse ordered her to fetch the security guards.

Casey twisted Phyllis's arm behind her back. "Why did you kill Mac?"

Phyllis's body went rigid. "I didn't. It was an accident! He wasn't supposed to die. Gave me a job, he did."

"Then why overdose him?"

"He was going to take it away. I wanted Mac to lose his job, that's all. To know what it felt like to be robbed of control."

Casey's heart pounded so hard, she could scarcely breathe. "Winson saw you in Mac's office that night, didn't he? He started putting two and two together."

"Another accident. Thought the ambulance would get there in time."

"Was Kendal supposed to be an accident as well? And how will you make that claim stick when I—"

Two security guards ran into the room.

"This woman tried to kill my friend with something in a syringe!" Casey yelled, adrenaline rushing through her body.

Phyllis's mouth quivered as the guards restrained her, yet there were no tears.

"You okay?" one of the guards asked Casey.

"Yeah." She turned to Kendal. "Are you all right? Did she inject you with anything?"

"No. I'm fine."

Casey turned to the nurse. "Any idea what's in the syringe?"

The nurse held it close to the light. "Nothing. I think she was going to inject her with air." The nurse looked at them. "If she'd hit an artery, it could have been fatal."

"I didn't know that," Phyllis said.

Was she freakin' out of her mind? "Like hell you didn't."

The second nurse reappeared. "I've called the police."

"Good," her colleague replied and then turned to the guards. "Get that woman out of here."

"Wait," Casey said. "I have a question." Turning to Phyllis, she took a deep breath. "Why did you push Kendal into the pool?"

Phyllis glanced up at her, a glint of hatred in her eyes. "I didn't."

"It wasn't a button she was returning, was it?" Casey said. "It was a pill. One that had become lodged deep in the corner of your sweater pocket, until you shook out the sweater after it had become trapped under the wheel of your cart."

"I don't know what you're on about."

"You leave the sweater at work, don't you?" Casey glanced at Phyllis's open coat, noting that she didn't have the sweater on now. "I often forget to bring home clothes that are kept in my work locker, which means they don't get washed often. That's why the pill was still there."

"That's what you say, but they're only words."

"I'm sure that forensics experts will find traces of digoxin in the pocket." Casey felt her anger surge. "Kendal will get her memory back, and between the two of us, we'll see who really controls your fate." She looked at the guards. "Get her out of my sight."

After they left, Casey lifted the book off the chair and plunked down. She leaned forward, elbows on her knees, and tried to clear her head. She heard voices talking out in the hallway—mention of the syringe and the police being on their way.

"Did she really want to kill me?" Kendal asked.

Casey looked up. "I think so. I guess you didn't recognize her?"

"She seemed vaguely familiar." Kendal paused. "Who are Mac and Winson?"

"I'll tell you later." She opened the book. "Right now, I'd rather focus on fiction."

As Casey turned to the first page, she tried not to think about what had just happened. The police would be here soon, then back to reality. She looked at her friend's blank expression and tried not to let discouragement and sadness overwhelm her.

Looking down, she read, "Last night I dreamt I went to Manderley again."

THIRTY-FOUR

JUSTIN PERCHED ON THE EDGE of Amy's desk while Amy sipped the coffee Casey had brought from the lunchroom. This was the happiest and most relaxed Amy had looked in a long time, but she had good reason. Given that Cruz had initiated the idea to involve Justin in his drug ring and Mia had helped make it happen, the charge regarding Justin's escape had finally been dropped.

"How does it feel to be free?" Casey asked him.

"Good, but kind of weird."

"I heard that Amir's running Fraserview now that Mia's officially been charged for her role in Cruz's operation," Casey said.

"He won't make that place any better," Justin replied.

"If you ask me, the adults behaved more badly than the kids," Amy said. "Look at that horrible woman who murdered two people and kept trying to kill your friend, for heaven's sake."

"Yeah, well, I think Phyllis went off the deep end some time ago."

Casey wished she'd realized that something more sinister than elderly eccentricity was rattling around Phyllis's brain. Mac's plan to fire her must have set Phyllis off. She decided that he was no better than her father and husband when it came to controlling her life. Only this time, she'd done something about it.

Casey cringed. She shouldn't have told Phyllis that Kendal was improving. If she'd figured out the pill connection sooner, Phyllis would never have gotten near Kendal. Worse, she'd completely underestimated Phyllis's need for vengeance, not to mention a disturbing cleverness that Casey wished she'd picked up on. It had been a huge mistake to let the woman's age and odd remarks distract her.

"I assume you won't be volunteering at Fraserview anymore?" Amy asked.

"No. Amir doesn't like volunteers, and I have enough data for my term paper anyway." Casey turned to Justin. "Have you heard from Tanya?"

He hesitated. "She's doing good. Wants to see me, but I dunno."

"I guess you're mad at her for not telling you about Didi's phone recording."

He shrugged. "Wouldn't you be?"

"Yeah, I'd be furious. Tanya's approach was wrong, but she wanted to keep you in her life. As Phyllis demonstrated, desperation drives people to do outrageous things."

"Tanya doesn't have your best interests at heart," Amy said to him. "Think about what I said this morning. If you want to break up with her, now's the time. She's in a safe place with professionals who can help her through it, right, Casey?"

Amy's expression made it clear she expected Casey to agree. "There's never a good time to break up," Casey replied. "But if it needs to be done, then it's better not to prolong it."

Amy gave Casey a brief nod and sipped her coffee. Yesterday, Amy confided that Justin's dad couldn't cope with the responsibility of parenting a teenager right now. His mother, not surprisingly, said he couldn't live with her either. Amy, however, was thrilled to have Justin move in with her.

Stan emerged from his office and handed Amy some loose sheets of paper. "I've been working on the quarterly report and it sounds stupid. Can you fix it?"

"Certainly."

Stan looked at Justin. "How goes it, buddy?"

"Good."

"We're heading up to Whistler for the weekend," Amy said. "Justin wants to get a little snowboarding in before winter's gone."

"Which reminds me, I need your vacation schedules for the summer." Stan glanced at the accounting and human resources staff at the other end of the room. He moved closer to Casey and murmured, "Have you and Lou set a wedding date yet?"

Stan and Amy were the only people at MPT who knew about the engagement. She'd asked them to keep it quiet until she and Lou came up with a date. "We've decided on August. Lou's mom is consulting an astrologer for the exact date." Casey tried to say it with a straight face and failed.

"Can't hurt, I suppose," Stan said with a grin. "I'm taking all of July off, so you'll be in charge."

"Really?" He'd never left her in charge for a whole month.

"Think you can handle it with all the wedding preparations?"

"Sure, I'll have lots of help. Lou's mom has already started an invitation list, so I guess we're off and running."

"How's your friend doing?"

"Getting stronger." Since Phyllis's arrest a week ago, Kendal had started to remember her job and her apartment, although she still didn't remember Casey, which was hugely discouraging. "I'm seeing her again tonight," Casey added. She would be finished the book soon, and after that? She supposed it was up to Kendal.

→   →   →

CASEY ENTERED THE private room, happy to see Kendal's welcoming smile. At least she recognized Casey now, but as a new friend who'd been visiting nearly every day for a week, not someone with a long shared history.

"You look good today," Casey said.

"No headache for a change."

The color had returned to Kendal's face, and her eyes were more alert and expressive. Her head was still bandaged, but Deanne said the doctors were amazed by her progress.

Casey pulled up a chair and pulled *Rebecca* from her bag. "Ready to begin?"

Kendal rolled onto her side so she was facing Casey. "Yep."

Casey had read only a couple of paragraphs when Kendal blurted, "She's about to realize the truth, isn't she? That Maxim really does love her."

"Yeah, it's my favorite part."

Casey read two more lines before Kendal again interrupted with, "Love is everything, isn't it?"

An odd comment. "Yeah. I think it is to most people, whether it's romantic love, or love for friends and family, or a pet." Kendal stared at her, her expression unreadable. Casey returned to the paragraph she was reading. She got through a couple more lines before she was interrupted again.

"You're engaged," Kendal said, nodding to Casey's ring.

"I am, yes."

"Congratulations."

Casey gave a quick smile. "Thanks." She started reading again.

"I always knew Lou was crazy about you."

"Yeah well, it took me a while to see it." She noticed the familiar smirk, something she hadn't seen in a long time. "Wait a sec; you remember Lou?"

"How could I forget a cutie like him?"

Casey's mouth fell open. "Have you always remembered him?"

Kendal shook her head. "Came to me this morning, right after I remembered everything about you."

Casey jumped up. "That's wonderful! What else do you remember?"

"A lot. After Phyllis tried to kill me, fuzzy images started appearing later that night . . . Friends, family, coworkers, and then Fraserview residents . . . Mac. I couldn't home in on them at first, but then things began to gel. I even remembered why I didn't want to go home during that awful camping trip. It was because of those cute guys in the camper across from us."

To see her old friend become herself again brought tears to Casey's eyes. "What about what happened in the pool room? Any recollection there?"

"That part's still fuzzy." She paused. "I do remember holding a white pill."

Casey nodded. "Police confirmed that it was digoxin."

"I don't remember how I wound up here."

"You don't need to." Casey swept long strands of hair away from Kendal's face. "Was the pill your last memory before you fell?"

"I kind of remember going into the pool room. At least I remember the cold, and Phyllis's face . . . how it changed from surprise to irritation to a strange stare."

"She apparently confessed to stealing one or two pills at a time until she had enough to overdose him. Phyllis ground the pills into a fine powder, though she didn't put the power in his thermos like I thought," Casey said. "It seems that Mac was fond of bringing enormous homemade sandwiches stuffed with deli meats and cheeses. She sprinkled powder between the meats and cheese, which were lathered with mustard and mayo. Between all the flavors and the way he apparently wolfed down his meals, he probably didn't notice the medication."

"Think she really intended to kill them?" Kendal asked.

"She's still insisting that Mac and Winson were accidents, but I have my doubts. The job and the casinos were all she had in her life. Without a paycheck, Phyllis would have lost everything. From what I understand, she has no children, and no relatives in Canada."

"Well, she's not our problem anymore," Kendal said, "So, let's talk about fun stuff, like your wedding."

Casey chuckled. "It seems I'll need of a maid of honor. Are you up for the job?"

"Only if you don't put me in some shitty dress with ruffles."

"No ruffles." Casey gave her a quick hug. "I promise."

Acknowledgments

The idea for this book was inspired by my volunteer work many years ago at a detention center that no longer exists. Fraserview Youth Custody Center and its staff and residents are strictly products of my imagination.

Many thanks to Kemal Khan, retired director of Burnaby Youth Custody Services, for kindly answering questions about current youth custody centers. I also had the pleasure of meeting Gordon Cruse, author of *Juvie: Inside Canada's Youth Jails*, whose experiences as a youth supervisor brought back a lot of memories and filled some gaps about things I'd long forgotten.

It has been a privilege to work with Ruth Linka, Taryn Boyd, and the talented people at TouchWood Editions, including editor Cailey Cavallin, designer Pete Kohut, and publicists Emily Shorthouse and Tori Elliott. Once again, I'm indebted to the always enthusiastic editor, Frances Thorsen, who's worked with me on all four of my Casey Holland books. Thanks as well to proofreader Sarah Weber.

Where would I be without my Port Moody writers' group? They've stuck with me for years and still give me many ah-ha moments with their insights. Also, heartfelt thanks to my family, whose support means the world to me.

DEBRA PURDY KONG's first Casey Holland transit security mystery, *The Opposite of Dark*, was released in 2011, the second, *Deadly Accusations*, appeared in 2012, and the third, *Beneath the Bleak New Moon*, in 2013. She is also the author of the Alex Bellamy white-collar crime mysteries, *Taxed to Death* and *Fatal Encryption*, and has written more than one hundred short stories, essays, and articles for publications such as *Chicken Soup for the Bride's Soul*, *BC Parent Magazine*, and the *Vancouver Sun*. In 2007, she won an honorable mention at the Surrey International Writers' Conference for her short story "Some Mother's Child." Debra has a diploma of associate in criminology and has worked in security as a patrol and communications officer. She lives in Port Moody, BC, with her family. More information about Debra and her work can be found at debrapurdykong.com. Follow her on Twitter at @DebraPurdyKong.